STAR GLORY

Book One of the Empire Series

T. Jackson King

Other King Novels
Mother Warm (2017), Battlecry (2017), Superguy (2016), Battlegroup (2016), Battlestar (2016), Defeat The Aliens (2016), Fight The Aliens (2016), First Contact (2015), Escape From Aliens (2015), Aliens Vs. Humans (2015), Freedom Vs. Aliens (2015), Humans Vs. Aliens (2015), Earth Vs. Aliens (2014), Genecode Illegal (2014), The Memory Singer (2014), Alien Assassin (2014), Anarchate Vigilante (2014), Galactic Vigilante (2013), Nebula Vigilante (2013), Speaker To Aliens (2013), Galactic Avatar (2013), Stellar Assassin (2013), Retread Shop (2012, 1988), Star Vigilante (2012), The Gaean Enchantment (2012), Little Brother's World (2010), Judgment Day (2009), Ancestor's World (1996).

Dedication
To my wife Sue, my son Keith and my dad Thomas, thank you all for your active duty service in defense of America.

Acknowledgments
First thanks go to scholar John Alcock and his book *Animal Behavior, An Evolutionary Approach* (1979). Second thanks go to the scholar Edward O. Wilson, whose book *Sociobiology: The New Synthesis* has guided me in my efforts to explore a future where humanity encounters life from other stars.

STAR GLORY
© 2017 T. Jackson King

This is a work of fiction. All the characters and events portrayed in this novel are either fictitious or are used fictitiously. All rights reserved. No part of this book may be used or reproduced in any manner whatsoever without written permission except for brief quotations for review purposes only.

Cover design by T. Jackson King; cover image by Luca Oleastri via Dreamstime license..

First Edition
Published by T. Jackson King, Santa Fe, NM 87507
http://www.tjacksonking.com/
ISBN 10: 1-54682-033-7
ISBN 13: 978-1-54682-033-8
Printed in the United States of America

CHAPTER ONE

  I never expected to be homeless in the galaxy. To be afraid to return to Sol and Earth out of fear that a return would bring the dreaded Empire fleets and subjugation for Earth. Course, I'm not really homeless. Not on the *Star Glory*, which has 369 humans on board and small private rooms for a petty officer like me. Still, homeless is how I feel now. It all began right after the *Glory* exited from Alcubierre stardrive and arrived at the outer edge of the furthest star yet visited by humans, a place called Kepler 37, which lies about 215 light years out from Earth.

  "PO Nathan Stewart! Are your antimatter injector tubes ready to feed the thrusters!" yelled Chief Engineer O'Connor from the other end of the giant room that houses our Alcubierre space-time graviton generators, our stern fusion reactor and my post.

  I looked up at the flare of nine flexible metal tubes that feed negative neutrons to the deck below, where it will be spit into the star flame of our fusion pulse thrusters. The shimmer of the rainbow colors that indicated perfect functioning of the containment magfields that enclosed each tube told me the system was ready.

  "Chief O'Connor! The tubes are ready to feed antimatter to our thrusters, sir!"

  The barrel-shaped man twisted his wide shoulders and looked my way. Beady black eyes squinted. "You don't have your goggles on! How the hell do you know your magfields are operational!"

  "Sir, I don't need the goggles." I looked up again. "The color shimmer matches exactly what they taught us to expect at NS Great Lakes!"

  The stocky, short man grimaced. "I don't give a damn that you have super-duper eyes. Put on your goggles anyway and report!"

  I did as ordered, even though Robert O'Connor was just being official for the overhead videyes that record the active duty behaviors of every human doing anything anywhere on the *Star Glory*. He doesn't object to my special eyesight. It just isn't in the Engineering operations manual, so he had to insist I put on the goggles. That was to ensure no EarthGov official could gig Captain Neil Skorzeny for "irregular" crew function. And the captain was a fair man, unlike Lieutenant Commander Mehta Nehru, the Second Watch line officer. Nehru had been a real bent shitcan all the days of our FTL transit. The man from India did not like Colorado country boys who raised cows to eat, he being Hindu and a lover of cattle wandering through one's streets, dropping turds everywhere they went. The man had made it a point to gig me for improper uniform appearance. Spots of oil and clumps of Teflon fibers are hard to avoid in Engineering. Plus I wasn't a Marine, a line officer or an academic and thereby deserving of his respect. So he dumped on me every time he saw me in the Mess Hall, in Recycling or anywhere else on the twelve decks of the ship. I shook my head and decided to pay attention to the job I liked doing. That meant ignoring the amused looks from the three Spacers and petty officer who sat beyond us at the fusion reactor station. I pulled my head strap tight and looked up through the goggles.

"Chief O'Connor, checking by way of goggles confirms the magfield shimmer colors meet regulation criteria," I said, hoping the words fit what I recalled from my years spent studying antimatter engineering at Naval Station Great Lakes, on the north side of Chicago.

"Good." The man looked away and focused on his own control panel, which held the controls for the ship's three fusion pulse thrusters. Then my fellow American tapped his seat's right armrest, activating his comlink with the Bridge. "Captain Skorzeny, Chief O'Connor reporting from Engineering. Thrusters are a go! Antimatter injection tubes are a go for afterburner push! Sir."

A nearby bulkhead vidscreen, presently filled with the white star dots of interstellar space, changed to an overhead view of Skorzeny as he sat on the command pedestal in the middle of the Bridge. To the man's left and lower down sat the XO, Commander Nadya Kumisov, whose black hair now held several white streaks. Like the captain and everyone on the Bridge and elsewhere in the ship, she wore a vacsuit with helmet thrown back, in case of deck pressure loss. This being First Watch, she looked very alert. As did Major James Owanju, commander of all the Marines on the *Star Glory*. The man's deep black skin seemed to soak in the yellow-normal lighting of the Bridge. Beyond Owanju, and to the lower right of the captain, sat the only civilian on the Bridge. Strapped in but appearing bothered by the tightness of his vacsuit was Doctor Magnus

Bjorg, expert in stellar cosmology and planetary systems. The Swede represented the Science Department geeks who partly filled a deck lying between Bridge and Engineering.

"Acknowledged, chief," Skorzeny said, his broad hands resting on his seat's armrests, the gloved fingers hovering just above the control patches on each armrest. The man nodded his head at the front vidscreen, which lay beyond the pickup range of the ceiling mounted videye. "All Ship! We have arrived at the edge of the magnetosphere of Kepler 37. Our sensors tell us we are in the outer portion of this system's Kuiper Belt of comets. As you can see," he said, tapping an armrest control patch, "ahead of us is this system's G8V yellow star. An outer gas giant is present, as are four very small inner worlds that Kepler documented. They lie too close for liquid water to survive on their surfaces. There are also two asteroid belts between us and the gas giant."

I looked away from the bulkhead vidscreen to a different vidscreen that was close to the chief's duty station. It showed the tiny round dot of a yellow star. To one side of the true space image was a system graphic image that showed an overhead plan view of the system, with the circular orbits of the five planets and two rock belts showing as dotted lines. The outer Kuiper Belt of comets showed as a blue zone that began at 38 AU and reached out to our position at 45 AU. The spot where we had exited stardrive. That spot now lay behind us as our ship and our two sister ships raced inward at one-tenth lightspeed. As I had learned at Great Lakes, whatever inertial speed a starship had when it entered Alcubierre was the speed it had upon exit. Hence the chief's yelling at me. The man wanted to be sure the *Star Glory* could fire her thrusters for maneuvering, and then speed up to eleven psol thanks to antimatter injections from my tubes. The tubes connected to the antimatter reservoir on the deck above Engineering. Feeding the reservoir was the particle accelerator coil that wrapped around the stern of the *Star Glory* and every other starship of EarthGov. The extra thrust provided by the antimatter injector tubes helped when any Earth ship was chasing pirates in Sol system, or was faced with the need to move faster than usual thanks to an incoming rock or comet.

"Captain!" yelled Kumisov. "Our bow sensor array reports stationary and moving neutrino emissions from three large moons above the gas giant! Tactical, give me a readout on those emissions. Are they asteroid rebels or generation ships?"

"Negative XO!" called Hilary Chang from Tactical. "The flavors of the neutrino emissions do not match any Earth fusion reactor or fusion pulse thruster. Sir!"

"Heidi," called the captain. "Do the neutrino emissions match *anything* ever recorded from Sol system?"

"They do not," responded the ship's AI, her normal light-hearted tone gone and replaced by a seriousness that sounded almost masculine.

"Aliens then," Kumisov said firmly. "Captain, suggest we go to Security Protocol Alpha Zed Forty-three. And that we advise our sister ships to do the same."

In the vidscreen near my work station the captain nodded, his curly brown hair bright in the light of the Bridge. "Communications, connect me with the captains of the *Dauntless* and the *Pyotr Velikiy*."

"Neutrino comlink established," said Jacob Wetstone from his Communications station in front of the command pedestal. "Incoming imagery and voice. Sir."

The nearby bulkhead vidscreen split now, with the overhead view of the Bridge moving to the left and two images filling the right side. I recognized Leslie Jacobsen, captain of the *HMS Dauntless* and Gregorii Nutsov, captain of the Russian battlecruiser *Pyotr Velikiy*. Both men looked darkly serious.

"Neil?" called Jacobsen.

"Comrade Skorzeny, these are aliens, yes?" muttered Nutsov.

"So it seems. Captains, go to Security Protocol Alpha Zed Forty-three." The captain pursed his lips, then spoke again. "Heidi, eject a comsat to handle our radio and neutrino communications with whomever that is down there. Apply Security Protocol—"

"Launching. Protocol applied," the AI said quickly. "Firewall established between our ship and the comsat."

"We're doing the same," reported Jacobsen.

"Same for us," Nutsov said. "Activating our electro-optical telescopes. Tactical! Get me imagery of those three moons!"

I saw the captain nod again. "Tactical, get us a feed from our scopes."

"Captain, our scopes are pulling in true light from the inner system," Chang said hurriedly.

Whispers came to my super-sensitive ears from the Spacers over at the fusion reactor station.

"PO, have we finally found aliens?" called a young man who went by Gus.

"Looks like it," said Petty Officer Dolores Gambuchino in a low whisper that most people would not hear. "Shut up, you three! And be ready to feed max power to ship weapons and systems if the captain orders it!"

Real aliens were a surprise. A very big surprise. My profs at Great Lakes had said it was probable the Milky Way held other space-going peoples, but emphasized we were unlikely to meet them given the 90,000 light year width of the galaxy. Now here they were, in our own galactic arm of Orion, and just 215 light years from Sol! *Damn.* I looked over to where the chief sat, his vacsuit tight about his muscular frame. The man looked troubled. His hands were hovering above his thruster control panel, clearly ready to activate the ship's three fusion pulse thrusters. The action of the chief made me look down at my own antimatter control panel which stood on a pedestal in front of my seat. The automatic straps that had criss-crossed my chest upon our emergence from Alcubierre kept me from moving forward very much. But I could reach the touchpanel. And the control patches on the armrests of my seat were easy to access. What was going to happen? Would the captain order us and our sister ships to turn back to the magnetosphere, there to re-enter Alcubierre space-time and head back to Sol? Heading back would take a good hour since we would have to stop our forward momentum, then reverse ship orientation so we could head back to the edge of the magnetosphere. Explosive experiments in Sol system had confirmed that no starship could safely activate its Alcubierre stardrive within the magnetosphere globe that surrounded any star. Or would the captain allow our small fleet to continue inward, eventually to make contact with the first aliens ever found by any Earth ship? The questions made me wonder about my friends Bill, Warren, Oksana and Cassandra, who was my higher math tutor. Cassie had a master's in exobiology and was expert on the lifeforms found on our twelve colony worlds. She or her boss should be up on the Bridge, ready to help the captain. Old Magnus just knew planets and stars. This first encounter with aliens was not anything I could help with. Growing up on a cattle ranch outside of Castle Rock,

Colorado does not prepare one to go head-to-carapace or whatever with intelligent space-going aliens!

"Captain, scope imagery going up on the front vidscreen," reported Chang, her voice business-like. "There are 47 moons of various sizes that orbit the gas giant, which lies three-fourths AU out from the star. The three moons each have an oxy-nitro atmosphere, they range in size from Venus to Earth, and . . ." She touched her control panel. "The front sensor array is detecting extensive emissions from laser coms, masers, coherent gamma rays and stuff on the radio and visual channels. Sir!"

The captain touched gloved fingers to his clean-shaven chin. "Com, how long will it take a radio signal to reach those moons and the ships and structures emitting these radiations?"

"Sir, eight point three hours to reach them, the same for any return reply." Wetstone looked back to Skorzeny. "Captain, I could try sending unencrypted neutrino signals from the comsat? They're FTL in nature." Wetstone blushed, as he recalled the captain and everyone on the Bridge well knew that neutrino com signals passed through an alternate dimension that allowed for instant talk-talk with another ship no matter how far away it might be. "If there is a reply, the comsat will retransmit to us in AM radio. Which will be filtered by Heidi's firewall."

The captain looked to his right and down. "Doctor Bjorg, your Science Department people must have a standard First Contact package ready to go. Correct?"

The big-framed man, who took pride in blond hair that reached his shoulders, nodded quickly. "Captain, we have such a package. It's a mix of math sequences, followed by basic English words with visual imagery that match the words. Shall I make it available to Heidi?"

"Do so." The captain sat back and folded his hands in his lap, appearing thoughtful. "Heidi, transmit the audiovisual package to the comsat. Then remove your astrogation data files from any form of digital access through our optical fiber lines. Put them into the Secure Block in Astrogation Department. That should protect the files from signal hacking. Captains Jacobsen and Nutsov, you should do the same. Who knows what these aliens may be capable of doing once they contact us?"

I agreed with the captain's decision to segregate the astrogation data files into the Secure Block. That data held the stellar coordinates for Earth and for our twelve colonies. Whatever came of this first encounter with aliens, they would not be able to discover where humans lived. And if one of our ships was captured, there was a self-destruct sequence that was both digital and manual. And I had no doubt Captain Skorzeny would destroy the ship, if faced with capture. While it had been a remote possibility when I was drafted by EarthGov, the discovery of so many habitable worlds close to Sol meant the galaxy was filled with places where life could exist. The Great Lakes profs had made clear that First Contact was just a matter of time. And that time had now come.

"Files are segregated," Heidi said, her tone still somber serious. "Your Bridge astrogator can still maneuver this ship through normal space-time. But transit into Alcubierre space-time modulus will require physical access to the Secure Block and release of its data back into my ship optical fiber veins."

"Understood." The captain sighed, then nodded abruptly. "Com, emit the open neutrino comsignal from the comsat. Transmit the AV package. Let's see if anyone is listening to neutrino com chatter."

"Transmitting, sir." Wetstone's face looked grim in the image on my bulkhead wall.

Did I look like that? Did the Chief look like that? The imagery of the Bridge and the two other ship captains showed everyone looking somber, serious and worried.

Those looks were something I knew well. Delivering a calf from a cow in the early morning in our family's barn was something I knew all too well. But living in a big city like Denver or Chicago was not something I had ever done, until I got my draft notice right after high school graduation. While the notice had showed up on my Facebook page, my family's business page and by old-fashioned letter sent to our woodframe house, it had been a shock. While everyone knew America was one of the seven nations that made up EarthGov, and was a prime supplier of commercial spaceships and combat spacecraft to the rest of the world, the fact the President had agreed to make the Constitution subservient to the EarthGov unification document was still sinking in seven years after the fact. Yes, a majority of Americans had voted in favor of joining EarthGov. Yes, that joining had resulted in increased trade and the creation of many new jobs. And yes, the joining had given America an equal voice with Russia, China, India, Britain, the African Union and Japan. But joining also meant the American president was the EarthGov boss just once every seven years. In high school we had learned how EarthGov was modeled after the Swiss national government system, where the governors of each Swiss canton rotated the national leadership among themselves. In EarthGov the most powerful nations now rotated planetary control among themselves, with citizens being heard in the Global Parliament in Geneva. But forced conscription had come with EarthGov membership. And the White House now sent out draft notices to American youth. I shivered, then told myself to put the memories of my fear of big cities into memory hold. Meeting unknown aliens was more serious than a country boy adjusting to big city life.

"Captain!" yelled Chang from her Tactical station. "We've got moving neutrino emission sources *behind* us! Long ways back but they are between us and the magnetosphere edge."

"How many?" growled Skorzeny.

"Twenty-seven sources, sir." Chang tapped her panel, looked back to the XO, who gestured upward, then she faced the captain. "They are spread out in a dome that covers ten million miles. The dome reaches out to our starboard, port, foc'sle, keel and stern directions. We are surrounded. Except for the space directly ahead. The sources are going up on our system graphic. Sir."

"What is their speed?"

"Same as us, one-tenth psol." Chang looked back to her station, focusing her attention on a holo that showed the system graphic of planets, asteroid belts, cometary zone and the green dots of our three ships. Behind and around our ships were twenty-seven red dots. All the dots were moving inward, toward the local star.

"Range to the nearest alien ship?"

"Sir, the nearest ship is fourteen million, three hundred sixty-eight thousand kilometers directly behind us. Two other ships are at the same range."

That was equal to almost nine million miles. At our current speed of one-tenth psol, or eighteen thousand six hundred miles per second, our ship could cover that distance in about eight minutes. It began to sink in just how close these aliens were. Are. And can be.

"XO, how did we fail to detect those neutrino emission sources?" Skorzeny said, his expression worried.

"No idea, sir." Kumisov tapped on her own control panel, then looked at a system graphic hologram that sprang into view in front of her. "We passed through the middle of this dome formation. We should have detected those ships' fusion reactors and thruster emissions. Sir, even if they were on the other side of a rocky planet, the neutrinos would pass through. Nothing material can block neutrinos. We should have detected them. We didn't."

"Astrogation, put us on a vector track away from our sister ships. Move to position 195 degrees down from the ecliptic plane." Skorzeny looked to a different area of the function stations that filled the front of the Bridge. "Weapons, put our lasers, missiles and railguns on Hot Ready status."

"Sir, new vector set," called Louise Ibarra from Astrogation.

"All Weapons stations moving to Hot Ready status," muttered Bill Yamamoto, a Japanese-American from San Francisco I had met twice in the Mess Hall.

The captain touched his right armrest. "Chief O'Connor, fire up our thrusters. Give me flank speed in forty seconds."

I saw my boss's thick shoulders tense. "Sir, thruster containment fields going up. DT pellets injecting. Fusion implosions are nearing max plasma density. Exhausting!"

My feet felt the deck vibrating from the pumps that transported frozen deuterium and tritium pellets from our fuel bunkers down their feedlines and into the implosion chambers where they were hit by a dozen terawatt-power lasers, causing fusion and the creation of excess energy that became glowing yellow-orange plasma. The plasma was contained by each thruster's containment magfield. Then the Chief tapped another control to open the exhaust funnel of each thruster. Those funnels were enclosed in magnetic fields that kept the positively charged plasma from touching the metal walls of the three implosion chambers and exhaust funnels. At the outer edge of the exhaust funnel for each thruster were three antimatter injector ports. They would shoot negative antimatter into the positive plasma exhaust when the Chief ordered an afterburner push. No such order came.

"Astro, move us ten thousand kilometers away from the *HMS Dauntless*." The man looked up. "Captains Jacobsen and Nutsov, I suggest you do the same. Let us adopt formation Victor Unity. The sudden appearance of these alien ships is not welcome news."

"Moving out," called the captain of the *HMS Dauntless*.

"*Pyotr Velikiy* is moving to its formation position," the Russian said bluntly.

Since the Chief had not told me to open the antimatter injector tubes to feed AM to the thruster exhausts, I could not help visualizing the new formation. It was basically a triangle, with the *Star Glory* at the apex and the other two ships at the lower angles. Each ship lay just beyond the 10,000 kilometer range of our carbon dioxide and proton lasers. The point of the formation was to prevent blue-on-blue collateral damage from laser firing, while being close enough to allow each ship to use its railguns in defense against incoming missiles and Smart Rocks. The formation allowed for mutual defense while maximizing the laser targeting angles.

"Captain, do we launch some x-ray thermonuke warheads?" called Kumisov.

"Not yet." Skorzeny hands hovered above his armrest control patches. "Let us see what response we get—"

"Incoming neutrino signal!" cried Wetstone. "Going up on the front vidscreen. Also going out on All Ship vidfeed. Sir, the signal perfectly matches our ship-to-ship neutrino comlink!"

How had this alien learned our neutrino comlink frequency? That was the signal that even now conveyed the images and voices of the other two captains. It was not the same signal frequency which Com was using to communicate with the comsat. Unease filled me. I looked up at the nine shimmering antimatter tubes that flared down from the overhead deck, spreading out like the spines of an umbrella and then heading straight down to our floor deck. And through the deck to the three thruster funnels. The reactor Spacers had teased me about hiding inside a cage of antimatter tubes while they sat 'in the open' at the control panels that fronted one side of Engineering's fusion reactor. I wasn't confined, not really. There was a meter between each tube, which left plenty of room for me to pass out from my station, and to return later. It didn't matter. The rainbow colors of the tube magfields were beautiful. A beauty I had long ago come to need since I was not good at being sociable. Putting aside my yearning for something meaningful to do, I focused on the nearby bulkhead.

The vidscreen grew an image in its middle, forcing to either side the overhead view of the Bridge and the images of the other two captains. A creature that resembled a black-furred otter took form. White fur stripes swept down to either side. The otter alien stood on two thick legs. Its two slim arms hung down to its curving hips. The shoulders flowed straight into a curving neck that supported an otter-like head that held two black eyes, a brown nose, sharp white teeth and flaring whiskers. The dome of a large braincase rose up above the creature's eyes. Looking lower I noticed a black-furred tail hanging from its rear, its smooth fur shiny under a white light. The tail moved lazily from side to side. To either side of the creature and behind it were nine other aliens, their forms far more bizarre than a giant walking otter. The creature's mouth opened. Inside a pink tongue moved.
    "Greetings to Captain Neil Skorzeny, manager of the Earth starship *Star Glory* and leader of two sister ships that have now reached the limits of your formation Victor Unity." The words stopped as shock filled me at the conversational English being spoken by an exotic creature from who knew where. It lifted an arm and gestured sideways with a black-furred hand that held four claw-tipped fingers. "As you can see, the bridge of my starship *Golden Pond* contains crew working at their function stations, much like your own bridge. My cohort name is Smooth Fur. Tell me, are your three vessels prepared to surrender to the Empire of Eternity?"

CHAPTER TWO

I will give the captain credit for not cussing out the alien critter. My Chief was not so restrained.

"Fuck the bastard," O'Connor muttered loud enough to be heard by me, the Spacers and PO Gambuchino.

Ignoring low comments from his XO, the other two captains and some of his Bridge crew, Skorzeny instead acted as if the alien's demand to surrender the *Star Glory*, the *HMS Dauntless* and the *Pyotr Velikiy* was simple Sunday morning go-to-church chatter over coffee.

"Captain Smooth Fur, how do you speak our English so easily? Or use our encrypted ship-to-ship neutrino comlink? And just what is your Empire of Eternity?"

Squeaks, chirps and low moans came from behind the otter-like alien. They appeared to be reactions from its bridge crew. Those reactions were not translated into English.

The alien's whiskers spread out from its muzzle, forming a brown halo around its toothy mouth. "Simple are the answers. First, your English was encoded in the primitive First Encounter program broadcast by your comsat. Second, you earlier spoke to your fellow ship captains using this particular neutrino comlink frequency. We detected those communications. The encryption was easy to break." The alien lifted its left hand and snapped two opposing fingers. A meter-high hologram appeared to its left side. In the holo was an overhead view of the Milky Way galaxy, appearing far more detailed and colorful than anything I had seen in my studies at Great Lakes. "The Empire of Eternity is the controlling body of this galaxy. You call it the Milky Way. The Dominants who reside closer to the center have given it the name of Warm Swirl. The Empire directly rules every space-traveling species in the four primary arms of Warm Swirl. My fleet is here because we are extending our rule out to the stars and nebulas of the fifth arm, which you call Orion." The critter's whiskers moved back until they barely stood out from its muzzle. "What is your response to my demand?"

"Captain," called Heidi the AI. "My firewall is registering 3,142 attempts to enter my digital abode. The attacks are arriving by way of this neutrino comlink and by riding atop the radio emissions from the comsat."

"XO, analysis."

"Sir, recommend we move to flank-plus speed and exit this star system," Kumisov said. "Also suggest we isolate the neutrino comlink receivers from all other ship systems."

"Heidi, isolate," the captain said.

"Isolating," the AI said, her tone sounding worried.

The black fur above the two eyes of the otter-like alien rose. "Human, your efforts to resist entry by our non-material probes will fail. The Empire has long experience in dealing with new and recalcitrant species."

The captain sat back, raised his right fist and gestured at the alien. "How long has your Empire existed?"

"Ninety-three thousand Earth years," Smooth Fur replied.

"How many species does your Empire control?"

"At the time we left our fleet base in Sagittarius Arm, the Empire consisted of 14,331 member species," the alien said. "Member rankings range from Dominant to Masterful to Associate to Intended to Novice and finally Servant." The alien waved one arm at some nearby crew aliens. "The pink floater belongs to an Intended species. His world is similar to your Jupiter. The scaly reptile nearby comes from an Associate species. His planet is similar to your Mercury in its heat, but has the oxygen-nitrogen air common to most Empire species. To my rear is crewbeing Zorta, who is a hunting cat similar to your tiger. She belongs to the Toka, which is a Novice species. Her world is very similar to your Earth. These three and the others you see are all respectful members of the Empire. As am I. My species is Notemka, a Masterful level member of the Empire of Eternity." The whiskers spread out in a brown halo. "What is your response to my demand?"

"Magnus," the captain grunted. "How the hell does this alien know about the planets in Sol system?"

Amidst the silence that ruled the Bridge, and a similar silence from the captains of our sister ships, the boss academic spoke.

"Captain Skorzeny, the First Contact audiovisual packet included visuals of all Sol system planets. Those visuals included closeups from recent visits to each world, plus digitized data on air, temperature, size and gravity field."

"Exactly," Smooth Fur said. "Your packet was basic but it has given us the essential data about your human species. Though it lacks data on your twelve colony stars. But the older image 'Earthrise' was quite useful. The starfield there will be examined to determine your home world's location within this Orion Arm."

"Fuck!" growled Major Owanju.

"Captain!" yelled Chang. "The alien ships are speeding up! They are at eleven psol and still increasing. They will overtake us within minutes."

"Engineering, move us out at flank-plus speed," Skorzeny said calmly.

"PO Stewart, activate—"

I slapped my control panel touchscreen. "Antimatter is flowing down all nine tubes, Chief O'Connor."

The deck floor vibration increased as the negative antimatter hit the positive fusion plasma. A digital readout on my panel slowly rose from 10 psol to 10.4, 10.6, 10.9 and finally eleven psol.

"Chief, we are moving at maximum flank-plus thrust," I called out.

"Chief," called Gambuchino. "Our fusion reactor is feeding ninety terawatts power to each thruster. Similar full power flows going out to Weapons stations, Environmental and to our gravity plates."

"Captains Jacobsen and Nutsov," Skorzeny called. "Follow us at flank-plus speed."

"Following," Jacobsen said, his tone sounding angry.

"The same," responded Nutsov. "I am ejecting Hunter-Killer mines. The People's Republic of Greater Russia will defend humanity from these satanic creatures!"

Laughter came from the image of the otter alien.

"So you use antimatter to supplement your basic fusion pulse spacedrive? Such a waste," Smooth Fur commented casually. "Truly your ships are primitive." The alien shifted its posture. "Zorta, take us to prey chase-down speed."

"Oh god," murmured Chang. "Captain, the twenty-seven alien ships are *all* speeding up. The three directly behind us are now moving at fifteen psol. They . . . they will intercept us within eight minutes."

"Astro, put us on a vector that will bring us to the edge of this star's magnetosphere."

"New vector laid in," Ibarra said softly. "Sir, it will take us ten minutes to reach the magnetosphere. Since we cannot reverse course I had to choose a vector track that takes us south of this system's ecliptic plane but keeps us away from the pursuing ships. The vector chord is rather long. Sir."

"Smooth Fur, are there any species in your Empire who are independent of your control?" Skorzeny said.

"None still exist," the alien said, sounding arrogant and confident. "Those species which resisted Empire control have no home worlds left. Any colony worlds were cleansed. Surviving members may roam the stars of Warm Swirl, but they are irrelevant to the life of the Empire."

"Captain," called Magnus. "The 'Earthrise' image does include a starfield behind the Earth image. But the stars that show do not include Cepheid variables, red giants or other marker stars. The starfield could be from anywhere in the Milky Way."

"It matters not," Smooth Fur said slowly. "Your home star is a yellow one. Yellow stars are less common than red or blue stars. We will find your home world. It will be offered the chance to join the Empire. If it refuses, all life on it will cease to exist."

"That is a crime against existence!" cried the XO.

More laughter came. "Hardly, subservient one. Warm Swirl contains four hundred billion stars. One hundred billion planets exist within its boundaries. We have not visited every planet. Which is why my fleet was resting . . . what is your phrase? Lying doggo? Anyway, this system contains a thriving Empire outpost of three life worlds above the gas giant. But it is on the frontier of our expansion into your Orion Arm. Earlier other Empire fleets crossed at the spot where your Orion Arm touches Sagittarius Arm, near to Nebula W51, which shelters our fleet base. That was three thousand Earth years ago. We have moved up the length of this short arm since then. Eventually we will control the full 10,000 light year length of Orion. And then the conquest of Warm Swirl will be complete." The critter's whiskers went flat against its muzzle. "You have short moments in which you may still live. Will you surrender your vessels and accept Servant status in the Empire?"

I glanced toward the Chief. Beyond him was the bulkhead vidscreen that showed the system graphic image. The twenty-seven red dots that were these Empire aliens were closing in on the three green dots of our small exploration fleet. We had weapons. We would fight. But no one in EarthGov or at Great Lakes had ever expected humans to encounter a body that ruled the Milky Way. From such lack of an imagination now arose desperation.

"Captain Smooth Fur, what is the meaning of Servant status in your Empire?" the captain asked.

Black eyes blinked slowly. "All species that are new to the Empire are assigned Servant status," the alien said casually, as if its attention were elsewhere. "It means your eight billion humans will follow any orders given by any Empire representative. Your EarthGov managers will answer to that representative. And you humans will provide food, minerals, unique biologicals and anything else the Empire desires to transport on ships of the Empire. After one or two millennia, and consistent obedience to Empire directives, your species may be allowed to advance to Novice status."

The captain gave a finger to the alien. "No thank you. As in, hell no! No human will ever be subservient to any alien!"

Behind the otter alien some of his crewbeings moved. They touched things with tentacles, pseudopods, clawed fingers or chomped on some kind of controls.

"Resistance is pointless," the giant otter said, his white-streaked black fur shiny in the white light of his bridge. "No species has ever successfully resisted the Empire of Eternity. If you cooperate now, it will be considered when my fleet arrives at your home world."

"And you tell your Dominants to go fuck themselves!" the captain yelled, his gloved hands gripping his seat armrests.

The otter alien's brown whiskers flared out into a halo. "Your death will be swift."

"Com, kill this comlink," the captain said firmly.

The image of the otter alien vanished, replaced by a true space image.

"Neutrino comlink connection killed," Wetstone said. "Sir, what about the comsat?"

"Detonate it."

A small yellow spark glowed in the true space image on the bulkhead vidscreen.

"Detonated," the Brit said.

"Five minutes to intercept," Chang murmured. "Magnetosphere edge is still seven minutes distant."

"All Ship! Go to General Quarters! Seal your helmets!" Skorzeny said loudly.

The overhead lights went to blinking red. Three loud horn hoots sounded. My seat straps tightened. I pulled my clear globular helmet over my head and down until it locked into the vacsuit's neckring. Then I looked up and aside at the rainbow shimmer of the AM tubes. The fields were showing perfect shimmer. Liters of antimatter were flowing down to join the yellow-orange plasmas of our three thrusters. My ship was moving as fast as it could. A new vibration told me the Astro woman had begun sideways jinking to make harder any targeting of the ship by lightspeed weapons. No doubt the other two ships were doing the same. A glance at the nearby bulkhead vidscreen showed the otter alien's image had vanished, leaving the overhead Bridge view and the faces of captains Jacobsen and Nutsov. They looked as worried as I felt. Were we all going to die before we could escape into Alcubierre space-time?

"Weapons, launch Hunter-Killer mines," captain Skorzeny said. "Eject six x-ray thermonuke missiles. Target them at the three closest alien ships. Detonate their warheads once they are in range of the targets."

"Launching mines and missiles," Yamamoto said quickly. "Mines are spreading to all sides. Missiles are moving at planetary escape velocity. Estimate they will arrive within target range in four minutes. Sir."

"Tactical, advise me on range to enemy ships."

"Sir, closest enemy ships are at ten million kilometers out and closing," Chang said, her voice shaky. "Three minutes thirty seconds to intercept point."

I wished I worked at the stern proton and CO_2 lasers. While their range was just 10,000 klicks, still, the enemy would not see the coherent green and red beams until they hit their ships. Or did the enemy have a stealth spysat now transmitting vidimages over a neutrino comlink? And what kind of weapons did this Empire enemy have? Surely they at least had our kind of lasers. Did they bother with slow-moving mines and missiles? Did they have a plasma beam? I recalled a Weapons course at Great Lakes where it was reported the

CERN scientists were working on a way to create a coherent plasma beam. Which was hard since pure plasma would dissolve any solid focusing lens. At the time I assumed the science geeks would use magnetic field focusing, if they could even generate such a beam. Now, theory was irrelevant. We were about to discover what this Empire of Eternity used to dominate thousands of space-going species.

"Reverse course!" growled Nutsov from the *Pyotr Velikiy*. "Leslie, Neil, we will do our best to delay these attackers! Neil, take care of Nadya."

Shock filled me. The Russian ship captain had flipped his fat spearhead of a ship to face rearward, toward the three closest Empire ships. His ship resumed thrusting at eleven psol, using antimatter from his tail particle accelerator coil to supplement the basic fusion pulse thrust. While his inward momentum continued, his ship's three thrusters were slowing it. Eventually the Kirov-class battlecruiser would achieve null velocity in space. Before that happened, the attacking ships would reach its position. The meaning of Nutsov's final words hit me, displacing mental images of spaceships rushing toward us. Nadya had to be the XO, Nadya Kumisov. Were they a couple? Had to be, otherwise Nutsov would not have spoken.

"Captain Nutsov, your defense of your comrade ships will be shared with all of EarthGov," Skorzeny said, his voice somber. "Nadya is here. She understands. She sends her love." The captain paused. "Gregorii, there is no need to repeat the battle of Leningrad here. We can all escape."

The short, stocky man laughed sharply. "This will not be Leningrad. It will be Kursk. My crew and I are ready to kill these animals!"

"Three minutes to interception. Five minutes to magnetosphere," murmured Chang. "Nutsov's range to enemy ships is three million kilometers and closing fast."

The green dot of Nutsov's ship drew away from the green dots of the *Star Glory* and the *HMS Dauntless*. It grew closer to the three red dots that were directly behind us.

"Nutsov range is one million kilometers. Enemy ship speed is still 15 psol," Chang said. "Intercept to us is two minutes forty-seven seconds. Four minutes fifty-one seconds to magnetosphere."

"Launch our Tsar Bomba," Nutsov said to someone on his bridge.

A fourth green dot appeared next to Nutsov's ship dot. Slowly, ever so slowly, it drew away from Nutsov's green dot.

"Heidi, filter all incoming space imagery," Skorzeny said bluntly. "And is your firewall still resisting their probes?"

"Filtering," the AI said, her tone now feminine. "My firewall is holding. I assigned four million worm-bots to fight the signal intrusion attempts. Which now number one million fourteen thousand and twelve. Neutrino comlink receivers are isolated. The Secure Block is intact."

The vidscreen image of the captain showed him nodding. "Good. Astro, get one of your people on Astrogation Deck to access the Secure Block. Obtain the coordinates for Kepler 22." He looked up. "Leslie, you should do the same. That is where I plan to head. But do not load the coordinates until we are at the magnetosphere edge. This bastard is listening to everything we say over this comlink."

"Will do, Neil," the red-headed British captain said, turning to speak to his Astro person.

Louise Ibarra tapped her control panel touchscreen. "Captain, I've got an Astro yeoman pulling those numbers. He will bring them here very soon."

"No need for the footrace," Skorzeny said. "Have him tell Heidi the numbers when he hears my order. The AI can set the ship orientation."

"Yes sir."

A brilliant yellow-orange sun filled the true space image that was the middle of the bulkhead vidscreen. Plasma streamers flickered and spread outward. What was this? The red dots of the Empire ships were the same number as earlier. With three drawing closer.

"Sir," called Chang. "The Tsar Bomba just detonated with 56 megatons of energy. The rad field from it is now hitting the three Empire ships."

I looked away to the system graphic image over by the Chief. It still showed three green dots surrounded and being pursued by twenty-seven red dots.

"No effect," Chang said. "Nutsov range is one hundred thousand kilometers. Enemy ship speed is still 15 psol. Intercept to us is two minutes twenty-seven seconds. Four minutes thirty-one seconds to magnetosphere."

Red, green and orange beams now streaked through the true space image of the nearby vidscreen. Where they ended there flared tiny yellow stars.

"Empire ships are firing lasers!" yelled Chang. "They are proton, CO_2 and . . . and *plasma* beams. Sir, the beams are hitting the Hunter-Killer mines launched earlier by Captain Nutsov. Also hit are the missiles he fired. The missiles had not yet launched their x-ray thermonuke warheads."

My gut churned. The Empire weapons range was ten times that of any Earth ship. While I had never trained on ship weapons, I knew the basics. Every Earth starship possessed proton and CO_2 lasers at the stern and bow, port and starboard-launching railguns and missiles that ejected from stern silos. That was it. Which meant this alien enemy could stand off at a hundred thousand klicks and melt down every weapons housing on any Earth ship, while staying far beyond the range of our weapons. Or the intense radiation front of the Tsar Bomba giant thermonuke, let alone the shorter range of our x-ray thermonuke warheads.

An electro-optical scope image of the Russian ship now appeared in place of the true space image. The 340 meter length of the fat spearhead was a powerful combat craft. Besides the lasers, missiles and railgun launchers that were common to all three ships, the *Pyotr Velikiy* possessed twelve decks manned by 381 crew, two dozen missiles, short-range pellet dispensers to kill any incoming Smart Rocks, active and passive sensor arrays on the bow, stern and keel, four dozen lifepods that would allow the entire crew to obey an Abandon Ship order, plus four space-to-land shuttles that could land on any planet we encountered. In size and shape it resembled one of the old *Gerald R. Ford*-class aircraft carriers, now long-retired and replaced by the *George W. Bush*-class carriers, which held 100 fighter and surveillance craft. While neither the *Star Glory*, the *Dauntless* nor the *Velikiy* held fighter craft or armed shuttles, still, they were a third of a kilometer long and were the peak of human spacecraft ingenuity. Now, this product of the Novosibirsk orbital shipyard was racing toward three enemy ships, its aim to delay them so its two sister ships could escape.

Red, green and purple beams hit the bow of the *Velikiy*. They struck the emission ports for its CO_2 and proton lasers, then the topdeck railgun launchers. Next hit were the stern lasers and missile silos. Large areas of the ship showed blackening. Several hull spots were warped or penetrated, with white air and silvery water globules spurting out. Now all three Empire ships concentrated their beams on the Russian ship. As best I could tell from the true space image and from following the beams back to their source, each enemy ship was firing four CO_2 lasers, four proton lasers and two plasma beamers. And that was from just the bow of each Empire ship. Which the scope now revealed to be dumbbell-shaped ships composed of a bow globe connected by a thick middle tube to a stern globe. The metal color was red-brown. Black and white streaks ran across the ship hull, similar to the pattern of Smooth Fur. Were all three Empire ships captained by otter-like aliens? Black smoke showed in the image of Nutsov and his bridge.

"Neil, we've got nothing left to fight with. Twenty-three of my crew are dead from hull punctures." Nutsov tapped his right armrest. "Captain Smooth Fur, the Russian battlecruiser *Pyotr Velikiy* surrenders to the Empire of Eternity. Will you allow my crew to live?"

The true space image of the *Velikiy* and the enemy beams that still struck different parts of the ship disappeared. The black-furred face of the otter alien appeared. It gestured aside to one of its crew.

"Earth ship *Velikiy*, cease your thrusting. An Empire craft will come alongside you. Do not resist our boarders if you wish to preserve the lives of your crewbeings. And you will address me as Manager Smooth Fur!"

"Understood, Manager Smooth Fur," Nutsov said. "Ship thrusters shutting off. Our mid-body hangar will open. It can accept your shuttle. Or whatever your ship sends over."

I looked to Chief O'Connor, not able to believe in the quick surrender of the swarthy-skinned Russian. He caught my look. As he also caught similar worried looks from Gambuchino and her Spacers. He shook a finger at us.

"Be silent! Let the captain handle this."

I turned back, checked the antimatter flow rates on my control panel, then looked back to the bulkhead vidscreen. As did Gambuchino, Gus and the other two Spacers. The image of Smooth

Fur was replaced by a true space scope image of the *Velikiy*. Blackened spots covered a third of its hull. Five areas had punch throughs with gas and water escaping. It looked badly damaged.

"Captain," Chang said. "Nutsov range is two thousand kilometers to nearest Empire ship, which is slowing to match its vector." She tapped her touchscreen. "Remaining two enemy ships are still approaching us at 15 psol. Intercept to us is two minutes four seconds. Four minutes five seconds to magnetosphere."

The captain looked tired. And sad. And thoughtful. Captain Jacobsen of the *Dauntless* looked the same. Neither said a word about the surrender of Nutsov.

The true space image of the *Velikiy* now expanded until the ship was a quarter of its size in the first image. To the right there approached a dumbbell ship, moving without exhaust thrust. I wondered at that. What did the alien ship use to move its craft through space without use of fusion pulse thrusters or chemical maneuvering jets? Then the angle changed and I saw the faint glow of fusion pulse thrusters. But how could they make 15 psol?

"Tactical, advise me on range to enemy ships."

"Sir, closest enemy ships are at three million kilometers out and closing," Chang said, her voice shaky. "Two minutes to intercept point."

In the vidscreen, the Empire ship drew up alongside the *Velikiy*. It was the same length and width as the Russian ship, best as I could tell. It stopped its approach.

"Captain," called someone on Nutsov's bridge. "Empire ship is within three kilometers of us. Engineering is opening the midbody hangar."

"Understood," Nutsov said, his voice gravelly. "All crew, carry out my instructions."

The image of the silvery Russian ship did not move. Nor did the image of the red-brown Empire ship.

A yellow-orange star flared in the middle of the Empire ship.

"Eat my antimatter!" yelled Nutsov. "Ship AI Nadya, comply with my final order."

The Empire ship disappeared in a spreading plasma glow as somehow, someway, Nutsov's particle accelerator coil ejected streams of negative neutrons at the enemy ship. Those streams of antimatter ended in a yellow star that filled the space where the alien ship had once floated in the cold void of space.

"Complying."

A new yellow-orange glow filled the spot where the *Velikiy* had just floated, making it two small stars that brightened a part of the void that lay at the far edge of the Kepler 37 star system. This was the place where the *Velikiy*, the *Dauntless* and the *Star Glory* had come in the hope of finding habitable planets for humans. Instead, we had found deadly aliens who ruled the galaxy. Nutsov had killed one such alien ship, at the cost of himself, his crew and his ship.

Death in space is always violent. And always silent.

"Goodbye, Gregorii," the captain said softly. "Tactical, how close are we to the edge of the magnetosphere?"

"Sir, we are still three minutes, twenty-five seconds away from the magnetosphere," Change said, sounding shocked by the sacrifice of Nutsov and his people. "Two enemy ships are at one million kilometers out and closing," Chang said, her voice shaky. "One minute forty seconds to intercept point."

I swallowed hard. Nutsov's sacrifice had not slowed the approach of the other two Empire ships.

"Neil, we are a bit closer," called Jacobsen of the *Dauntless*. "We are launching x-ray thermonukes. We will do what we can."

Our captain waved to the other captain. "I'm sure you and your crew will do your best, Leslie. Let us all fight!"

The bulkhead true space image now showed the silver spearhead of the *Dauntless*. It had flipped over so its bow was facing the two incoming Empire ships. It was not reducing speed, unlike Nutsov. But clearly it was preparing to fire lasers and to jink sideways. Tiny red flares said it was doing just that as maneuvering thrusters moved it further away from the *Star Glory*. Its actions made me wonder at the intent of its captain. That wonderment brought back the visual image of Captain Gregorii Nutsov and how he had suckered in the Empire ship, only for it to die in a cloud of antimatter. After which Nutsov blew up his own ship. My mind wrapped around the actions of Nutsov, then spun out a solution to our deadly dilemma.

I looked to my boss. "Chief O'Connor, I have an idea for attacking the Empire ships," I said over my vacsuit comlink. "Will you come here?"

The descendant of Scottish immigrants looked my way, frowned, then released his accel straps. He stood and walked over. Gambuchino and her Spacers watched us.

"What's your idea?"

I gestured at the shimmering tubes that surrounded me. Then I held up two gloved fists. "My left fist is the *Star Glory*. My right fist is the two Empire ships. See what happens if we shut off the thrusters?"

Surprise filled his face. Then he nodded. "I do. But we can't tell the *Dauntless* to do the same, can we?"

"Nope. The aliens will understand anything we send over the neutrino comlink."

"Pity. But combat is like that."

The Chief walked fast back to his thruster control station. He sat back down, sat back as the automatic accel straps criss-crossed his chest, then he tapped his armrest control patch.

"Captain, I am shutting off all three thrusters," he said over his link to the Bridge. "Trust me. This is the only way we will survive!"

On the bulkhead vidscreen the captain frowned. "We lose any ability to dodge incoming beams. Engineering, are you sure of this?"

"I am." The Chief tapped his control panel. "All three thrusters are shutting down. DT pellet feed is stopped. Sir, we *will* escape!"

Captain Skorzeny nodded. "Understood. All Ship, prepare for combat. Enemy ships are approaching."

I looked quickly to the system graphic vidscreen near the Chief. It showed the two closest Empire ships closing in on us and the *Dauntless*, with the Brit ship being slightly closer to the enemy. Maybe forty thousand klicks closer. The Victor Unity formation had gone dead with the death of the *Velikiy*. Now, it was every ship for herself. Which was why I had not spoken aloud my idea to the Chief. Who knew if these aliens could tap into the within-ship coms?

Red, green and orange beams shot from the two Empire ships and ended in space not far from the *Dauntless*. Bright red sparks showed at the end of each beam.

"They're taking out our mines and missiles," Jacobsen said, sounding strong and determined. "Bow lasers, fire on them. Don't give a damn what the range is. Fire on them!"

A pair of green and red laser beams shot out from the *Dauntless*, one beam aiming for the starboard enemy ship while the other beam aimed at the portside ship. The beams flickered out far from contact.

"Range of enemy ships to *Dauntless* is 22,000 klicks," Chang said. "Intercept to us is forty seconds. Magnetosphere edge is one minute twenty seconds out."

Two black beams shot out from the two Empire ships. They touched the bow of the *Dauntless*.

A yellow-orange star formed at the front of the British battlecruiser. That star quickly ate its way down the length of the ship, growing larger as the black beams ate into the *Dauntless*. In less than two seconds it was gone. A yellow-orange star glowed where once an ally had existed.

"Tactical! What is that black beam!" yelled the captain.

"Sir, sensors say it is antimatter! Negative neutronic antimatter, just like what we use for our afterburners. But it is coherent," Chang said hurriedly. "And its range is 20,000 klicks!"

Sadness filled me at the death of the men and women on the *Dauntless*. They had been good allies during this confrontation. I had never met any of her crew or her captain, but times spent chatting with other crew in our Mess Hall had conveyed what some of them knew from rousting with the *Dauntless* crew during our Earth orbit fueling. But maybe we could gain some vengeance for them.

A new yellow-orange star filled the space where the starboard enemy ship had been. It glowed in the vast blackness of deep space, outshining the distant stars for a moment.

"Yes!" I yelled. "Our antimatter afterburners killed that sucker!"

A new image appeared in the bulkhead vidscreen. It was the otter alien.

"Divert!" it said loudly. "Move up!"

I looked over at the system graphic image by the Chief.

On it were the single red dot of the closest Empire ship. Which now moved away from the ecliptic plane and upward, off of our inbound track. And thereby away from the dispersed cloud of antimatter that had been shooting out from our stern for the last minute. Kilos and kilos of black antimatter had shot out, dispersing slightly, but filling the space between us and the two Empire ships.

While the antimatter did not move at lightspeed or even planetary escape velocity, still, the widening cloud of antimatter filled our vector track. The track that the two Empire ships had been following in their determined effort to close on us and then kill us all.

Well, one of them had died from being too close to our stern vector track. And the surviving ship was now rising up and curving away from our vector.

"Range to closest enemy ship is increasing!" called Chang. "Distance is one million four hundred thousand klicks and increasing! Magnetosphere edge is just twenty seconds out!"

Relief filled me. My gut stopped churning. Chills ran down my neck and back. I closed my eyes, ignoring the excited words from Gambuchino and her Spacers. We were alive. And our chances for escaping death were good. Depending on what happened in the next twenty seconds.

"Astro yeoman!" called Captain Skorzeny. "Release the Kepler 22 coordinates to Heidi!"

"Releasing coordinates," came a man's voice that I did not recognize.

"AI Heidi, orient ship toward Kepler 22."

"Orienting. Astrogation will regain ship control momentarily."

"Good." The image of Captain Skorzeny showed him bumping his gloved hand against his clear helmet as he tried to wipe sweat from his brow. "Engineering! Activate the Alcubierre space-time engines!"

"Activating Alcubierre engines," the Chief said loudly as his hands touched those controls.

The bulkhead vidscreen's image of true space changed to gray. Only the overhead image of the Bridge and its crew people now showed. Across the room the system graphic vidscreen lost its image of twenty-five red dots that had been all too close to the *Star Glory*. Now, that enemy could not reach us. While the direction of our departure was easily visible from any Empire ship, they had no knowledge which star was Kepler 22. Or how far away it was. The Empire ships and Manager Smooth Fur just knew that one human starship had survived their sneak attack. And that ship had fled somewhere. And since our orientation had not been toward Sol and Earth, the Empire aliens had no way of knowing in which direction lay Sol, our colonies and eight billion humans. But how long would that ignorance last?

I didn't know. I just knew that my idea of releasing raw antimatter into the vector track behind us had bought us our lives, and time in which to figure out how to deal with this Empire of Eternity.

CHAPTER THREE

"You're a hero," Warren said from the other side of the table he shared with me and our friends in the Mess Hall. Which was very busy with lunch service. My Marine buddy had several sushi wraps on his plate, plus a sweet potato.

"Bilge water." I poked at the baked chicken breast that occupied most of my plate. Mashed potatoes, snow peas and a precious orange occupied the rest of the plate.

"Nate, you really *did* save us all," murmured Oksana from my left, where she had finished her meal and was sipping from a glass of ice tea. Our Russian émigré looked somber, as if the death of the *Velikiy* still bothered her.

"You're no hero," muttered Bill from my right side. The redheaded dairyman from Tennessee speared a piece of guinea pig steak which dripped with brown sauce. "But Oksana is right. Much as I hate to admit it, your antimatter fart idea saved us when it killed that Empire ship and forced the survivor off our track."

The last member of our hang-out team laughed softly. "You did good, Nate, and that is *not* bilge water. For a member of the Black Gang, you do have some good ideas now and then," said Cassandra Murphy, the only civilian at the table. Even though she was a Brit from Portsmouth, she acted unaffected by the loss of the *Dauntless*. Instead, the woman who was a foot shorter than me sprinkled garlic powder on the spaghetti and veggie meatballs pile that filled her plate. "And your math tutoring session is set for 1400 hours. Hope that doesn't mess with your sleep."

I winced. It had been six hours since our escape from Kepler 37 and the Chief had only released me from my shift an hour ago. Which had given me enough time to hit my Residential cabin, shower, shave, put on fresh black pants and khaki shirt, check to be sure my name badge was properly aligned atop my right shirt pocket, then head to the Mess Hall for this lunch with the only people on the *Star Glory* who gave a damn about me. Even Bill, a proton laser gunner from Weapons Deck who regularly torqued me, supported me when any enlisted or other NCOs talked down Engineering. Or called me a

Bilge Rat or Bilge Turd, terms that I had had to look up while at Great Lakes since they dated to old-style submarine and water ship days. Now I was going to miss half my sleep period thanks to the news from the only person at the table who owned a Ph.D., an M.A and a B.A. Her fields of expertise were cosmology, exobiology and anthropology, in that same order. She was my assigned tutor for the higher math I had to conquer in order to earn a master's in antimatter engineering while on this cruise. Which now was surely going to last longer than planned.

"I'll manage. Have you geeks on Science Deck figured out how those Empire ships can move at right angles without showing a drive flare?"

"Nope," Cassandra said as she lifted a fork of red-dripping noodles to her lips. "Maybe Oksana knows. Intelligence knows everything important there is to know, right?"

Everyone at the table laughed, including Oksana herself. She had emigrated to the U.S. at age ten to live with an aunt and uncle in New York City, then had joined the Navy at seventeen. She was now 28, held a master's in systems management and was a Chief Warrant Officer Two, thanks to her years at DIA and with EarthGov's Orbital Defense Systems directorate. She had volunteered to be part of the *Star Glory's* Intelligence crowd, though why an armed exploration vessel needed Deep Black intelligence types had always escaped me. Still, she showed a friendly smile to everyone, was patient with people outside her department, and at six feet was the only person at the table who came close to my own six foot five tallness. Shapely even in her NWU Type III blue and gray fatigues, I would have asked her for a date. She was outside my staff chain of command. But she was not Cassandra, whose curly black hair framed an oval face that I had fallen for shortly after we boarded the ship in Earth orbit. It did not matter that Cassandra was a foot shorter than me. But it mattered to Cassandra that her objective in civie life was to become top dog professor in the cosmology department at Stanford, the place where she'd earned her Ph.D. She had no time for romance. So I accepted the hour every other day she allocated to me for my study of tensor quadratics equations and similar crazy math.

Blond-haired Oksana gave a shrug. A sign to all of us who knew her that she did indeed know something. "Well, the XO *did* ask us to figure out that no drive-flare maneuvering the last two Empire ships did. First to pull close to the *Velikiy*, then later to move off their vector track at a right angle." She sipped her glass of tea, then put it down. Her bright blue eyes scanned the four of us. "My boss Lieutenant Gakasaki said he recalled a recent experiment by DARPA that tested a magfield spacedrive on a spysat out by the Moon. It was a proof of concept thing. DARPA wanted a spysat that could move without emitting any kind of drive thrust. Well, the experiment worked. It showed a small sat like that could either latch onto, or push away from the Sun's solar magnetic field. Which as we all know extends out to the edge of the magnetosphere. That might be what the Empire aliens were using. And how they were able to move at 15 psol, with their magfield drive supplementing their fusion pulse thrusters."

"Hmpph," muttered Cassandra. "That's the kind of basic research which should have been shared with great universities like Stanford. Or MIT. Or GWU. They've all got Defense contracts. We're loyal."

Oksana gave a sly smile. "Of course you are loyal. Otherwise you would not be on this ship. But civie universities and colleges are known to leak tech stuff. Which was why this experiment was tagged as Top Secret Compartmentalized." She reached out and grabbed a coconut cookie that sat on the sweets platter in the middle of the table. "Anyway, that's what my boss told the XO. As for how those ships moved at right angles to their vector tracks, that's obvious. They have inertial compensators just like we do."

"Bet you they don't have Marines!" growled Warren, an Aussie who hailed from Darwin. He was a full corporal in the ship's Marine platoon and proud of it.

"They don't *need* Marines so long as they have lasers with ten times our range, let alone that fucking antimatter beam!" grunted Bill, hunching his shoulders as if ready to pound anyone who said a Petty Officer Third Class like him was no better than a basic Spacer.

Bill's grouchy temperament was something we all accepted. It was part of who he was. As was his fixation on proving to anyone who would listen that being a farmer, a dairy farmer, was more important work than being a rancher, like me, who *only* raised cattle for the export market. Still, he didn't give a damn for rank of any sort. Which was why he sat at a table occupied by a civie research scientist, an Intelligence chief warrant officer, a Marine scout and a

Black Gang petty officer like me. Around the Mess Hall were dozens of tables occupied by men and women who had been released from First Shift. But close review of the tables showed that line and staff officers sat together, NCOs and Spacers sat in another grouping, the civilians sat in a third group and the Marine folks hunkered down in one corner of the large room. The groupings were not formally required. Captain Skorzeny sometimes sat with the civies and even the Marines. Still, naval traditions were something everyone had pounded into them at Great Lakes, at Annapolis or at fleet anchorage in San Diego and Norfolk. The fact we all flew through space in a starship the size of a supercarrier, guided by astronautics that were more properly the domain of the Air Force, that mattered not. The Navy had won the fight in Congress to have humanity's military spaceships labeled as the Star Navy. One admiral had even laughed at a hearing and said "Who ever heard of a Star Air Force, when there is no air in space?" No one on the committee pointed out there was no water in space either.

"Folks," I said, hoping to head off a pointless debate over tactics versus weapons. "The reality is that this Empire of Eternity exists. They control most of the Milky Way. They killed two of our ships. They are a threat to Earth and to humanity." I looked around the table, hoping for someone to bring up a light-hearted topic like whether Brazil would win this year's world soccer championship. No luck. People were either focused on food, or frowning or looking ready to snap at anyone who said the wrong thing. Which was likely the mood at the other Mess Hall tables, considering how we had just loss more than 700 humans in two starships that we had thought powerful enough to stand up to any group of Asteroid Belt rebels or long-lost generation ship colonists. But they had not been strong enough to defy the aliens who ran home galaxy. I looked over to Cassandra, who was munching on a veggie meatball. "Cassie, what's your take on those aliens we saw on the bridge of that spaceship? And their leader, Smooth Fur."

She licked her pale lips clean, put down her fork and sat back in her chair, her expression thoughtful. "They are predators, maybe even apex predators. They breath or need oxy-nitro air. They need gravity, though the floater alien that resembles a giant jellyfish may be a high atmosphere occupant. The reptile alien resembled a Komodo dragon sitting on its back legs. The hunting cat alien at the back of Smooth Fur's bridge was a tiger with manipulating tendrils under its chin. The other aliens on its bridge were equally dangerous looking. To me, that Empire bridge was filled with omnivore or carnivore apex predators. Not a touchy-huggy herbivore to be seen."

Oksana lifted her eyebrows. "And Smooth Fur? What do you think of him? He looked like an overgrown river otter to me."

"Okie, he's the most dangerous of that crowd," Cassandra said, pushing away her half-empty plate and grabbing her own glass of ice tea. "You saw his black fur with white stripes on it? That mix of black and white stripes is a warning sign to any other predator, or prey. It's the aposematic principle. Bright colors warn that you are dangerous, so best to leave you alone." She sipped some tea.

"Isn't that judging a thinking person by their looks?" Bill muttered low, as he too pushed away his empty plate. "I grant you they attacked us with no provocation. But why do we assume they are individually dangerous, rather than just following the orders of these Dominants?"

"Because they *are* dangerous!" Cassie said loudly, then looked around to see if she had drawn attention from nearby tables. She hadn't. The nearby NCOs and Spacers were arguing over who would win the ship's lottery for liberty when we hit a safe port. Assuming such existed. "Here's some examples. The honey badger has a mix of black and white fur, and it is a predator known for taking on other predators three times its size. Same for the skunk, whose black-furred spine is flanked by two white stripes. With white fur on its head. And the same white on black skin pattern is found on killer whales, who hunt in packs and are often called the wolves of the sea." She pointed at Bill. "So, Mr. Professional Skeptic, *you* go for a swim off the coast of Alaska when a killer whale pod is cruising nearby!"

Bill held up both arms, which showed his natural hairiness thanks to the NWU sleeves being folded back to his elbows. "Okay, okay. So I guess that means the reptile alien's red and yellow spotted scales, the red and black bandedness of the floater and the black stripes on yellow fur of the Zorta cat alien are all signs of natural born predators?"

"Exactly correct, my friend Bill." Cassandra's tone had eased its sharpness. She looked around. "People, there may well be aliens out there who are friendly herbivores, or relaxed omnivores who are not like our wolf packs on Earth. The galaxy is a big place, like

Smooth Fur said. And this Empire has not visited every planet. Or found every space-going species, since they missed us. And since they still have half of Orion Arm yet to explore." She folded her arms over her service khaki shirt. "But we've just found out that home galaxy is a jungle occupied by critters who will eat us for lunch, and then some."

Warren leaned forward. "Cassie, you make a lot of sense to me. So we ran into the galaxy's top apex predators. Well, humans are the apex predator of Earth. Do you think there's a chance there are other predator species out there who oppose this Empire? Who might become our allies?"

"It's possible," Cassandra said, then looked past me and Bill to Oksana, who sat next to Warren. "Okie, why is the captain taking us to Kepler 22? No human ship has ever been there, according to what Magnus shared with the rest of Science Department. Kepler 22 is 406 light years out past 37. So why go there, versus anywhere else?"

The woman with the highest naval rank at our table gave another shrug, this one different. From the few months I had known her it seemed to reflect thoughtfulness.

"The XO did not say. Nor has anyone from the Bridge said why," Oksana said, her hands spinning her empty glass in place. "But I think the captain is hoping to find either the underbelly of this empire or a rebel outlier. Every empire on Earth has had a criminal underbelly. And there were always outlying rebels who figured out how to escape the empire's attention." She grabbed another coconut cookie, in keeping with her love of chocolates, nougats and anything sweet. "And the XO did say we needed to get more intelligence info on this Empire before we head back to Earth. Plus heading to Kepler 22 takes us further into the territory already controlled by this Empire. That star is closer to the nexus of Sagittarius and Orion arms."

The Russian's speculations made sense. But they added to my concerns. "Well, then we either find help or we die on the vine. We've only got so much DT fuel. And just three months of food, even with the fresh output from the Farm Deck and Forest Room."

Bill looked to me, his smooth-shaven face somber. "You going to help raise more crops on the Farm Deck, rancher boy?"

I shrugged. "Might do that. But the food output of the Farm Deck, the fruit trees, grape vines and berry shrubs in Forest Room and the algae steaks we harvest from the hydroponic tubes in the Recycling Deck will not feed us forever. We recycle very well. And our oxy output from growing stuff is sufficient to support our crew. But we do not have endless DT fuel, which runs our fusion reactors and gives us normal space thruster power. The limits on any starship's range have always been air and DT fuel. Unless we can buy fresh deuterium and tritium fuel pellets somewhere, either we head back to Earth within three months, or we die in deep space."

Warren looked down at his empty plate. The sushi rolls and sweet potato had gone down fast. His big appetite did not surprise me. He pursed his lips. "And this trip to Kepler 22 will take sixteen days, right Nate?"

I nodded. "Yes. Or actually it will take sixteen and a quarter days. Our best Alcubierre speed is 25 light years a day. As you all know."

All four of them nodded, their expressions a mix of worry, somberness and thoughtfulness.

Faced with the sudden silence, I poked my fork into the lukewarm mashed potatoes and chowed down. My food might not be freshly hot, but a thing my Mom and Dad had taught me on our ranch was to eat what was put before me and my two sisters. Including veggies like broccoli sprouts, the taste and smell of which I hated. At least the snow peas were buttery flavored. And I looked forward to eating the orange, one of the limited outputs of the fruit trees in our Forest Room. When the cooks of the Mess Hall had to prepare three meals a day for 369 people, plus lay on fancy wine and scotch for the captain and senior officers, well, that limited what made its way down to the plates of Spacers, petty officers, other NCOs and civilians. Those limitations made smuggled aboard chocolate bars and chocolate chips the food of romance, or at least intimacy. Guys and gals were very willing to spend intimate time with someone who had a stash of nougats or Hershey bars. Plus, time to connect with others was essential on long voyages like the trip we had begun. We'd already spent almost nine days traveling from the outer limits of Sol to Kepler 37. Now we faced nearly twice that time in the captain's search for the criminal underbelly of this Empire of Eternity, or for covert rebels who had never heard of humans. It seemed a long shot, what we were now doing. But I wasn't in charge. Nor was my Chief.

The captain was. His orders we all followed. I just hoped he had good instincts for hiding places.

♦ ♦ ♦

At 4 a.m. the next day I showed up on Engineering Deck and headed for my station in the center of the cage of vertical antimatter flow tubes. Passing by Gambuchino and her three Spacers, I waved to them. The PO was trained in inertial confinement fusion reactor functions, while the Spacers were all graduates of the A-Schools at Great Lakes. Gus was an Electrician's Mate, while Cindy was an Electronics Technician and Duncan was an Operations Specialist. They did jobs assigned them by the PO. They waved back at me, their expressions friendlier than before our escape. Clearly I was on their list of Good Guys. Stepping through the rainbow shimmer of the AM tubes, I dropped down onto my cushioned seat, waited for the accel straps to criss-cross me, then tapped on the Systems Diagnostic checker program that was the first thing I did every time I began my shift. Green bars showed for all systems. Power flow, green. Tube magnetic fields, green. Antimatter containment field on the deck above, green, thank the Goddess. Inflow of new antimatter from the particle accelerator coil that wrapped around our stern was green. Replacing the AM we had spent to get away was exactly—

"PO Stewart!" called Chief O'Connor from where he sat at his control panel for the thrusters and the Alcubierre space-time modulus generator. "Leave that be. Come with me. The captain wants to see us. Both of us."

"Yes sir, coming." Surprise filled me. Then curiosity. I tapped the diagnostic program to automatic function and looked up at the overhead. "Heidi, please take over monitoring of my station."

"Assuming monitoring of antimatter flow station," she said, her tone lightly musical.

Giving thanks the AI was not in the mood to try out one of her practical jokes on me, I released my straps, stood up and stepped out past the shimmering tubes that made a cage around my station. The Chief stood there, hands on his hips, his wide shoulders stretching the fabric of his brown khaki shirt, while his black pants looked newly starched. He did not look up at me. Which forced me to look down at him. I saluted.

"Petty Officer Second Class Stewart is ready, sir."

His beady black eyes met mine. "Follow me to the gravlift. We have an invite to the officers conference room up top."

The short, stocky man twisted in place on his black-shining shoes, then began a quick march to the center of the room where the gravlift stood, a gray metal shaft that ran from the deck up to the overhead and through it, all the way up to the Bridge Deck at the top. The gravlift was one of three on the ship. The other two lay on the starboard and port sides of the ship. They served as backup in case one shaft's gravity repulsion plate failed. There were also stairwells on two sides of the ship, in case all power was lost to the gravlift shafts. In keeping with Navy, Army and Air Force tradition, there were multiple backups to all vital systems. Like fire extinguisher tubes hanging from each chamber's walls as a supplement to the automated halon gas extinguishers that ran across every overhead ceiling. And like how the ship's four orbit-to-ground shuttles could also function as space tugs to move the *Star Glory* into or out of orbit in the event she lost all fusion pulse motive power. Chief O'Connor stopped before the gravlift shaft, reached out and pushed hard against the Call patch that glowed red on the right side of the metal door that would slide to one side when the gravlift plate arrived at our deck. At that point the patch would turn green. Which it now did. The three meter wide slidedoor swished to the left. No one was inside the gray walled tube.

"Get your butt in there!"

"Aye, aye, Chief O'Connor."

Stepping in and then moving to the right, I turned and faced the shaft's exit door. Which now closed as the Chief clomped in, his booted feet causing the plate metal to echo softly. He twisted in place and face the same way.

"AI Heidi, take us up to Bridge Deck," the Chief said. "Do not stop for anyone short of the captain. Obey per security code Alpha Romero Twelve."

"Transporting you up to Bridge Deck per security code Alpha Romero Twelve," the AI said brightly.

The Chief's order surprised me. While Heidi would respond to any rating or officer on the ship, she would only obey orders given by line officers. Which the Chief was not. He was the staff officer who ran Engineering Deck. As were all the other people who ran the other eleven decks of the ship. As I had learned at Great Lakes, the AI had to know whom to obey as first priority, whenever any humans were present on the ship. Clearly the captain had given the Chief a security code that required the AI to obey his orders. This order was intended to prevent any stopping at intervening decks per service calls by other crew people. But why were we going to the officers conference room? I had never been there, nor had most ratings and NCOs on the ship. The man at my side did not act upset with me, just preoccupied with something. Anyhow, discipline due to an enlisted, a rating or an NCO would be delivered by his staff officer, not by the captain. Which fact was only a slight comfort. I did not like uncertainty in life. I'd had enough of that after Dad died, Mom had been forced to sell the ranch and she and my two sisters had gone to live in a condo apartment while I went to Great Lakes. Certainty in life was something I strove to achieve. Most people I spent time with seemed to appreciate that about me. But did the captain value me? Or was I about to find out how I had screwed the pooch somehow?

Since the Chief chose silence rather than filling me in on why we had been called topside, I watched the vertical transport bar that glowed waist high on the shaft's wall, just left of the exit door. Engineering was at the bottom of the 340 meter-long spearhead that was the *Star Glory*. Next deck above us was the Antimatter Fuel Deck, which occupied most of the deck. Only a single inspection hallway lay outside the shaft, since the massive doughnut that was the AM fuel bunker filled the entire deck. Next up was the larger DT Fuel Bunkers Deck. At thirty meters high, the several DT fuel bunkers needed only supercold refrigeration to maintain the integrity of the frozen DT fuel pellets. Feed tubes left each bunker and ran down the inside of the hull to feed Engineering's fusion reactor and our three fusion pulse thrusters. Other feed tubes ran upward to feed the mid-deck and topside reactors. The red bar that represented our position rose up steadily, passing through the Medical, Mess Hall and Recreation Deck, then the roomy Residential Deck where everyone slept, snored or studied independently in the hope of future advancement in their ship function. We now passed through Supplies Deck, the place of empire run by the ship's Quartermaster. It was rumored that anything could be found on Supplies Deck, if you gave the Q-master a proper inducement. Our red bar now crossed Armories and Weapons Deck where Bill and Warren had their stations, then

Recycling Deck, followed by Farm Deck with its Forest Room. That was a place I enjoyed visiting, both to see the chickens, guinea pigs, goats and small pigs that provided the meat protein for our meals, and to breath in the smells of a living forest. Magnolia shrubs and yellow pine trees put out competing scents in the Forest Room. I loved those scents and the musty odor of dry dirt leavened with green grass smells. It all reminded me of the big ranch that had been my home. Next we passed through Science Deck, where Cassandra worked among her fellow academics. We were almost there. The red bar passed slowly through Astrogation and Intelligence Deck, which reminded me of Oksana's insights about the captain's choice of Kepler 22 as our next place to visit. The plate came to a stop as the bar hit the top level of Bridge. The slidedoor slid open. The Chief clomped out.

"Follow me."

"Following, Chief."

My short, stocky and determined boss turned right, walked a few feet, then stopped in front of a smaller slidedoor. Above the door was painted Officers Conference Room. The Chief spoke.

"Heidi, open this slidedoor per Security Code Alpha Romero Twelve."

"Complying," the AI said in a sing-song voice that sounded almost like something from a *Singing With The Stars* televid program.

The door slid open. I followed the Chief inside. The big round room had control panels and flat screens on several sections of its gray metal wall. In the center was a rectangular oak table that had to be five meters long. Seated at the far end was Captain Neil Skorzeny. On his right sat XO Nadya Kumisov. On the captain's left sat Lieutenant Senior Grade Martha Bjorn, another Swede who had joined America's military forces. Sitting next to Bjorn was Major James Owanju, who was Bill's boss and the man who told other Marines what to do. The Black man was wide-shouldered, big-chested, sharp-jawed and had a shaven head. Like the rest of them he wore brown service khakis. Apparently the Type III blue and gray MARPAT camo fatigues were just for the lower ranks.

"Chief Warrant Officer Four Robert O'Connor reporting, sir," the Chief said firmly, his right hand lifting to salute the assembled brass.

I saluted too. "Petty Officer Second Class Nathan Stewart reporting, sir!"

The captain looked us over. His brown eyes were bright and intense. His smooth-shaven face was trim with not a jowl to be seen. His collar tips had silver eagles on them. No one at the table wore shoulder boards, let alone stripes on a dress blue jacket. Clearly this was intended to be a working meeting, not a public display.

"Welcome to both of you. Sit over by the XO. There's plenty of room on that side of the table," the captain said calmly. He gestured at the water pitcher in middle of the table. "Help yourselves to a drink as you wish."

I followed the Chief, who sat next to XO Kumisov. She nodded to him, her expression somber, as if the loss of her lover and the *Velikiy* still weighed on her. The Chief nodded back to her, then laid his elbows on the table, clenched his fists and sat silent. I sat to the Chief's right, just across from Major Owanju. The major lifted his black eyebrows a bit as his eyes looked deep into me. I licked my lips and gave him a quick nod.

"Thank you both for coming," the captain said. "Lieutenant Commander Nehru is standing in for me on the Bridge. I pulled these other folks in here, including Third Shift's Lieutenant Boxley from her sleep, for a simple reason. This ship should have died back in Kepler 37. The Empire ships had the speed and armament advantage on us. We didn't die. Thanks to a timely counterattack concept put forth by PO Stewart." The captain looked directly at me. "Tell me, PO Stewart, how did you arrive at the idea of releasing antimatter along our vector track?"

CHAPTER FOUR

Oh crap. "Sir, it just came to me. Sir."

Four sets of eyes watched me. The Chief turned and looked, adding a fifth set. The captain looked me over, ignoring the glass of water in front of him. From the ceiling and walls came a low hum. It was the hum I heard everywhere on the *Star Glory*. My blasted super hearing would not let up, even when asleep. Any unexpected sound in my cabin brought me awake with a jerk. Nobody else seemed to notice the low hum. Just as no one else had thought to do what seemed obvious to me. There I was surrounded by AM flowing down the tubes to the thrusters. We were not able to move faster than the eleven PSOL we achieved with the antimatter afterburners. We could not enter Alcubierre space-time. Our weapons could not reach the two Empire ships before their weapons creamed us. So it had come to me, as if the antimatter itself had spoken.

Bjorn's right hand tapped the oak table top with unpainted nails. Her blue eyes peered at me. Intently. "PO Stewart, what you proposed to Chief O'Connor, in a way that avoided vocal description and thereby the chance you would be overheard by Manager Smooth Fur, has never before been done in the history of the Star Navy. I know. A sideline interest of mine is the combat history of the Star Navy." The slim, trim woman who appeared to be in her late thirties angled her head to one side, causing her blond curls to flare out. "So. Did the antimatter just talk to you?"

My face felt warm. Had it flushed red? I hoped not. "Lieutenant SG, no, it did not." Mentally I searched wildly for something, any idea that would get me off this hot seat. "Ma'am, I'm just good at seeing what is wrong with a piece of machinery. Like when our tractor on our ranch in Colorado began jerking, then moving unsteadily. I realized it was the power feed from the photovoltaic panel on top of the electrocoil that feeds power to each wheel's rotary electromagnet." I did not say that I had seen a shimmer above the hood whose color did not look right. "Anyway, it seemed obvious to me that we were not going to escape on thruster power. Turning off the fusing of DT pellets in each thruster in order to allow the antimatter to flow unimpeded out into space seemed obvious. The ship would retain its forward momentum of eleven PSOL. And the loss of maneuvering power would not matter since the killing of the *HMS Dauntless* had shown the ability of the Empire gunners to adjust their beam fire to her jinking and jerking. Ma'am. Uh, Sir."

The captain looked over to his XO. "Commander, was turning off the three thrusters obvious to you at the time?"

The petite veteran of the Russian Space Force, who hailed from the Siberian city of Irkutsk according to comments from Oksana, looked the picture of high brass, with her silver oak leaves shining on each collar tip. She shook her head. "Captain, no, it was not obvious to me. In fact, such an action went against all my training at Annapolis and later at Moon Base. No line officer should ever deprive her ship of its maneuvering power. Sir."

Captain Skorzeny gave her a brief smile, his slim lips lifting as if by habit. Then he looked to both sides of the table. "Major Owanju, Chief O'Connor, did shutting down the thrusters seem like an obvious tactical option to either of you?"

"No sir," Owanju said, his jaw muscles clenching. The man looked away from the captain and fixed on me. "It would be like a Marine killing the blowers on his hovercraft lander and relying on the waves to take him ashore. Sir."

My boss slowly shook his head, reddish-brown curls not moving at all due to how close-cut his hair was. The man who had always been fair with me from the time I boarded the *Glory* now looked intently at me, his eyes almost glowing. "Sir, it was not obvious to me. And I have served time as an AM instructor at the antimatter engineering A-school at Great Lakes. PO Stewart has always been outstanding in the performance of his duties as the operator of the AM flow tubes. This morning, as usual, he began his shift by activating the antimatter systems diagnostic program that is standard on every Star Navy ship that uses a particle accelerator coil to feed AM to its thruster afterburners." The Chief paused, poured himself a glass of water and took a sip. He put the glass down. "But Stewart's actions in the last minutes of our time in Kepler 37 were . . . unique behavior. He called me to his station. I went over. He spoke briefly, then used his fists to show how closely the Empire ship was following directly along our vector track. With a nod of his head he indicated the AM tubes. I understood quickly what he meant. To do this counterattack required shutting down the thrusters. Which I advised you of by comlink. You approved that action. The thrusters shut down." The Chief, still watching me, gave a half smile. "Liters of antimatter flowed out, creating a thick stream of negative neutronic antimatter along our vector track. The Empire ship did not detect the AM. It ran into the antimatter and kept plowing through it, in the way a wet navy ship might encounter the wall of water created by a tsunami. The Empire ship quickly exploded. Smooth Fur's ship escaped solely because it was able to shoot off the vector track at a right angle." The Chief sat back and looked to the man who ruled our ship. "Captain, later as I thought about it, after we made it into Alcubierre space-time, I realized shutting off the thrusters allowed us to create our own antimatter beam, similar to what the Empire ship used against the *Dauntless*. Our beam was not coherent or guided. But it did not need to be. The close pursuit of the Empire ships guaranteed they would run into our beam. The PO's suggestion was a stroke of genius that saved us all. Which is why I sent you the email recommending him for a combat commendation. Sir."

The Chief had recommended me for a commendation? No boss I had ever worked for, either at Great Lakes, on our orbital training flights or during my deployment to Moon Base for six months, had ever commended me to a senior officer. They had all liked my work. Why had the chief done this?

The captain gave the Chief a nod, then sat back. He reached out one hairy arm to hold his glass of water but did not lift it. The brown curls of his head almost glowed under the overhead's yellow lights. Or were my eyes playing tricks on me? I saw deeper into the electromag spectrum than any person I knew, or had read about. I could see ultraviolet at the far end, far infrared at the other end, and even see the flutter of microwaves as they escaped from a Mess Hall reheater. So my ability to directly see the rainbow shimmer of the antimatter tubes without use of goggles was not unusual. To me. Clearly the captain thought otherwise.

"PO Stewart, this morning I approved the combat commendation for you and sent that approval to your digital file. The Quartermaster will deliver to you a ribbon, plus a sword pin that you can add to your rating badge." I did not look down to where the eagle, anchors and two red chevrons sat on my left shirt sleeve. Making it to an E-5 Petty Officer Second Class in just a year after graduation from

Great Lakes had seemed outstanding to me. Clearly the captain liked what I had done. But he had not called us here to confirm my commendation. What did he have in mind?

"Sir, yes sir. I will add the ribbon and pin to my service khakis. Thank you, sir."

The captain's face moved from amiable to intensely thoughtful. His eyebrows pulled together as he squinted at me. "PO Stewart, as captain of the *Star Glory* I make it a point to know the backgrounds and abilities of each person on this ship. Which is how I came to be aware of your remarkable eyesight. You do not need to wear the magfield goggles in order to see the rainbow shimmer of each antimatter injector tube, do you?"

"Sir, no sir, goggles are not necessary. But the Chief insists I wear them so . . . so some reviewing party at Moon Base does not have cause to cite this ship for irregular crew behavior. Sir."

The captain nodded slowly. "Yes, you do what is needed in order to keep me out of the gaze of the electron pushers at Moon Base. I appreciate that. Some enlisteds and NCOs are not so careful in their performance." The man lifted his water glass, took a sip and put it down. "You are also different in other ways. It has been reported to me that you can hear whispered conversations from a mile away. Or you did so on the parade field at Great Lakes. And from the far side of the Farm Deck here. Is that correct?"

Oh crap. I licked my dry lips, wishing for my own glass of water. "Sir, yes sir. That is correct."

Nadya Kumisov now turned and stared at me. As did Martha Bjorn. Major Owanju gave a low sigh.

"Wish my Marines could hear the enemy moving over the terrain that well," the large man said.

The captain raised his right hand. He showed two raised fingers. Now he raised a third. "Lastly, I saw a vidrecording of you lifting up Corporal Warren Johnson at Orbital Base Trinity, then also lifting up Spacer Third Bill Watson. That was outside the Barnacle Bill tavern on the station." The man leaned forward and folded both broad hands on the table. "Then you *ran*, while carrying them both, at a speed estimated to be thirty-seven miles per hour down the corridor, arriving at a corridor intersection in time to avoid the arrival of the naval MPs. That's as fast as a gray wolf or a spotted hyena. Is that vidrecord correct?"

Oh, may the Goddess save me! "Sir, captain, the vidrecord is correct. Uh, I got muscles from my cattle ranch work during my teen years. And I learned to run fast across our acreage. Sir."

The captain slowly shook his head. "PO Stewart, stick with the truth, as you have done so far. Do not attempt to decoy me with peripheral data. I've been subjected to lots of decoy maneuvers during combat trials above Moon Base. You can't decoy me."

Major Owanju chuckled. Lieutenant Bjorn nodded slowly. Commander Kumisov kept her black eyes on me and squinted. Her look was very intent. As if she were trying to figure out the puzzle that was me. Well, I had spent most of my life doing my best to hide my special abilities. Clearly those efforts had not worked with this captain.

"Sir, uh, I've always been good at anticipating problems and having ready a needed solution." I grabbed an empty glass, then just held it as pouring water from the pitcher while under the gaze of five people way senior to me did not seem smart. "That was how I figured we could use an antimatter stream to hit back at the Empire ships, before they got in range to laser zap us. Didn't need to do the math to know the AM would hit them before they got in range to zap us. Just knew it. Sir."

The captain blinked. "That comment is interesting, but not really relevant to the issue at hand." The captain sat back, stiffened his shoulders and looked at me the way a brown eagle had while I was birthing a baby calf. As if the sight of blood had aroused it. "PO Stewart, you have unusual abilities beyond a sharp mind. That means you are a tactical tool who may prove useful in future dealings with Empire aliens. And any other aliens we may meet at Kepler 22 and elsewhere. I expect to need *every* human tool at my disposal in order to obtain intelligence on this Empire, and to find a way to obtain DT pellet refueling, which as you noted to your friends was the controlling factor in how long this ship can stay away from Sol. Correct?"

"Uh, correct, sir." This captain was a leader unlike any I had ever before met. Somehow he had had Heidi call up the vidrecord of my lunch chat with my friends. Hopefully the captain had not called up records of my toilet time. "Sir, how can I help you and the ship?"

A brief smile showed on the man's lightly tanned face. "A good response. I can see why all the Great Lakes profs liked your work." Then somber seriousness replaced it. "PO Stewart, as your friend Chief Warrant Officer Two Oksana Rutskaya told you and your table mates, I ordered this ship to Kepler 22 in an effort to obtain intelligence on the Empire. Perhaps we will meet there what she called the Empire's underbelly, criminals to be specific. Or maybe we will find people who have rebelled against this Empire. That is less likely, in my judgment." The captain took a sip from his water glass. "You have unusual insights, in addition to unique physical abilities. What would you suggest this ship *do* upon arrival at Kepler 22?"

Wasn't it obvious? "Captain, sir, I recommend we remain in the outer reaches of that star system, beyond the edge of its magnetosphere. That way we can jump to another star if an Empire ship suddenly decloaks off our starboard beam." Another thought hit me. "Or, if our arrival spot is empty of other ships and people, we could make a short Alcubierre jump to the other side of the system. In fact we could do multiple mini-jumps to different parts of the star's magnetosphere globe. Sir."

Kumisov nodded slowly. Bjorn gave me a thumbs-up sign of approval. Owanju sat still as a rock, though a low rumble of musing came from his throat. My hearing again. The captain lifted his eyebrows.

"Good tactical suggestion, PO Stewart. What else? What other possibilities do you see in our arrival at Kepler 22?"

I knew I should have hidden from the draft. Mom's cousin Aunt Agatha owned a small farm in Manitoba. I could have gone there and pretended to be an autistic youth who had been passed over for the draft. It had been an option I'd considered in the last year of high school. But running from trouble, or from my duty, were never options I chose while growing up. Which morality had landed me here, under the steely penetrating gaze of a combat starship captain who was clearly far more thoughtful than the usual run of ship commanders I had heard about. Or maybe what I had heard at Great Lakes had been bogus bilge turd, if Captain Neil Skorzeny was a good example of the women and men who captained EarthGov's starships.

"Sir, the Forest Room on Farm Deck has some unique biologicals from the Amazon jungle. Medicinal herbs, sir. I've heard they were planted by Doctor Indira Khatri of Med Hall." The Chief now joined the intense visual watch of me. "Sir, our tech is likely to be of low value to any star-traveling species. But unique biologicals might have commercial value. Smooth Fur mentioned them as something Earth would have to supply to the Empire." I licked my lips. "We might trade some of our biologicals for DT fuel pellets. Since large gas giants contain hydrogen isotopes in their upper atmospheres, there might be some gas giant miners who pull DT isotopes from an outer gas giant and then sell them to ships that arrive at the edge of the magnetosphere. Sir."

The captain frowned. "Now that is insightful. XO Kumisov had earlier suggested to me the need to stay at the edge of the magnetosphere, though the option of doing mini-jumps had not been mentioned by her or by Tactical's CWO Hilary Chang." He glanced at Kumisov, then over to Bjorn, before fixing back on me. "The offer of biologicals as trade items has not been suggested by anyone. Including Lieutenant Gladys Morales of Farm Deck. That's two insights. You got a third?"

Wracking my brain while under the intense inspection of the ship's senior officers was not an exercise I welcomed. At least Nehru had been left out of this assemblage. Though no doubt the man would watch the vidrecord of me and the Chief when he went off shift. If the man did not ask for the vidrecord, it was clear to me now that Captain Skorzeny would order Nehru to review it. This captain missed nothing. I had thought grabbing my two badly drunk friends and running them to a cross corridor had been unseen by anyone in authority. After all, it was just what a friend would do for another friend. Now, all my friends might avoid having a meal with me in view of the fact our latest lunch had been monitored by the captain. I hoped not. Romance had evaded me. I dance poorly. I'm too literal in my thinking. And I'm socially inept, compared to other people my age. Keeping Bill, Warren, Oksana and Cassandra as friends was vital to me. Maybe the Chief would not tell them about our lunch table monitoring. That musing gave me a third idea.

"Captain, Doctor Cassandra Murphy mentioned during our recent lunch that all the aliens on the bridge of Smooth Fur's ship appeared to show bright skin colors. She called it aposematism, as in warning signs that this critter person is dangerous." I paused. The captain's intent look had not wavered. Lieutenant Bjorn was looking interested. The major was thoughtful. And Commander Kumisov continued to watch me intently, as if I were an antique Rubik's Cube puzzle she strongly wished to figure out. Great. "Anyway, Cassandra observed that all the Empire aliens resembled apex predators. If that is correct, then we can assume this Empire is run by other apex predators like these Dominants who seem to be in charge." I smiled quickly. "And Smooth Fur told the hunting cat Zorka to move his ship to 'prey chase-down' speed. Well, if the Empire bosses are intelligent predators, there have to be intelligent prey people. Whether they are herbivores or omnivores like us, it does not matter. What matters is that anyone viewed as prey by the Empire could be, or become, our allies. Sir."

"Nicely put. Better than Magnus himself put it last night." The captain looked right to Kumisov. "XO, what is your view of this little lesson in evolutionary biology?"

The Russian native frowned, then poured water into her glass. She took a sip, then set it down. "Sir, the observations of Doctor Murphy and Dr. Bjorg give us some idea of how to view other peoples in this Empire of Eternity. And you cannot run an empire the size of Milky Way galaxy without making enemies, and without motivating other species to hide from you, undercut your influence and seek every possible ally in that species' resistance to the Empire's authority." She nodded to me, then faced the man in charge. "Captain, I suspect there will be plenty of space-going alien people who will be just like us—tech weak and weapons weak species who are seeking help from other people just like us."

The captain looked to me. "PO Stewart, I like your insights. Continue your studies with Dr. Murphy. Learn from your Chief. Ignore Lieutenant Nehru's verbal jabs. I for one like a good steak. And when we emerge from Alcubierre space-time, make sure you are on duty and watching our All Ship video transmission from the Bridge. If you see something important, speak up! Immediately." The man looked back to Kumisov and smiled easily. "XO, I think the actions of young Stewart in Kepler 37, which happened thanks to his watching of our Bridge feed, are the best justification I can come up with for continuing to share live, unedited audiovisual feeds from the Bridge with the rest of the ship. Do you agree?"

"Yes sir, agree most strongly." Kumisov looked aside to me. "And while some of PO Stewart's suggestions are matters we have heard from other parties, they do reflect his rather . . . unique insight ability. Who knows, maybe we can cross-appoint him as our Alien

Ambassador?" She chuckled and her cheeks went red with the laughing.

The captain laughed also, as did Bjorn and my Chief. The major just shook his head at the mention of politics in a combat threat situation. I did not know what to make of the captain calling me up here to admit to personal issues I had worked hard to hide from public view, let alone to offer tactical suggestions. He had a fine Tactical officer in Chang, and a well-trained combat officer in the Marine major. My thoughts did not seem unusual to me. Most of it was obvious, given our status at a lone surviving starship on the run from the bosses of the galaxy.

The captain stopped laughing. His expression went serious. "Chief O'Connor, PO Stewart, you two are dismissed. Attend to your shift duties."

My boss stood up slowly and saluted our boss. "Captain Skorzeny, this has been most interesting. Thank you for approving my commendation suggestion."

I stood hurriedly, pushing back my wooden chair with a scrape against the metal of deck. I too saluted. "Sir, thank you for the commendation approval!"

Skorzeny saluted back, then reached out for the water pitcher. "Get out of here you two."

We got. A quick tap on the gravshaft wall's Open patch brought us our ride home. I followed the Chief onto the gravplate, then listened and watched.

"Heidi, take us down to Engineering."

"Descending," the AI said softly, her soprano sounding nicely musical.

I watched the red bar of our gravplate moved down past Astrogation, Science and Farm decks. Next came Recycling Deck. It always had a pissed-on odor the few times I'd entered it. Course maybe that was my imagination. Our descent slowed and stopped. The red bar held steady at Armories and Weapons Deck. The slidedoor slid open.

My best friend Warren stood there, looking distracted. But as soon as he looked up at the door opening, surprise showed on his face. "Hi there Nate. Uh, hello Chief O'Connor. Thought you folks would be stuck down in Engineering since this is the start of First Shift." He walked into the gravshaft interior. "Heidi, take me down to Residential," Warren said hurriedly as the slidedoor closed.

I nodded to him. "Warren, great to see you! Thought you'd be asleep by now. Why up so early?"

He shrugged his shoulders. "The major assigned me and five other platoon folks to work on installing a nose laser gun on two of the GTO shuttles. Before we arrive at this Kepler 22. He believes in being prepared. And he does not like the idea of visiting a strange ship in a weaponless shuttle."

The Chief shifted his position as the red bar slowly descended. "Good action by your major. Best to be prepared for the unknown."

Warren nodded, then looked to me, his relaxed look going serious. "Which reminds me of something I've been thinking I need to share with you, Nate. Okay?"

The red bar slowed as it crossed into the Supplies Deck region. "Sure Warren, what's on your mind?"

My friend glanced at the Chief, who stood stiff and focused on the slidedoor exit. Warren looked back to me.

"Nate, you may not get this cause Western and modern Asia folks are used to saying 'See you tomorrow!' to a friend they part from. But I've served in Somalia, Sudan and Yemen. In those places, people see death every day. They do not count on being alive the next day. So they never say what is normal to you and me." My friend paused, as if the presence of the Chief bothered him. With a shrug he spoke. "Well, everyone on this ship now looks forward to the next day of life. But with a change. They no longer take it for granted that they *will* live to see the following day." He smiled. "Your part in this is well known. So you'll probably get laid before we arrive at Kepler 22."

"No way," I said hurriedly, not liking this turn into my private affairs.

"Yes, way," Warren said very soberly. "Just keep on having your life-saving hunches, Nate. I owe a guy at Barnacle Bill's tavern a round of drinks. I sure would like to be alive to buy them for him. Okay?"

The red bar stopped at Residential Deck. The slidedoor slid open.

I nodded quickly. "Sure. I'll keep on being lucky in my guesses. Your bunk calls now."

Warren smiled at me. Then he lifted both hands and passed them along the sidewalls of his short brown hair. "Who the hell says I'm heading to Marine quarters to *sleep*?" He turned and walked out quickly, a lift to his steps I had not noticed.

The slidedoor closed. The gravplate resumed its downward fall. The bar passed into the Medical, Mess Hall and Recreation Deck. The Chief looked over to me, his beady black eyes bright. "Your friend is right. Lots of folks appreciate what you did to save this ship. Probably you will get laid sometime in the next two weeks. Don't let it go to your head. Focus. Focus on your job and on your antimatter systems. PO Gambuchino will take care of our reactor. And I will manage the thrusters and Alcubierre systems. We're a team, young man. Stick with the team!"

"Sir, uh Chief, I will!"

The stocky, wide-shouldered man leaned forward, his shoulders stretching the brown fabric of his khaki shirt. "Good. Now follow me out to our work. And don't worry, I will not tell anyone about the captain listening in on the lunch chatter of you and your friends. In truth, they are smart young folks. Stick with them. And like the captain said, speak up if you have another smart idea on dealing with these Empire aliens!"

"Chief, I will. Thank you, sir."

I followed him out into the warm, humming space of Engineering. It mattered not to me that no one else could hear the distinctive humming of each ship system, like the fusion reactor, or the Supplies elevator or the microwave units in the Mess Hall. So what? So yes, I was a little bit special. But no one person can ever be the savior of a group. It's up to the group to save itself. To be a united team. As I passed by Gambuchino, I waved to her and to her three Spacers. They waved back, their expressions happy to see me. That was something new to me. Something I really really needed, I now realized. My four best friends were the folks I knew I could rely on. But now, it seemed there would be other friends, other team members, on whom I could rely. It made my feelings of unease over our uncertain future easier to bear.

CHAPTER FIVE

Sixteen days go by fast. Now, we are just a half hour short of emergence from Alcubierre space-time. We will arrive at the outer edge of the magnetosphere of Kepler 22. A star which the Kepler survey of early this century documented as containing a single planet twice the size of Earth in its habitable zone of liquid water. Would there be more planets? Asteroids? For sure there would be comets. Every system visited by humanity had an outer ring of Kuiper zone comets, with a larger ring of Oort Cloud comets extending further out. A star's gravitational reach always extends past the edge of its magnetosphere. That was Cosmology 101, as Cassandra might say.

"PO Stewart! How's the antimatter flow look?"

I looked at the surrounding nine flow tubes. Their rainbow shimmers reminded me of a spring rainbow just after a rainstorm swept over Castle Rock. In short, the shimmers were perfect. "A-Okay, Chief. Ready to feed to our thrusters." With a mental curse I lifted the goggles that regs required me to wear and put them on. "Verified by goggle check. Sir!"

"Good." At one end of the room the Chief sat before his thruster and Alcubierre control panels. Like all of us, including Gambuchino and her Spacers, he wore a vacsuit with helmet thrown back. He tapped a control patch on his right armrest. "Captain Skorzeny, Chief O'Connor reporting from Engineering. Thrusters are a go! Antimatter injection tubes are a go for afterburner push! Sir."

I looked right at the nearby bulkhead vidscreen. It was live, in color and gave a top-down view of the Bridge. As before the captain sat in his seat at the top of the command pedestal, with XO Kumisov, Major Owanju and Dr. Bjorg seated below him. In front, arranged in a half circle, were the six function stations of the Bridge. Those stations were Communications, Astrogation, Power, Life Support, Tactical and Weapons. Seats for visitors ran along the back half of the circular room that lay at the front of the *Star Glory*. While it lacked quartz portals for directly viewing external space, its front vidscreen was large, measuring five meters long by three high. The screen edge stopped just below the overhead's gray metal. Beyond that overhead lay the inner hull metal, a water barrier to impede external radiation, and a thick armored outer hull. That outer hull was festooned with front and rear sensor arrays, the ship's electro-optical telescope for true space views, neutrino com transmission nodes and, to either side of the rounded bow of the ship, lay the laser stations. A proton laser sat on port side while a CO_2 laser station adorned starboard. At the ship's stern were similar laser stations, with four missile silos and the funnels of the ship's three fusion pulse thrusters filling the space between the laser stations. On the spine and belly of the outer hull were located sideways-shooting railguns. The Smart Rocks that shot out of the railguns were part of the ship's final close-in defense against small meteors and Hunter-Killer mines. During lessons at Great Lakes, and fleet maneuvers above Moon Base, I had thought the *Star Glory*, the *HMS Dauntless* and the *Pyotr Velikiy* were unbeatable warships. Now, I knew better. Now I knew why people crossed their fingers before they set off on a dangerous trip. Or just before they went into battle.

"Acknowledged, chief," Skorzeny said, both vacsuited arms lifted to hover just above the control patches on his seat's armrests. "Astrogation, what's the count?"

"Twenty-three minutes until emergence," Ibarra said softly, her Spanish-accented English reminding me the woman hailed from northern New Mexico. Her dark brown face looked young, though I'd heard from Cassie that she was in her mid-thirties and had a hubby and young kids back home in Chimayó. It had been founded in the 17th century by Spanish settlers, Oksana had added during our discussion.

"Life Support? How are we doing on the oxy-carbon dioxide balance?"

"Captain, the balance is Earth-normal," replied Becky Woodman, an Aussie who hailed from Alice Springs, according to Cassie. "The Forest Room and all of Farm Deck are doing great in producing fresh oxy . . . as are the hydroponic tubes," she added belatedly.

I didn't blame her for neglecting the hydroponics, which lay on Recycling Deck. Nothing good came out of recycling, including the algae steaks that the Mess Hall cooks mixed with soy protein to give the vegetarians on the ship an alternative to real meat. As someone who had seen real hot dogs being made in Denver from meat scraps, I understood her attitude. It was similar to mine toward hot dogs. A real T-bone, New York Strip or Ribeye steak were the real deal. As I had told Bill many many times.

"Power?" the captain said. "How are the reactors? And the energy flow to the containment fields on the Antimatter Deck?"

"Captain, all three fusion reactors are producing power at rated levels," responded Diego Suárez y Alonso, whose home was the seaside town of Fortaleza, Cassie had mentioned. "Neutron embrittlement of reactor vessel walls is miniscule. The armor metal is holding up fine. Power output can be increased with increased DT pellet feed. Sir!"

"Good to hear that," said Captain Skorzeny, his tone thoughtful.

Was the man planning to run the reactors beyond their rated levels? That was dangerous, or so I had learned at Great Lakes. But so was running the thrusters at more than their rated levels of ten percent of the speed of light. The captain continued his function station inquiries, listening to what Wetstone at Communications, Yamamoto at Weapons and Chang at Tactical had to say for their stations. It was normal command behavior just prior to emergence from Alcubierre space-time. Every starship captain wanted to know his ship could operate at its full rated capabilities. Including the ability to fight off pirates, asteroid rebels and now, aliens of the Empire. Would we find friendly aliens at Kepler 22? Would there be Empire starships hiding behind their sensor cloaking field? Would we be fired upon the moment we emerged? Course, when we emerged, we would be heading in toward the local star at eleven psol. That was our exit speed as we escaped from the Empire in Kepler 37. So it would be our emergence speed here.

"Ninety seconds," called Ibarra.

What? Had I nodded off? Where had more than twenty minutes disappeared to? Shaking my head I told myself to stop mental wool gathering and meandering among memories. I was part of a team. The same team that included the Bridge function stations and the top brass up there. My friends would be at their stations right now. Cassandra would be seated somewhere on Science Deck, watching her own image of the Bridge. Not far away was Oksana, in the Intelligence portion of the deck. Below them were Warren and Bill in Weapons and Armories Deck. Hundreds of other crew filled the other decks, all waiting and wondering about what we would find at Kepler 22.

"Heidi, if you see an immediate threat before I do, take action to protect the ship," the captain said firmly.

"Understood. I am prepared to protect this vessel," said the AI, her tone becoming half-masculine.

The captain's order to the AI was something I had never before heard, or heard reported from other ships. But as I considered it, the order made sense. The AI's senses were lightspeed-functioning. They included direct inputs from our sensor arrays and the true space electro-optical scope. If any being on the *Star Glory* would be the first to know of a threat, it would be the AI.

"Heidi, advise me on the status of our sensor arrays. Is everything operational?" the captain said, clearly needing to pass time.

"Ship external sensors are fully functional," the AI said in a sing-song voice. "Sensors for x-rays, ultraviolet, infrared, far infrared, stellar wind, yellow light, ranging radar down to millimeter wavelength, beta and gamma rays, plasma sources, neutrinos, gamma rays and microwaves are all activated," Heidi said. "In the realm of imagery, the ship's electro-optical telescope has its aperture open. With it we can perform speckle interferometry and high-resolution near infrared spectroscopy, in addition to true space imaging of planets and moons. Other systems include radar pulse compression ranging, PAVE-PAWS phased array radar, and ultrawideband imaging radar."

"Good. Maintain your active observation in all spectrums!"

"Emerging," called Ibarra.

The bulkhead vidscreen now changed. The Bridge image moved left while the right side became filled with an image of black space. White star dots filled that image. At its center was a tiny yellow orb that glowed brightly. I looked over to the other vidscreen by the Chief. Its imagery had changed from the gray of Alcubierre space-time. Now it held a system graphic image, with the yellow star located at the far left side of a top down view of the local system of star, planets, comets and anything else we might detect from our sensors and the electro-optical scope.

"Tactical!" the captain called sharply.

"No moving neutrino sources, sir," answered Chang, sounding anxious. "No stationary neutrino sources near us either. Sir, it looks as if this part of space is empty of starships."

"Understood." The captain looked to the left side of the arc of function stations. "Astrogation! Reorient this ship at a right angle to our current course. We have to avoid passing into the magnetosphere! Set us to cruise parallel to the sphere's boundary."

"Activating port nose thrusters," Ibarra said. "Sir, even if we thrust along this new vector track, our current track will still be headed inward until we counter our current momentum."

"Understood." The captain tapped his right armrest. "Engineering! Full power on the thrusters. Add antimatter flow to them. I want us up to eleven psol within a minute or less!"

"Activating all three thrusters," the Chief said. "PO Stewart, turn on—"

I pulled my hands back from my AM control panel. "Chief, antimatter is now flowing below our deck and into the afterburner nozzles. Antimatter is now combining with the three fusion pulse plasma flares. Sir!"

"Captain, this ship is now moving sideways at eleven psol," the Chief said, ignoring my anticipation of his order.

In the nearby vidscreen the captain nodded. "Tactical, talk to me about this system. What's here?"

Hilary leaned forward to stare at her control panel and at a holo now glowing to the right of the panel. She brushed her black bangs away from her eyes.

"Sir, Kepler 22 is confirmed to be a yellow, G5V main sequence star. Electro-optical scope true space view shows five planets! Positions are going up on the system graphic on our front vidscreen." The slim Chinese-American woman sat back a bit. I looked away from her image and over to the vidscreen next to the Chief. Its system graphic now grew a yellow star orb, with silvery dots for five planets.

"Details, Tactical," Skorzeny said quickly.

"Sir, planet one is a Venus-size world orbiting at half an AU out from this star. Planet two is the known super-Earth located at 0.849 AU, in the middle of the system's habitable zone. Planet three is an Earth-size world lying at 1.1 AU. It also lies in the habitable zone. Planet four is Mars-size. It's at three AU out, which is beyond the habitable zone. Planet five is a Saturn-sized gas giant! It's located at seven AU. There's an asteroid belt at ten AU. Uh, the local Kuiper Belt of comets begins at 38 AU and extends out to 43 AU. The magnetosphere edge is at 45 AU. We are at 46 AU, in the lower range of this system's Oort cloud of dispersed comets. Sir!"

The system graphic vidscreen grew dotted lines to show the circular orbits of all the planets and the outer belts, plus the edge of the magnetosphere. Our ship's green dot showed just beyond the sphere's boundary line. Our dot moved inward very slowly. To my surprise seven purple dots showed up one-third of the way around the edge of the magnetosphere. An eighth purple dot showed just above the gas giant. Ships!

"Captain!" called Chang. "There are eight stationary neutrino sources now going up! Seven are at the magnetosphere edge about a hundred degrees beyond us, while the eighth is orbiting next to the gas giant. They are shown as purple dots, sir."

"Tactical!" yelled Kumisov. "Give me a readout on those emissions. Are they Empire ships? Or asteroid rebels or Earth generation ships?"

"Negative XO!" called Chang. "The flavors of the neutrino emissions do not match any Earth fusion reactor or fusion pulse thruster. Nor do they match the emissions from the Empire ships that hit us in 37. Sir!"

"Heidi," called the captain. "Do the neutrino emissions match *anything* ever recorded from Sol system?"

"They do not," responded the ship's AI, sounding like Aunt Agatha on a cold winter day.

I recalled Agatha telling her grown sons to come inside, but only after knocking off the snow on their boots. The woman was older than my Mom by twenty years, and her sons had children of their own. But in keeping with the tradition of her tight-knit family, all three sons had returned to her small farm to put out bales of hay in the nearby corral for munching on by Aunt Agatha's four cows and one bull. It was a memory I cherished.

"Doctor Bjorg," the captain said abruptly. "I see no one to talk to or trade with at this location. Nor do I see any sign of the Empire in this system. I propose we do a mini-jump to the spot where those seven ships are clustered near the edge of the magnetosphere. Those ships seem to be holding formation there, neither moving inward nor outward. What is your opinion?"

The Science Deck chief cleared his throat. "Captain, recommend we travel to where those seven ships are located. By now they know we have arrived here, assuming they have the same neutrino FTL sensors that we have. Let's go there and see if their translator software is as good as the Empire's."

I looked to the Chief. Who was already looking my way. "PO Stewart, kill the antimatter flow."

I tapped my control panel. The shimmer of the nine injector tubes remained the same, but the flow rate sensor froze at its record of 2.1 liters expended so far. "Chief, antimatter flow stopped."

"Engineering, shut off the thrusters and the antimatter feed," called the captain. "Once that is done, give me a verbal countdown to re-entry into Alcubierre space-time. Astrogation, provide Heidi with the coordinates to those seven ships. Heidi, feed those coordinates into the Alcubierre space-time modulus formation program!"

"Sending coordinates," called Ibarra.

"Coordinates entered into the formation program," the AI said softly, sounding far more relaxed than when we had arrived.

To my left the Chief put out his hand to just above his Alcubierre control panel.

"Captain, going Alcubierre mini-jump on the count of five. Four, three, two, one—"

The bulkhead vidscreen showed the gray of Alcubierre space-time alongside the image of the Bridge.

"Exiting Alcubierre space-time," said Heidi.

The black space and white dots of normal space-time filled the side of the vidscreen that had held grayness.

In my mind I finished my count. The mini-jump had lasted just 41 seconds and some nanoseconds. Which seemed right considering we were traveling maybe 50 AU to get a third of the way around this system, measured at its plane of planetary ecliptic. I did not compute that distance number. It just seemed right, based on my mental intuition for where we had to go, based on the system graphic image and its depiction of this system. It was the kind of thing that my Great Lakes profs had marveled at. Before telling me to use my tablet to work the numbers and verify what I told them.

"Tactical, report!"

"Sir, seven very large starships are clustered about 900 kilometers from us." Chang tapped her control panel. "I'm putting up the electro-optical scope image of them on the front vidscreen. Sir!"

The bulkhead vidscreen's true space image was replaced by a different true space image. In this image there were seven red starships that resembled long pencils with rounded ends. No fins showed. Exhaust funnels were apparent at one end of each ship. But the scale at the right of the image was what shocked me. Each of those pencil ships was ten kilometers long! And two klicks wide! Each was larger than any ship ever produced by humanity.

"Damn," muttered the captain. "Those are biggies. Doctor Bjorg, is your First Contact program cleansed of the EarthRise starfield?"

"It is, Captain Skorzeny. The package is ready to transmit," the Swede said in a low rumble.

"Send it to Heidi."

The Swede tapped a control patch on his left armrest. "Sending."

"Heidi, transmit the program by both neutrino comlink and AM radio. Route any incoming response to Mr. Wetstone."

"Transmitting," the AI said in a low soprano.

Seconds passed. Then a minute. Then two minutes. I glanced around. Dolores and her three Spacers were all watching a bulkhead vidscreen near their station. The Chief was watching his vidscreen, which now had the same multiple images as the Bridge's front vidscreen. Those were the system graphic, the true space image of the seven ships and the overhead Bridge view. Which were also the images now showing on my vidscreen.

"Incoming neutrino comlink signal!" called Wetstone eagerly. "Sir, it is audiovisual and matches the frequency of our outgoing neutrino signal. Putting it up."

My bulkhead vidscreen now grew a fourth image next to the ship imagery.

Five beings who resembled orangutans stared at us. They had reddish-brown hair all over, leather straps that crossed their shoulders and which supported brown bags that held silvery metal objects, and a forward-leaning stance that seemed natural to all of them. The room in which they stood was half-filled with brown-barked trees whose thick limbs supported fat green leaves. Yellow balls that might be fruit dangled from some limbs. Beyond the trees that filled the room's middle were metal walls adorned with vidscreens and green vines, cupped seats before each screen, and six other orang-type beings who either moved from one station to another, or sat on a large branch, holding something that resembled an old-style iPad in their laps. No one was wearing clothes other than the leather straps and carrybags.

"Com, sound off," the captain said. "Doctor Bjorg, what are we looking at here? As in what kind of people are these folks?"

The big-framed man leaned forward against his accel straps. "Captain, they are bipedal vertebrate primates with stereoscopic vision who appear to be arboreal in heritage. Like us and like the orangutans they resemble, they have very long arms, short legs and five digits on each hand and foot, with opposable thumbs showing on each limb." The man gave a sigh. "I could speculate they are mammals and sexually dimorphic like us, but that will have to wait until they talk to us. Assuming they use acoustic sounds to communicate."

"How else would they communicate than by sound?" the XO said, sounding puzzled.

"Doctor Kumisov, they could communicate using pheromones like our ants and wasps, or by using skin color changes like our octopi, who are chromatophoric animals," Bjorg said. "Given their dense body fur, I would rule out skin color changes as a communication medium. They might also use sign language of a sort."

The captain pursed his lips, his expression thoughtful. "Communications, activate sound from this side."

"Activated sir."

"Hello. I am Captain Neil Skorzeny of the starship *Star Glory*. We call ourselves humans. We come from a world with trees that orbits a yellow star. We are peaceful. Who are you?"

The five orang aliens looked to each other. That was when I noticed one of the five was shorter and less bulky than the other five. That being stood at the far left of the line. The other four now faced forward. The central one moved its thick brown lips.

"Are you of the Empire? A Novice or Associate people?" the being asked.

"No!" the captain said loudly. "We just escaped from an attack on us by Empire starships at another star system. Are you a member species?"

Brown eyelids blinked quickly. All five orang-beings leaned against each other, brushing shoulders. As if in reassurance. Or some kind of group behavior normal to these people. I could not help wondering how similar they might be to Earth orangutans. Then memories from an evolutionary biology class at Great Lakes reminded me that bipedality is not restricted to humans, monkeys and the great apes. Birds roost on two feet. Some reptiles stand and run on two feet. Still, the resemblance was startling.

The central orang-being slapped its bare forehead with a left hand. "Never! We are the Melanchon. We refused to join the Empire. The creatures of the Empire destroyed our home world. We escaped with seven habitat ships. The only Melanchon still alive reside inside our ships. We use them to travel from system to system, seeking trade with those willing to exchange items peacefully." The orang-being stopped talking a moment to accept a red tablet from an orang-being who came up from the rear of the room. That person walked away, then climbed up a nearby tree to sit on a thick branch. "We avoid the long-settled parts of the Empire. We try to stay at the edge of the Empire's frontier, or even beyond among stars not visited by the Empire. We hope to find a system far from the Empire that we might make into a new home for the Melanchon." The being paused again. "I am a Mother, name of Hatsepsit. Beside me are three other Mothers and one Father. Do you humans also have Mothers and Fathers?"

The captain smiled. It was the first full-bodied smile I had seen on him since the Empire encounter. "Yes! We humans are male and female. We join together in families to have children. Those who produce children are called mothers and fathers. Some humans do not produce children, but study knowledge. They are elders. While we have hair on parts of our bodies, we come in different colors. Our heritage on our world of Earth shows we too first lived among the trees. Your trees are beautiful. Do you have many on your ships?"

Hatsepsit's lips drew apart and lifted, showing white teeth that were a mix of canines and molars. Her nose had a strong ridge much like that of humans. She also had ears on either side of her head, though they were partly covered by head hair. Whether she possessed nipples or small breasts could not be seen due to the thick reddish-brown fur that covered her broad chest.

"We have many. The trees are as much a part of us as are our children, who come singly after a long time inside the Mother. Each Mother brings forth her egg child to rest in warm sand." The female leader shifted her head, her brown eyes scanning her image of the Bridge and its people. "I see you humans come in two basic shapes. One form that is flat-chested and tall while the other form has a bulging chest and curved hips. Which is Mother and which is Father?"

"Captain," whispered Bjorg. "These Melanchon are monotremes. A type of mammal. They birth their young in eggs that later hatch. Two Earth examples are the platypus and the echidna."

The captain gestured down to the academic to shush. "Mother Hatsepsit, I am a Father or male. Below me on my left is a Mother or female. Some of my people that you see are Mothers and Fathers with children. Others have yet to mate for children. Uh, why are you holding place here, at the outer edge of this star system?"

Hatsepsit snorted, a sound that was translated as laughter. "We hold here because if we travel to the worlds inside, we could be attacked by an unseen Empire ship. While the gas mining ship that swings above the fifth world tells us no Empire ship is in the system, we have learned to stay at the edge of each star's attraction field, the better to escape into the grayness that allows travel to other stars," she said. "So we waited for the gas ship to come to us to trade gas fuel that we need for power and movement. Clearly you have learned the same lesson."

"We have," the captain said. "How did you pay for the gas fuel?"

Hatsepsit's shoulders rose up then down. "The usual way. We gave the gas ship items they desired. They gave us a small lake of frozen gas fuel."

"Does this gas ship accept minerals in payment? Like gold, silver, diamonds and such?" the captain asked.

Mentally I gave thanks for the superior translation program of the Melanchon. Clearly they had done the same as the Empire ship, taking our First Contact math and English words and then converting them to Melanchon speech. It made me wonder if we could obtain the device or software that allowed such outstanding translations.

Hatsepsit's eyebrows rose. A rim of white eyeball showed around the brown pupil of each eye. "You consider those things of value? Strange. They are common among the asteroids of every system. No, the gas ship people accept payment in unique biologicals, in what they call rare earths that are used to make special devices, and in technology they do not possess."

"Barter trade," murmured Bjorg.

The captain ignored the Science Deck chief. "We have the first two. Tell me, will you give us the neutrino frequency by which we may call the gas ship? We have need of gas isotope fuels."

The Mother flapped her elbows against her body. "Yes." She tapped on the red tablet she held in one hand. "It is sent. Do you enjoy the fruits of trees? We have many types of such fruits available to trade. Your teeth show you eat soft plant foods, like we do."

"We do enjoy fruits of the tree," the captain said. "We have several such fruits. We call them oranges, apples, pomegranates, mangos, more than I can name. We would trade with you while we wait for the gas ship to arrive. What do you need?"

"A new home," Hatsepsit said. "Do you humans know of worlds beyond the Empire? We came here from lower down on this arm of stars, hoping to find a warm world with trees not already occupied by people." She sighed, much as a human might sigh. "My family here are skeptical we will ever find a home beyond the reach of the Empire. But I must try. We have too many children who know only the closed in spaces of our habitat ships."

The captain frowned. "We cannot give you the location of our world of Earth. I belong to our protector group and we are sworn to keep our home world safe from this Empire," he said. "But if we could provide you with some stars that we know possess worlds, stars that lie farther out on our Orion Arm, what would you give us in return?"

Hatsepsit's standing posture changed. She leaned forward more than before, as if eager. "Tell me, your device for travel through the grayness to other stars. How long does it take you to travel? Our device is as efficient as the Empire grayness devices."

The captain looked down to the XO, then to Doctor Bjorg, before facing forward. "We travel 25 light years in one of our days."

The female's brown eyes widened. "That slow? You must be very new to star visiting. The standard in the Empire is a grayness device that covers 100 light years in a day cycle."

That was four times the efficiency of our Alcubierre stardrive! The prospect enticed me. And the need of the Melanchon for a new home world brought to mind an idea. Did it fit the captain's criteria for interrupting him?

"Chief, tell the captain I need to talk to him about this new stardrive deal! He needs to know what I know."

The Chief glanced my way, frowned, then tapped his armrest. "Captain, Engineering here. PO Stewart says he has info you need to know about this new stardrive trade thing. Will you listen?"

The captain's image showed him frowning, then he looked up. "Mother Hatsepsit, give me a moment to speak with my people. We may have the information you need."

"A fruit break is welcome," she said, looking back and catching a thrown yellow globe that must be some kind of fruit. "I await your proposal."

"Stewart! Spill it fast."

CHAPTER SIX

My heart beat fast as I realized I was talking to the entire ship, not just the captain, thanks to his order of an All Ship broadcast of what happened on the Bridge.

"Captain, Doctor Bjorg and Doctor Murphy can provide you with lists of stars that have known exo-planets in the upper part of Orion Arm," I said quickly. "Those lists will get you the fast Alcubierre stardrive device. But these Melanchon, and we humans, need *more* than a place of refuge. When you offer the star lists, why don't you suggest these Melanchon put out a neutrino signaling satellite above the world they occupy? If the Empire ships show up in their new system, they can send out an FTL call for help to us. And to any other refugee aliens we encounter in the Empire space." I licked my lips. "Call it a NATO of the Stars. At Great Lakes I learned how NATO prevented World War III during the last century and into this century, until the collapse of the Putin Era made it less essential. That's my idea, sir."

The captain squinted. "A good idea, Stewart." He looked ahead. "Communications, are there unused neutrino comlink frequencies?"

Wetstone looked back from his station. "There are plenty, captain. There are billions of neutrino comlink frequencies. That is why we never heard these Empire ships talking with each other. And why they have not heard Earth ships talking at our colony stars. These Melanchon copied our signal frequency to talk with us. Surely they have their own frequency they use among their ships." The Brit frowned thoughtfully. "And since neutrino comlink signals travel faster-than-light through an alternate dimension, we could hear a call for help as soon as it was sent. Sir."

"Doctor Bjorg," the captain said looking down and to his right. "How many stars with confirmed exo-planets do we know of that lie uparm, beyond Earth and Sol?"

"Hundreds," the Swede said quickly. "While the Kepler survey documented more than 4,000 exo-planets lying in the downarm part of Orion Arm that we now know is controlled by the

Empire, other surveys documented hundreds of other stars with planets in the uparm direction." The large man shifted in his seat to look up to the captain. "The major surveys labeled stars as HD or SAO with a number, for the Henry Draper and Smithsonian Astrophysical Observatory surveys. Other observatories in Chile, Hawaii and by way of orbital scopes documented other stars with planets. Sir, we have a major trade item of great value to these Melanchon folks."

Captain Skorzeny slapped his hands together. "Yes! We can get a quadrupling of our Alcubierre speed and maybe create this NATO of the Stars that Stewart suggests." He looked down. "XO, your thoughts on the NATO thing?"

Kumisov cleared her throat. "Captain, I like the proposal. We can ask these Melanchon to put up such a neutrino sat when they find a new home planet. It costs them nothing and allows them contact with us, and maybe with other refugee peoples. If EarthGov does not endorse a mutual defense treaty with aliens, well, at least we have a means of talking to them that is faster than a starship trip."

"Those are my thoughts too," the captain said. "Com, activate sound on our side."

"Activated."

"Mother Hatsepsit, my people tell me we have records of hundreds of stars with known planets that exist further up this arm," the captain said slowly. "Many of those worlds lie within the liquid water habitability zone. Some stars are yellow, some white-yellow and some orange, which we call G, F and K-class stars. How do we do this trade?"

The orang leaned forward eagerly. "Wonderful news! While we have our own star watchers, we have been too busy just surviving and avoiding Empire ships to undertake a careful survey of the upper part of this arm. We are most interested in yellow stars with warm worlds and trees, as you can see from our Leaders Chamber." She looked right. "The Father of my family is there, at the end of this row. His signifier is Woktaken. Like most males he is an explorer and innovator, while we Mothers have created the world culture that led us into the dark cold spaces between stars. I will send him to your ship with the plans for our grayness device. Maybe he can adapt your own device to work like ours. If not, he will show you how to build a more efficient one. Would this satisfy you?"

"It would," the captain said. "I have a female who is not yet a Mother but she is an expert on stars and nebulas of Orion Arm. Her name is Cassandra Murphy. I will send her and her leader, Father Magnus Bjorg to your ship. They will bring devices with the needed information for you to locate these stars with planets. In some cases our data includes the size of the planet, how far out it orbits and the nature of its home star. Will that satisfy you?"

"It will," Hatsepsit said. "And since you humans enjoy fruits of the trees, I will send a container of our fruits with Woktaken when he travels to your ship. Is this agreeable?"

"Most agreeable," the captain said, slapping his ribs with his elbows in imitation of the pleased gesture of the orang-being. "Our trade of star locations with you offers you and us more than an equal trade. We humans have a history of banding together for mutual defense. It has worked well to preserve peoples and cultures through our history." He tapped a patch on his right armrest. A holo took form to his right. It showed a slowly rotating Earth. "This is our home world of Earth. We hope to protect it from attack by the Empire. You will surely find a similar world for your Melanchon people. I suggest you put in orbit a device that sends out neutrino signals on a frequency unknown to the Empire. If the Empire arrives at your new home, you can ask us for help in fighting them. If the Empire arrives at Earth, we would ask you for similar fighting help. Perhaps we can find other peoples fleeing the Empire who would do the same. Do you like this mutual defense idea?"

The five orang-beings bumped shoulders. Then Hatsepsit leaned forward. "We like this idea. It is similar to what our Fathers did early in our history when we settled new lands and had to fight off animal predators. The Empire is a group of terrible and hungry predators. No other people should lose their home world like we did."

"Thank you," the captain said softly. "When I send our Father and Mother-To-Be to you, they will provide you with this special neutrino frequency. Perhaps you will let us know when you arrive at a warm world."

"We will call you. Now, your star people are welcome to visit us. Our trees will welcome them."

The captain smiled again. "I am sure they will enjoy giving your trees a hug. That is something we humans do with our trees."

"Most welcome that is!" Hatsepsit said, sounding surprised. "We Melanchon bring our newly hatched children to their family heritage tree to see the marks on it from their ancestors. The children always hug that tree. Do you have trees on your ship?"

"We do, in what we call our Forest Room," the captain said. "You and other Mothers are welcome to visit and see our trees. Perhaps those who study trees and other living things can each visit the other's ship?"

"Very most welcome that is!" Hatsepsit looked to her right. "Woktaken, go obtain the grayness device tablet. Take it and our fruit out to these humans." She looked back forward. "Our small transport device will visit you in one-tenth of our day cycle. Your own transport device may come when you wish to send it."

"I suspect our people will be eager to visit you," the captain said. "While they are visiting you we will call the gas mining craft to come visit us. We have need of gas isotopes. But we are even more in need of finding friends like you Melanchon. Let us trade together and both benefit. I end this discussion for now. Call me whenever you wish. And we look forward to the arrival of Woktaken."

"He will come soon. Perhaps with the help of another Father, and one of our family Mothers to keep the males from arguing too much!" she said.

I almost laughed. This Mother who led her people sounded so much like Aunt Agatha! My aunt was the boss of her family and a person who knew how to get things done in the family. Clearly these Mothers knew how to use their Fathers to the best advantage of both genders.

The captain did laugh. "Woktaken and helpers are welcome here. For now, I close this discussion so I may prepare our team to visit you. Until . . . until we speak again."

"Until we speak again," Hatsepsit said, touching the tablet in her hand.

Her image vanished, leaving only the true space image of her seven ships. On either side were the system graphic and the overhead Bridge view. The vanishing of the orang-beings left me feeling eager. And exposed. While the captain had liked my NATO of the Stars idea, I had spoken before the entire ship. For sure Lieutenant Commander Nehru would have something to say about me being a "show off".

"PO Stewart."

I looked back to the Bridge image. The captain was looking up at the overhead videye. I gulped. "Captain? Uh, sir, how many I assist you?"

The man's thoughtful expression did not change. "*You* will leave with Doctor Murphy and Doctor Bjorg for the trip to the Melanchon ship. Along with Lieutenant Morales who bring some Farm Deck stuff for our new friends. Chief O'Connor can handle the Alcubierre upgrade chat with this Haktoken without your help. I want you over on that big ship as my eyes and ears. And to alert me to anything unusual you may see there, or any tech devices we might need beyond this fast Alcubierre device. Get moving!"

That order meant I had to rendezvous with the two star geeks at the ship's midbody hangar, where the four GTO shuttles were stored. "Sir, yes sir." I stood up. "Captain, may I suggest a Marine or two accompany us? It would give our people a chance to learn a few things about how these Melanchon people fight. And the kind of ship weapons they possess. Sir."

He frowned. "So you want another of your lunch friends to go with you besides Doctor Murphy? Fine. Grab Corporal Johnson." The captain looked down. "Major Owanju, go with these people. And take Chief Rutskaya of Intelligence with you. Might as well have another Mother-To-Be on this visit!"

The Marine boss unsnapped his straps and stood up. He faced the captain and saluted. "Sir, heading out! I'll grab the people you mentioned."

I unsnapped my accel straps, stood up and looked over to my boss, whose beady eyes had been watching me the whole time I was shelling out my NATO scheme to the captain. "Chief, may I leave my post?"

"Of course you may short-circuit your shift! I'll get Heidi to monitor the antimatter containment fields. Get moving! The captain expects performance over jawing."

I turned and ran for the gravshaft pillar. There was a recording tablet I wanted to take with me, along with a change of clothes, a snack and a bottle of water. Who knew how long I would be over there? I just hoped I could repay the captain's faith in my off the beaten path ideas. Which brought to mind another idea. The reason our ship could not directly contact EarthGov via a ship-to-ship neutrino comlink frequency was because that frequency was changed on a daily basis by EarthGov, to avoid hacking or jamming of our communications by remnants of the Asteroid Belt rebels or by roaming pirates. Well, maybe when we got back to Earth we could get EarthGov to always listen in on this NATO call-out frequency? That would allow other starships to warn Earth of events like the discovery of this Empire of Eternity!

The red bar of the gravplate rose up and up until it hit Residential Deck. I ran through the open slidedoor, turned left and headed for my cabin. While running I wondered if Cassandra would be appreciative enough of her inclusion in this trip to have a dinner date with me? But it would be just like my bad dating luck to have Oksana insist on joining us, thereby minimizing my chances for a kiss. Assuming Cassie even thought of me in those ways. Well, being with her on a strange alien starship might loosen her up. I hoped so. It was great she was one of my four closest friends. Having some romance in my life would be even better!

♦ ♦ ♦

The shuttle seemed crowded. There were only nine people in the ten meter-long cargohold. Me, Cassie, Oksana, Warren, Major Owanju, Bill who had been grabbed by the major, Doctor Bjorg, Lieutenant Morales from Farm Deck, and a Science Deck evolutionary biologist by the name of Evelyn Kierkgaard. But we all wore orange and white-striped vacsuits with our globular helmets sealed to our neckrings. Also filling the cargohold were two large cartons of fruit, which represented a week's worth of fruit normally served in the Mess Hall. The cooks had complained loudly, according to what Bill told me as we boarded. Clearly they had been overridden by the Farm Deck lieutenant, who had met us in the hangar bay with two floater cartons, smiling and eager for this visit to a new biome.

Now, we all sat silent, our eyes on a holo that floated in the middle of the cargohold aisle. It showed the cluster of seven red pencil ships that we were approaching. We could talk over the vacsuit radio comlink. But such was discouraged by the shuttle pilot. Who was not the rating normally assigned to this shuttle. Instead, Hilary Chang had somehow gotten leave from the captain and now flew us the 900 klicks to the giant pencil that was Hatsepsit's ship. Clearly the

Tactical chief wanted a first-hand view of the outside and inside of an alien starship. Which made sense given her Tactical role. Me, I didn't care. While the woman from San Francisco had been courteous to us as we boarded, she was not someone I had ever spent time with. Nor had I spent time with Major Owanju. Hanging with the Bridge crew was just not done by enlisteds, NCOs and civilian geeks. But now, here we were, a strange mix of ranks, expertise and hopes.

"Doctor Murphy, did you scrub the RA and Galco coordinates from our star list?" called Bjorg over the vacsuit radio.

"Of course!" my friend said, clearly irritated. "I know as well as you that Right Ascension and Galactic Coordinate numbers for each star are based on sightlines from Earth." Cassandra sat across from me on the bench that ran parallel to the starboard side of the shuttle. She crossed arms over her belly, a frown on her pretty face. "Instead I substituted numbers based on angle and declination relative to the Sagittarius A radio source at the galaxy's center. Would you have done otherwise?"

I looked right to where the Swede sat at the end of the line of people on the starboard side. The man had his thick blond mane pulled back into a ponytail. The hair detail reminded me of decades-old images I'd seen of people from early this century. Then, lots of men had ponytails, both genders had piles of tattoos on their arms and bodies, and their music was a grinding roar that hurt my ears the last time I had listened to it. My Mom and Dad had belonged to the Natural generation that rejected such additions to the basic human form. No tattoos for them. No artificial hair colors like purple, green or blue. No ponytails for the men. And women had gone back to ankle-length dresses, despite the functional utility of pantsuits. Thank the Goddess my generation was more sensible. People my age often had a small tattoo or two. Some men wore earrings of precious stones. A few women dyed their hair green or blue using food dyes. Women wore pants and shorts as they wished. But no one my age deformed their ear lobes with the giant rings that had been favored by the people called Gen X. Whatever that term meant. Bjorg's arms and upper chest were clear of tattoos, based on what I'd seen before he put on his vacsuit. Same for Major Owanju, although the Marine did have an anchor and trident tattoo on his left bicep. The chief of Science Deck looked toward Cassie, his expression impatient.

"Doctor Murphy, using Sag A as the coordinate reference point is what I would have done. I'm sure you did a fine job of filtering out location data relevant to Earth."

Cassie pursed her lips, still looking bothered. "Thank you, Doctor Bjorg. Now shall we discuss something new?" She pointed at the holo in the aisle. "I note the seven red pencil ships are all rotating about their central axis, like spindles. Do you think that means the Melanchon do not possess gravity plates?"

"Most interesting," the chief geek murmured as he leaned forward against the seat restraint straps, peering at the holo. "The image of their bridge showed them moving about as if they had normal gravity on that deck. Which reminds me, do we *know* what their normal gravity level is? One gee? Less? More?"

"Nine-tenths gee," interjected Hilary Chang from her pilot bubble. "And if case you have forgotten the basics about visiting new biomes, I confirmed their hangar has sterilization chambers that we all have to enter before we meet any live Melanchon. Check the holo." In the holo, one red pencil ship grew larger. Our vector track curved toward its front end. A big black hole showed in the middle of the rounded end of the ship. Clearly it was the intended entry point for us. "They do not want to take chances with any Earth bugs. They do the same as we do when anyone arrives from a colony planet, or someone visits a colony orbital station."

"Well," called Bill from my left. "Has there ever been a case of any colony world germ hurting a human? Or vice versa?"

"No such case exists," Oksana said from my right side. "But standard precautions make sense. For us and for them. They are the last survivors of their species. They surely do not wish to die from a human bug!"

"Shut up!" called Chang. "Time for me to link in with their hangar control. You can chatter later in the decontam chambers. That way you can pretend to not notice each other's flabby bodies!"

We all shut up. But Tactical's sarcastic comment reminded me this would be my first chance to see Cassie naked. Oksana too. I liked that. But what would they think of me? I was tall, had adequate pecs from stacking hay bales in our barn, and a bit of chest hair. No one at Great Lakes had ever teased me as being a skinny geek during our swims off the beaches of Chicago. Course the waters of Lake Michigan are cold no matter the season. Which had interesting effects on parts of both female and male anatomy. I told myself to stop being a voyeur. I'd shared mixed showers after unit marches at Great Lakes. It was something I could handle. But I'd never seen any of my lunch table friends without clothes on. Well, there was a first time for everything.

"Entering hangar now," Chang said, her radio chat with the Melanchon hangar people finished.

The holo showed us entering a very large chamber of gray metal. It had scattered portals on each wall that gave a view into the hangar, and a cluster of small oval craft that were about the size of our shuttle. They sat on one side of the hangar floor. Their support legs were clamped down to the deck by grapples that looked strong to me. Our shuttle moved on short spurts of chemfuel toward an empty spot with a ring of flashing yellow and green lights. The ring enclosed a cluster of grapples. The grapples were attached to chains, which would allow them to adjust to our shuttle's different shape. Our view of the hangar became steady. We'd landed. The hull's external videyes showed a ground level view. The inner wall of the hangar had a cluster of clear portals, behind which moved a dozen or more red-furred Melanchon. Their hangar control booth looked very similar to our midbody hangar booth. The outline of an arching door showed to the left of the booth portals. That door now dropped down on a hinge that connected the door to the metal deck. Out from the airlock now walked three Melanchon in bulky, padded vacsuits. Clear globular helmets covered their hairy heads. The three headed for our shuttle. I felt thumps through my boots as the grapples outside moved to latch onto our landing legs. Clearly the Melanchon automation was the equal of our own. Chang appeared in the open hatch from the pilot bubble. She was slim, trim and had short black hair that had no curls, unlike the hair of Cassie and Okie. Or the curling red hair of Kierkgaard, whose freckled face looked eager for our adventure.

"Up!" called Chang. "Major, perhaps you can be first out our airlock to say hi to our greeters? Or, sorry ma'am, Lieutenant Morales you have the rank in this group. Do you wish to take the lead?"

Morales stood up from her starboard seat as Owanju did the same. She shook her head, tight black curls bobbing inside her helmet. "Nope. Anyway, a major in the Marines is an O-4 rank, while my Navy lieutenant commission is an O-3 rank." The middle-aged woman gave a smile to the major.

"Chief Chang," called Bjorg as he stood up, exceeding her in height by a good foot or more. "The Melanchon are an obvious matriarchy that follows polyandry. As in a single male in a relationship with at least four females, as we saw in the group led by leader Hatsepsit. I suggest a female be first to leave our shuttle. In this case, Lieutenant Morales would do nicely."

The Marine major gave a sigh. "Goddess protect us from academics! Lieutenant, please, take the lead. Marines have no trouble following anyone, so long as we are first on the beach!"

Morales laughed brightly, her smile big and engaging. "Thank you, Major Owanju. Guess I will lead this crowd out to meet our first group of friendly aliens!"

The Farm Deck boss walked past Cassie and Owanju to the two large cartons that held apples, oranges, pomegranates and other fruits from her deck. She grabbed the front carton's leash and walked to the cargohold's inner airlock hatch. The two cartons, floating on gravplate repulsors, followed after her like little pups following their mother. She tapped open the hatch, entered, pulled the linked cartons in with her, waited for the major and Cassie to join her, then the hatch closed. The rest of us stood in the aisle, watching the holo. Floor vibrations told me when the outer airlock hatch opened and deployed its flexible ramp. The holo image showed Morales leading Cassie and Owanju down the ramp and out to the group of three waiting Melanchon. Which appeared to be made of two large and bulky females, with a single male of shorter stature and moderate build. I followed after Bjorg and Oksana as they walked toward the airlock hatch. Others followed behind us. We all heard the first words spoken by Morales.

"Greetings to all Melanchon!" she said brightly over her vacsuit's radio. "I bring fruit from our trees. I am Mother Gladys Morales. Trees and other growing plants are my area of life work. Beside me are Father James Owanju, a member of our Marine protection family, and Mother-To-Be Cassandra Murphy, who holds the star information we promised you."

The middle Melanchon leaned forward more than the lean common to all orang-beings. "Greetings to the humans from Earth. I am Mother Madamedura, sister to Hatsepsit. Beside me are Father Leksatok and Mother Yolomokden." Briefly I gave thanks for instant radio translation by the Melanchon software. Then the boss female looked up as I came down the ramp with Bjorg, Oksana and Bill. Behind us followed Chang, Kierkgaard and Warren. "So you are half Mothers and half Fathers? Most interesting. Our elder in family patterns is Mother Yolomokden. I am sure she will enjoy discussing your human family patterns. Now, will you follow me to the decontamination chamber?"

Morales stepped forward and bowed slightly. "We understand the need to protect your people from any ailments that might be on our skin. However, I present to you Earth fruits from my Farm Deck, where I work. On it we grow food plants, trees, fruit orchards and shrubs which give forth small fruit like strawberries. Shall I leave the cartons here?"

Madamedura slapped the front of her helmet. "Yes, that is wise. Other Melanchon will take your special gift and serve the fruit to our family elders. I see your cartons float. You humans must possess the pull-down device. We use similar devices on our family leadership space, where you saw Mother Hatsepsit and her family members." The big Melanchon, who was nearly as tall as me, stepped back and gestured toward the arched door they had come through. "Will you follow us to the decontamination chamber? You can leave your air clothing there. The clothing will be safe there. There are no small predators in that chamber."

"We follow," Morales said, moving to walk alongside Madamedura. "Mother Madamedura, we each carry small bags that contain our day clothing, water and some food. How do you wish to make safe those things?"

A low rumbled came over my helmet's comlink. "There is an opening in the wall of the chamber. You humans may put all your possessions into that opening. They will be decontaminated by special light, with no use of liquids. You can rejoin your bags after your bodies are cleansed."

Cassie held up her black tablet. "This is the electronic device that contains my star data. Will it be safe in this wall opening?"

"Hand your device to Father Leksatok. He will take it to a different chamber for safe cleansing," the Mother leader said.

I pulled my tablet from my backpack. Around me others did the same. We all handed our tablets to the Father orang-being. Who looked surprised, if eye-widening was surprise among the Melanchon. But he quickly loaded the ten tablets into pockets of his vacsuit. We entered the arch door, walking over the metal of the door as it lay atop the hangar floor. I had been expecting a different kind of door. Other species would not automatically have doors that open on side hinges, or that slide into a wall. This entry door was different, but made sense if you considered how the Melanchon evolved in the trees and clearly valued them as part of their daily life. Having doors that drop down out of the way leaves the long arms of the Melanchon free to grab branches, limbs, vines and whatever else they use inside their own personal quarters. The three Melanchon led us down a short hallway empty of people. But a line of lights that ran alongside both walls now changed from black to green.

"The air of life has returned to this walkway," Madamedura said over our radio comlinks. "Feel free to open your head protectors and breath the fresh air of Melanchon!"

"Thank you," Morales said, sounding happy. "We humans always prefer natural air to the stored air of our small transports."

"So do we," commented the orang-being Yolomokden

We all did just that as we followed the three orang-beings down a side hallway. It ended in front of a wall with the outline of an arch door. Yolomokden touched a brown bar to the right of the door. The door top began coming down.

"Enter the decontamination chamber," Madamedura said as she stood to one side. "The opening for your bags is to the left side of this chamber. After you have removed your air clothing, hang the clothing on a branch that projects from the right side of the chamber. In the middle of the chamber are round marks on the floor," the leader said with a gesture from her long right arm. "When you are without coverings each human will stand inside a round mark. Water and cleansing liquid will rise up from the floor and fall from the ceiling. Then special lights will shine on you. You may close your eyes if you wish, though the cleansers and the lights will not harm you, based on the information provided us by your Mother Indira Khatri."

"We will enter and be cleansed," Morales said quickly, waving to the leader. "Mother Madamedura, I hope we see you when we exit."

"You will see me and my family members," the Melanchon said in a low rumble. "It is our task to acquire your star data and to take you to any part of our habitat ship you wish to visit. We will await you on the other side of this chamber. Father Leksatok will return your devices to you when you emerge."

Morales led the way into a yellow-lighted room. I followed after her, Cassie and the major. They turned left and headed for a rectangular opening in the wall. As they put their backpacks into the opening, the base of which moved inward like a conveyor belt, I pulled off my backpack. When my turn came I stuffed mine into the opening. It had my name on the top of the pack, the same as the packs of other folks. When everyone had put packs into the opening, we followed Morales over to a low curving metal beam that had the angles and texture of bark. I stripped off my suit as Morales, Cassie and the major led the way. In two minutes all of us had stripped off vacsuits and hung them from the metal limb. Next came the vacsuit's skin protection unitard. Which left each of us naked. Doing my best to not stare at the five women, I moved toward an empty floor circle. Sucking in my breath, I stood inside my circle. Then I gave up and looked around.

Morales stood not far from me, her expression patient, though her eyes scanned the chamber, glancing at each of us. Her breasts were full and drooped a bit. Which fit the fact of her actually being a mother who had birthed children. Her motherhood was clear from the stretch marks on her stomach. But like all of us she was in good shape. She was medium tall, with muscles in her arms and legs. Her heritage of growing up on a farm in the Spanish city of Lérida, in Catalonia province, also showed in the dark brown tan that covered her entirely.

It was impossible not to look at the other women. I'm male, after all, and my hormones still work. Very nicely, thank you. Chang stood not far away from me, her oval eyes closed as she lifted her face to the warmth of the ceiling lights. Which not only shone yellow star bright, but also contained a secondary glow of infrared, my eyes told me. None of us were going to be chilled here. Looking down Chang's slim body I saw petite breasts with dark nipples, arms with nice biceps, flaring hips, black hair in her groin and shapely legs that ended in feet with trimmed nails. She was shorter than Cassie but clearly a runner judging by the muscles in her legs.

Beyond Chang stood Evelyn Kierkgaard. The evolutionary biologist from Science Deck was a classic Irish redhead with curly red hair that flared out and fell to her bare shoulders. The freckles on the woman's face covered her entire body, from her neck down to very full white breasts with pink nipples, then a flat tummy and on down her legs to her feet. Short red curls filled her groin. Her toenails were also nicely trimmed, unlike my own. She was taller than most women, a good six feet it seemed. While she was very shapely there was no flab on her, anywhere. Evelyn saw me looking. She smiled, waved a hand my way, then gave a wave to my buddy Warren, who seemed very entranced by the only redhead among us.

Oksana's blue eyes were remarkable as she stared at me. Then she gave me a grin as if to say "Hay, the gals can enjoy body watching just as much as the guys!" To add to the tease she shook her shoulders, causing her medium-sized breasts to jiggle a bit. Her blond curls also shook. Showing off like that brought a grin to my face. I waved back to her. She looked away and waved to Bill. I could not avoid finishing my lookover. Her groin hair was a nice patch of blond curls, while her hips were only slightly broader than my own. She might not have the Earth Goddess look of Evelyn, but Oksana looked very nice. Plus she was just four years older than me. And at six feet tall, she could meet my eyes. Whenever she chose to.

Cassandra stood between the large black frame of the major and beer bellied Bjorg, who was running fingers through his shank of long blond hair. Cassie was turned around so I saw her full-on, versus the profile of Chang. Her pretty face glowed under her short black curls. Her brown eyes switched between Owanju and Bjorg as she followed Chang's advice and chattered with the two men. Which left me free to appreciate her full beauty. Her skin was a classic British pinky white, with a darker pink on her neck and upper chest where her skin had been exposed to natural tanning. Her shoulders were as wide as mine, though her arms lacked the full biceps of our athletic ladies. Her breasts, though, were full, well-shaped and had dark pink nipples. Which were not cold-stiffened, an effect I had enjoyed back in the Great Lakes mixed showers. Her belly did not show the six-pack of muscles that were apparent on Owanju, and on my friends Bill and Warren. But it was nicely flat and led down to a patch of black curls in her groin. Her hips curved nicely but were in proportion to her shoulders. Her legs were even nicer, being gymnast fit and long. Like all the women her toenails were nicely trimmed. Trimmed toenails were one nice aspect of my enhanced eyesight. Another was the infrared glow from her chest and lower body. A glow which was common to all humans in the chamber. But on her it was special. Cassie was not petite like Chang. Instead she was shapely, well-formed and an enticement to dreams any male would welcome!

The rains came from above and below, interrupting my view. I closed my eyes, gave thanks for my special vision and hoped dear Cassie would say yes to a dinner date!

CHAPTER SEVEN

Dressed and wearing our backpacks, all ten of us stood in a normal room beyond the decontam chamber. The three Melanchon were already there when we walked out into the room and found our backpacks with our clothes waiting on low metal branches that were close to the chamber exit. Hurriedly we'd all dressed, aware of being watched by the three orang-beings. When dressing was finished, Leksatok had walked up to us, offered two handfuls of tablets to us and waited while we each grabbed our own device. Then he stepped back to join the two females of his family. Who were taller and bulkier than him, we now saw clearly since none of them wore vacsuits. All three did wear shoulder straps that ended in brown carrybags that held metal tools and red tablet devices. In sum, three alien orangutans covered in thick reddish-brown hair stood in front of us, their brown eyes watchful, their faces not moving or showing an expression in the human fashion. Leastwise based on what we could see of their faces, since the red hair covered their cheeks and chins, leaving only brown noses, eyes and foreheads bare of hair. All three seemed comfortable in the warm, humid temp of the room. Me, I felt glad I wore a Type III blue and gray camo short-sleeve like the rest of us, except for the three civies, who wore earth tone blouses or a Hawaiian shirt, like that worn by Bjorg.

"Would you like to see our Leaders Chamber?" asked Madamedura, who was the tallest of the three.

I heard her words thanks to a translator tube on my left shoulder. We had found tubes attached to each backpack when we arrived. A bit larger than an over-the-ear head phone and shaped like a fat ink pen, the tube translated what we heard from any Melanchon and picked up our words for transmittal to similar tubes attached to each Melanchon shoulder.

Morales nodded. "Oh yes! And as you may tell, we humans nod our heads forward in agreement with things said by other humans. Or by you Melanchon."

The big leader lifted her thick brown lips. "So we deduced from watching you relate to each other in the broadcast from the

Bridge of Father Neil Skorzeny. As you can see, we Melanchon smile in a way similar to you humans. Pleasant that we share these manners, is it not?"

"Very pleasant," Cassandra said. "Which way is it to your Leaders Chamber?"

"Down the hallway that lies outside this room," Madamedura said in her normal low rumble of barks, chirps and grunts that I now heard in addition to the English translation produced by my shoulder tube. "Our chamber lies close to the front of our habitat ship. You will enjoy the trees in it."

"I'm sure we will," Morales said, moving to walk alongside Madamedura.

Cassie moved to walk next to Yolomokden while Major Owanju moved to walk alongside Leksatok. The rest of us followed. In seconds we passed through another drop-down door, entered a hallway, turned left and began walking down a long metal hall. Unlike human hallways the overhead was curved, like the top of their doors. And green vines grew along each wall at shoulder height, the plants rooted in long shallow trays. The vines were festooned with red flowers that made the hallway a bright, nature-like venue. Yellow glowspots on the overhead provided illumination every three meters or so. The gravity felt almost Earth-normal to me as we walked, scattered out along the hallway. The lack of formation marching did not bother me. I had had my fill of military marching at the Great Lakes. I far preferred a meandering stroll down to the creek on our ranch property, or bouncing through null-gee in a room at an orbital station where we played three-dee soccer. Military discipline I accepted. But rigid marching for the sake of looking good to higher brass did not appeal to me. Or to any of the enlisteds, NCOs or civies I had met on the *Star Glory*. At the end of the hall we turned right and walked up a sloping ramp. A very large arch door lay at the top of the ramp. Madamedura reached out, touched a black spot, which turned green. The arch door lowered down. A whiff of flower scent and apple-citrus smells blew out from the room. Which was partly obscured by the brown-barked trees we had all seen in the first image of the Melanchon bridge.

"Come with me," Madamedura said in a quick series of barks.

We all followed her into the expansive room, looking to either side and ahead and finally up. And up. And up even more. This room was clearly the bridge for this alien generation ship, but it was more than that. The large trees we had seen in the vidscreen image rose up twenty and thirty meters toward a distant overhead that glowed like Sol on a Spring morning. The base of each tree was rooted in a depression full of dark brown and black soil. Which made me wonder just how far down the roots of the forest giants had to go. Course they likely went sideways below the metal floor we walked on. But still, this bridge was totally unlike any bridge on a human ship. The apple-citrus smell came from vines that crawled over the distant bulkhead that enclosed the bridge in a wall of metal. A metal half-covered in vines. Where the wall was exposed were vidscreens, below which lay cupped seats that were only knee high to a human. Five orang-beings sat in the cups. They were scattered about the room. Five more orang folks sat on lower limbs of the giant trees, holding red tablets in their furry hands. Each Melanchon looked our way as we entered, then they returned to whatever they were doing at their stations. Or in the trees.

"Do you like our trees?" Madamedura chirped lightly.

Lieutenant Morales walked up to a nearby trunk, which was as wide as she. It rose twenty meters above her, its limbs festooned with fat green leaves and red flowers. Yellow fruit balls hung here and there. The brown bark of the trunk was ridged in a way similar to juniper trees I often saw in drier parts of Colorado and New Mexico. She reached out a slim hand, touched the bark, ran her fingers over the trunk, then looked up.

"Amazing!" the Farm Deck chief said. "Do you have trees everywhere on your ship?"

"They grow in many places, and bigger than these," Mother Madamedura barked low. She walked up to stand beside the Spanish woman. Her red-furred fingers reached out, touched the bark near Morales' fingers, then reached up to wrap long fingers around a low branch. "We love our forests. We love the fruit that comes from them. When we knew our home world was doomed to death by the Empire, we put all our efforts into building these sevens ships and filling them with trees and other Melanchon."

Morales nodded and stepped back. She turned and faced a nearby wall which held a large vidscreen. On it glowed the red pencils of the six other Melanchon generation ships. "How many of you are there?"

"Seven million," the taller orang said, her voice tone low and sad. "A million Melanchon on each ship. We are all that are left."

"What a horror," said Bjorg, moving to stand on the other side of Madamedura. "We humans have a history of fighting among ourselves. But we have never killed the biome of an entire planet." The Science Deck chief turned to look at the orang-being who had met us. The Swede's blue eyes scanned the wide face of the Mother who was a sister to the ship commander. "Mother Madamedura, I am honored to provide you with star listings that we know will offer possible new homes for your people." The man waved to Cassandra. "Doctor Murphy, will you come over here?" The Swede turned back to the orang leader. "Mother-To-Be Murphy has—"

"Wait!" called Madamedura. Who lifted her head and let out a low rumbling howl that did not translate. The Melanchon Mother looked down. "Father Bjorg, I have called my sister. She leads us all. She must be here to see your gift of star homes."

Around them other orang-beings moved in the trees or on their cup seats. A few dropped from the trees and stood nearby, leaning forward with hunched shoulders. They stood beyond our group of ten humans. But close enough I could see the eagerness in their body stance and the brightness in their brown eyes. From beyond them came movement. Four large orang-beings came into view from behind thick tree trunks. They walked toward us, their short legs moving quickly. In seconds they stood close to Madamedura, Yolomokden and Leksatok. All seven rubbed shoulders. Then the four newcomers, whose reddish-brown fur was longer and stringier than the Melanchon who had met us, looked at us. That was when I noticed they also had shoulder translation tubes. One pursed lips.

"I am Mother Hatsepsit. Beside me are my family Mothers," she said. "Welcome Father Magnus Bjorg and Mother-To-Be Cassandra Murphy. Welcome also to your companions." The leader paused, her dark brown eyes blinking. "It is refreshing to see you in the fur. Especially this one," she said, turning to face Evelyn. "You are Mother-To-Be Evelyn Kierkgaard, who studies how plants and animals change over time. Your head hair is most appealing. Do many humans have hair like you?"

Evelyn laughed softly. "Only a few. I come from the island known as Ireland, or *Éire* to those of us who live there. Other redheads live elsewhere on Earth." The evolutionary biologist smiled widely. "I am most pleased to meet the leader of all Melanchon."

Hatsepsit tilted her head to one side, then scanned the rest of us before looking back to Cassie. "Mother-To-Be Murphy, can you show us these stars with worlds that lie beyond the domain of the Empire?"

Cassandra nodded, then held out her black tablet. "All the star and planet data is on my device. It can communicate with your tablets, I was told by our AI Heidi. You use the same binary signaling system that we use in our electronic devices."

Hatsepsit nodded slowly. She pulled out a red tablet from her shoulder carrybag and held it up. "We do use these devices the same as you."

Cassie smiled. Her thumb pressed the side of her tablet as she held it close to the leader's red tablet. "Done! Would you like to see imagery of these stars?"

"Yes!" squeaked Madamedura, joined by low squeaks from Mother Yolomokden and Father Leksatok. Similar squeaks of agreement came from the three older Mothers who made up Hatsepsit's family. Which reminded me their joint husband, Father Woktaken, was already on the *Star Glory*, hanging with Chief O'Connor. I hoped he and his fellow orang-beings were enjoying their visit as much as I was enjoying mine. Being on the bridge of this giant starship reminded me of groves of trees near our ranch that I had visited when I was younger.

"Well, then, here is the Orion Arm, with the locations of 294 stars with planets noted as blinking green dots," Cassie said, holding up her tablet and pointing one end of it outward. Three light beams shot out.

A hologram nearly as tall as Cassie took form in front of her. The holo was as wide as it was tall. That allowed us all to see the curving sweep of white, red, blue and yellow stars that make up Orion Arm. The lower left end of the star arm touched an inner curving arm, which was labeled as Sagittarius-Carina Arm. A dispersed scatter of stars blinked greenly starting halfway up the arm. The scatter reached out to the end of the uparm segment, a distance of 5,000 light years.

Cassie's left hand rose. It held a laser pointer. She shifted it until its red dot rested near a blinking green dot which lay close to the middle of the arm. "This is the yellow star HD 4203. It lies a good

450 light years distant from the Kepler 22 star. It has two very large gas giants orbiting it. The inner big world lies fully within the star's liquid water habitable zone. The outer big world lies about seven AU out from the star. While our star viewers have yet to see small worlds transiting this G5V star, it is likely the inner big world has dozens of large moons orbiting it much like our worlds of Jupiter and Saturn in our Sol system." Cassie moved the laser to put its red dot next to another blinking dot. "This is Gliese 3293, located about 280 light years from here. It is an M2.5 red dwarf star with four worlds in orbit, three of which lie within its habitable zone. The world 3293c is best located to be warm, though it is much larger than Earth. It is possible Earth-size moons orbit this world or the three gas giants known to orbit its red star." Our astrogeek again shifted her laser pointer. "Another promising star is BD-08 2823. It is a K3V white-yellow star similar to our Sol. It lies about 340 light years away from Kepler 22. It has two known planets, one of them in its habitable zone. While larger than Earth, this planet could host moons with air." She turned off her pointer and looked to the boss Melanchon even as she held out her tablet with its holo projection. "Mother Hatsepsit, there are many white-yellow, yellow, orange and red stars with planets, some of them with worlds like our Earth. Good hunting!"

The big Melanchon sighed. She reached out and ran her furry right hand through the holo arc of stars. "So many possible home worlds. So much to do. I will convey this vital news to our own star viewers. But it is encouraging to know so many possible worlds lie within only a few days travel time in the grayness." The boss Mother looked back to us all. "Father Bjorg, Mother-To-Be Murphy and Mother Gladys Morales, what else can *we* share with you in our gratitude?"

The lieutenant stepped forward. "What can you tell us about the Empire of Eternity? Are there other star-traveling people like you? Are there people who steal from this Empire? And do any other peoples possess weapons with the reach of the Empire ship weapons?" Morales looked aside to the nine of us, then back. "We know little of this Empire, other than how deadly and predatory it is."

Hatsepsit gestured to Madamedura. Who reached up and grabbed a cluster of yellow fruit balls. She tossed them to her sister, who caught them easily, holding them all against her long reddish-brown chest fur. "I will share what we know. But it will take some while." Hatsepsit tossed a fruit ball to Cassie, who caught it even as she looked surprised. The big Mother tossed fruit balls to each of us. "Eat of this sweet fruit. It will provide energy while we visit."

"Thank you," Cassie said after taking a bite of the yellow fruit ball. "Tastes like an orange. And smells better." She switched off the Orion Arm holo and lowered her tablet.

Hatsepsit moved to sit under a tree located in the middle of her bridge. We all followed her, taking seats on the metal floor or on the soil beneath the tree. "Yes, there are other peoples who sent out life ships like ours before their home worlds were destroyed." The orang-being pointed her red tablet at Cassie's tablet. "The locations of five such peoples who we met while traveling up this Orion Arm are now known to you." She lowered the tablet, her brown eyes big and bright. "And yes, there are beings in single starships who raid Empire outposts and then flee into gray space before Empire fighting ships arrive. Three locations where we met such people are included in the knowledge I shared just now. One of the locations is the site of a comet base where these raiders repaired the fusion pulse engine of one of our life ships." She took a deep breath. "As for the weapons and speed of the Empire fighter ships, we have learned that a few people in the Empire possess ships able to move as quickly as Empire ships. And some people even possess the deadly black beams that turn a ship into a small skyglow. Both can be found at the raider base. But no one understands how Empire ships can hide from detection. Like you we have devices that detect the invisible emissions sent out by power blocks and dark space engines. We are unable to detect Empire ships until they drop their concealment. By that time they are always within striking range. Which is why we and other traveling outcasts stay beyond any star's magnetic sphere, the better to disappear into grayness when a crowd of Empire fighter ships suddenly appears."

"So you have no way to detect the arrival of Empire ships?" called Hilary Chang.

"We cannot detect their presence. But their *arrival* outside a star system is possible." The big orang gestured to her sister. "Mother Madamedura is a specialist in the study of invisible radiations. She and other specialists on our other life ships watch for the sudden arrival of . . . of what you call gravitons. The particles that give weight to all substance." The orang took a big bite out of her fruit, munched it several times and swallowed. "We have noticed that while such particles arrive from all directions of space, when a ship is about to exit from gray space there is a surge of these gravitons. If your specialist people watch their devices closely, they will note the direction and rough distance at which an incoming ship will appear out of the grayness." Hatsepsit looked to Cassie. "Mother-To-Be Murphy, watching our graviton devices is how we knew of your arrival, even before you left the gray space. We saw you arrive at the other side of this system. Then we saw a closer surge of gravitons, which told us you had detected our power emissions and chosen to arrive here. We were ready to flee if you had been an Empire starship or a people allied with the Empire."

Cassie looked to Chang. "Tactical, you got that? Watching for this graviton surge will be vital to the captain, no matter what star he takes us to next."

"Would your Mother-To-Be Chang wish to see our records of these graviton surges?" Hatsepsit said in a low rumble.

"She would," Cassie said.

Hatsepsit gestured to Madamedura. "Take her to your study cup. Show her what we detect."

The big orang stood up. "Will you join me?" she said, looking to Chang.

"I will join you." Chang waved to the rest of us, then followed the red-furred Mother to a nearby cup seat that stood below a bulkhead vidscreen.

Cassandra looked over to Oksana. "Intelligence, check those star locations for people like these Melanchon. And note which star holds this pirate base."

"I will check their data," Okie said, pulling back her tablet from its closeness to Cassie's tablet. "This pirate base sounds promising if it can do ship repairs."

Cassie looked back to the boss orang. "Mother Hatsepsit, thank you for this information. And the news about the Empire weapons and ship speed. We lost two fellow ships from the deadliness of the Empire weapons. Do you have any weapons which might harm an Empire ship? And if so, would you share that knowledge with us?"

The big orang nodded slowly, then lifted her lips in a smile. "Your gift of these world locations is worth anything we possess. I would give you one of our ships if I could. But I cannot. Instead, our Father Woktaken now gives your Father O'Connor knowledge of how to move quickly through gray space." She gestured to one of the big females who were part of her family. "Mother Niktaktong is a manager of our weapons. Like you we possess weapons which shoot out deadly beams of light. We also possess a weapon that expels hard invisible radiation. You call these particles gamma rays. The Mother will take your specialists to see these weapons."

"Thank you," Morales said quickly, then looked to her side. "Major Owanju, PO Watson, go with this Mother Niktaktong. Learn what you can. Get the specs for these weapons." The Farm boss looked back to the orang leader. "Mother Hatsepsit, we appreciate your willingness to share weapons knowledge. While we do not know how to produce the black beams that turn a ship into a small star, our coherent laser weapons have a reach shorter than Empire beams. Do you know how the Empire shoots farther than our weapons?"

Hatsepsit took another yellow fruit ball from one of her family Mothers. "We do not know that. The reach of our light beam weapons is far shorter than Empire beams. And since our life ships cannot move faster through real space than Empire ships, we avoid visiting the planets of any star system. But the leaders of the raider base may know more. They offered us weapons but we wished only to have our engine repaired."

I watched as Bill left with the major and Mother Niktaktong. They headed for an arch door in a distant wall, passed through it and disappeared from sight. Which left seven of us. What else was going to happen? More importantly, were there other Melanchon devices which would be useful to the *Star Glory* and the captain?

"Mother Hatsepsit," Morales said, leaning forward. "I love these yellow fruit balls! I hope your people have enjoyed our cartons of apples, oranges, pomegranates, mangos, grapes and strawberries that we brought over."

The boss Mother smiled big, lifting her big brown lips high to expose her white teeth. Which like human teeth were a mix of front canines and rear molars. Though the molars appeared bigger than any human molar. Which made sense in view of how linked to trees and tree fruits these people were. While they might eat insects and eggs like the orangutans of Earth, it was clear they loved their tree fruits. That gave me an idea.

"Lieutenant Morales, perhaps Mother Hatsepsit would like to receive seeds from our apple and orange trees, if you have any in storage?"

The Spaniard lifted her black eyebrows in surprise, then gave another of her big engaging smiles. "Yes!" She looked back to the boss orang. "Mother Hatsepsit, among our trees on my Farm Deck there are fruit trees. They grow there and also inside our Forest Room. I have seeds of such trees in cold storage. Would you like some of our fruit tree seeds? To grow Earth fruit trees on your life ships?"

"Yes, yes!" smacked Hatsepsit as she leaned forward eagerly. "Variety in food is much desired by our people, especially our young ones," she said, her wide shoulders hunching together. "We will trade you seeds of our Mother Trees. Their yellow fruit grows in all seasons. We have other fruit trees and bushes. We will trade those seeds to you, Mother Morales. Do you have room to add new trees to your Farm Deck?"

"We do!" Morales said excitedly. "Thank you! I'm sure our Mess Hall cooks will enjoy these yellow balls, once we grow a few trees to an age at which they fruit. And if you have berry bushes like our raspberries, that will diversify our meals! After we return to our ship, I will have one of my Farm people come back with a container of seeds. She can receive your seeds then."

"This is all fascinating," murmured Evelyn from where she had sat silent during the discussions. The Irish woman looked to Gladys. "Lieutenant Morales, perhaps these Melanchon would like to see *our* forest giants. Do you have imagery of redwoods? And the sequoia trees?"

"Outstanding idea," Morales said, turning to face the Melanchon leader. She lifted her tablet and pointed it to the empty space where the Orion Arm holo had appeared. She touched a rim control. Light beams sprang out. "Mother Hatsepsit, look up on our giant trees! Their bark is as red as your fur. They are among our oldest trees, living far longer than any human. And they grow taller than any other tree on Earth."

I watched as a person-high holo took form in front of Hatsepsit. The image solidified into a line of red-barked leviathans whose trunks reached high into the blue sky. I thought I recognized a grove I had seen north of San Francisco, not far from the Oregon border. Or was it of the sequoia trees that grew near Yosemite

National Park in central California? I had visited both places with my Mom and my two sisters, just after my graduation from Great Lakes. It had been an amazing trip, giving life and substance to images I had seen only in three-dee holos. Or on my recorder tablet. Which had been silently recording this meeting in the Leaders Chamber of the Melanchon starship. Now, once more, I felt like I was close to the quiet life of a great forest. One from Earth and one from the home world of the Melanchon. It felt good.

"Ahhhhh," rumbled low Hatsepsit, staring fixedly at the forest of redwoods with trunks thicker than the reach of five people. "These resemble the ancient *bolo* trees of our homeworld. They grew larger than the *melong* tree under which we rest. Would you like to see our inner world? Where the rest of my people live?"

"Yes," said Bjorg, who had been thoughtful during the exchanges with Cassie and Morales. "Where is this inner world?"

"Through the door beyond and then past a vine walkway," Hatsepsit said, rising to her bare feet.

She wore no shoes, unlike the tennies we humans wore. But her feet were wide and long, with prehensile toes that could clearly grip a branch or limb. It was another puzzle which I had thought about before and since our arrival on this giant ship. Why were the Melanchon females larger than the males? Why did these orangutan-like beings have families of four females and one male? Where were the children?

"Follow me. And see the wonder of what our home world once was," Hatsepsit said, turning and heading for the exit.

Her two older sisters followed her. As did Yolomokden and Leksatok. Morales took the lead. Oksana, Cassie, Warren, Bjorg, Evelyn and I followed the boss females. What other mysteries did this giant ship hold?

CHAPTER EIGHT

After a long trip downward, which I guessed was aimed at taking us closer to the ship's outer hull, Hatsepsit stepped up onto a deck that lay at a right angle to the ramp we'd come down. As I followed the others up and onto this deck, I felt a change in gravity. My feet told me it was still the nine-tenths gee we had felt in the arrival hangar and on the bridge. But my head said different. Before I could ask about what I felt, Hatsepsit touched a black patch on a wall that held the outline of a large arch door. The door was the size of some aircraft hangar doors. The patch turned green. The big door slowly lowered down, coming to a clanking halt on the floor we stood on. Brilliant yellow light made me blink a lot. The smells of the yellow ball fruits hit my nose hard. A whisper of wind came out from the space beyond, sounding both far and near. My sensitive ears heard rumbling conversations from a far distance. Other conversations were closer. Hatsepsit stalked forward through the giant opening. We all followed.

Giant *melong* trees rose up before us, their brown bark ridged and showing loose strips here and there. Limbs thicker than my body reached out from the wide trunks of the trees. We all followed those trunks upward. Then upward more. Finally, far, far above us, we saw a bright yellow glow coming from a long tube that ran from the wall behind us out and down the long, open space into which we had stepped. It was this place's interior sun. Wilder still was what I saw beyond the tube. Beyond it lay groves of *melong* trees, green grassy fields, blue ponds, tumbling creeks and ridgelines that poked up above the tops of the *melong* tree groves. But it was all upside down! What I saw was identical to the space we stood in. But looking up past the tube sun we saw the tops of the distant trees, then the landscape in which they were rooted. It felt like one of those old-style circus spin barrels, where people were pushed against the wooden wall of the barrel as it spun. Then the barrel tilted so people were looking down at the ground below, but did not fall. They were stuck to the barrel wall by the force of what my Great Lakes instructors called spingee. Or the artificial gravity created by rapid rotation of an outer hull around a central axis. What I now saw was a gigantic version of that circus spin barrel.

"Damn!" yelled Warren, standing with arms widespread as he looked up. "They're upside down! And it looks like there are people up there!"

"There are," Hatsepsit rumbled low and slowly. "Follow the view further down. Inside the spinning shell of our life ship we have recreated the best parts of our home world. We have forests, freshwater ponds, croplands, ridgelines and manufactories where other Melanchon work to build what we need to survive."

"It's an O'Neill cylinder," Cassie said, her tone wondering. "We are inside a giant tube that spins on its central axis, which is that yellow light tube. The spinning creates spingee. Or centrifugal force. The spingee keeps the soil, water, trees and people firmly glued to the inner lands of this world. Amazing."

Cassandra's words brought to my mind the memory of an O'Neill cylinder that one of my Great Lakes profs had shown us when discussing orbital habitats. Except this Melanchon version had no strips of quartz glass, which would allow in solar light for something in Earth orbit. This life ship cylinder carried its own light inside, in the weightless axis area. That yellow tube shown super bright. Brighter than could be explained by a fluorescent light tube's gases. Whatever was producing the light glow, it was more powerful than a giant fluorescent tube. I shifted my view, following the long stretch of upside down land, trees and lakes. My memory of the bulkhead vidscreen image with its scale had shown each of these red pencil ships to be ten kilometers long. The distance to the topside had to be a good two kilometers. Which made this giant ship smaller than the five mile width and twenty mile length proposed by Dr. Gerard K. O'Neill. Still, this spinning habitat did what an O'Neill cylinder could not do. It moved through true space on fusion pulse thrusters, then jumped from one star to another using its own Alcubierre stardrive. Truly this life ship was a world unto itself.

"Where do your people live?" Bjorg said musingly.

"Half of our million live among the *melong* forests, which supply food and sleeping locations," Hatsepsit said. "The other half live in manufactories and enclosures that shelter devices. We Melanchon do enjoy meat, and our enclosures raise the limb-runners we call *dokteka*. They are the size of my foot or hand."

"We too raise small animals for food," Morales said, reaching out to grip the red-furred shoulder of Hatsepsit. "On my Farm Deck we have guinea pigs, chickens, goats, sheep and pigs. Our human biochemistry requires regular eating of meat proteins, in addition to vegetables and fruits."

"Do you humans enjoy spending time in lakes of water?" Hatsepsit said, reaching up to lay her large hand atop Morales' left hand.

"Oh yes! We humans swim a lot," Morales said. "At the beach where our oceans meet our continents. In lakes. In rivers that flow across our lands. And in artificial lakes we call swimming pools," Then she laughed brightly. "Bet we dry off faster than you Melanchon!"

Yolomokden chuffed, which came across as laughter. "For people who resemble hairless Melanchon, of course you will dry quicker than us. But our long fur keeps us warm at nights. You humans must wear dead coverings to keep warm. I do not envy you."

"Mother Hatsepsit," called Warren. "Why do you Melanchon spin your life ship? You have gravity plates on your bridge and in your arrival hangar. Surely you could use such devices to create gravity here. Can't you?"

I had wondered the same as my buddy. But I had kept it to myself. However Warren was a Marine corporal. He would of course be curious about power use and why something so artificial as this spingee was being used by these orang-beings. And maybe my friend was wondering at the difficulties involved in taking over a habitat ship that had an inner ecozone which spun like a top. We had yet to encounter any habitat ships run by the religious zealots who had fled EarthGov ten years ago. Presumably those ships had fled uparm, since the Empire people had not encountered other humans. But we might encounter them, when we headed back to Sol. Or if we traveled beyond Sol to an uparm star. While twenty Marines were too few to take over a large habitat ship run by zealots, still, Warren often thought about the combat implications of any place he visited. It was as much a part of his training as my awareness of the rainbow colors generated by the containment fields around our antimatter tubes was part of my training. An AM engineer like me never forgets the essential function of containment magfields, just as no Marine ever forgets about a platoon mate who might cover him in a live fire event.

"We could use such devices," Hatsepsit rumbled low. "But it would require most of the power generated by our power blocks. Those blocks require the isotope gases you and we use to drive our ships through black space. Relying on natural weightiness by spinning our life ship allows us to go long periods without refueling our power blocks. And if we lost power for some reason, this world would still be intact. For us, this was wisdom."

"Agreed," said Evelyn, looking down and outward. "Your *melong* trees are a beautiful wonder. How far back in time did you Melanchon live among these trees and eat their fruit?"

Hatsepsit looked down and stepped away from Morales' hand. "A long, long time. Our past-time specialists say we lived among the *melong* trees before we learned to make fires and tools. They fed us early in our history. They feed us now. And our wastes feed the roots of our trees. It is a cycle that always existed. Until the Empire came, made its threat, then later destroyed my world." The boss orang gestured ahead. "A village lies not far ahead. Do you wish to see it?"

"Oh yes!" Evelyn said eagerly. "I want to see your families at home. And see your children! They must be a delight."

"Our children are why we still travel through the black space," Hatsepsit rumbled low and slow. "Some of us might have stopped eating and drinking, were it not for the children. They give us the energy to go on. To search for a new home for them. Our children deserve a world with a sky that is endless."

The sadness of the loss of the Melanchon home world hit me hard. When I envisioned Earth turning from a blue and green lifeworld into a dead black marble in the darkness of space, my gut twisted more. What this Empire did to people who had never harmed them was worse than terrible. It was evil. An evil that had spread across the Milky Way. Was there any chance we could fight this evil? Any chance we could save Earth from the same fate?

"Wait!" yelled a human voice behind us.

I looked back. It was Chang, her strong legs pumping as she ran toward us. Madamedura followed her, moving quickly on her short legs but unable to keep up with Hilary's speed. Our Tactical chief slid to a stop near us. Then she looked up. And up.

"Oh, wow!" Chang said brightly.

"Yes, it is amazing," our Farm chief said. "We're inside a spinning cylinder. There are a million Melanchon living inside this life ship. Come, we're going to see a village."

"Sounds good," grunted Major Owanju as he appeared through the giant trees, with Bill walking fast beside him. "Lieutenant, we got the gamma ray laser weapons specs. And saw their installation. They also have proton and CO_2 laser blisters on the sides, bow and stern of this ship. I like how they have port and starboard laser mounts."

Morales nodded as she walked behind Hatsepsit. "Good to know. And as Corporal Johnson can tell you, these Melanchon use spingee for internal gravity in order to save on DT refueling needs. Come!"

We all followed after her, now back to our full ten person count. Madamedura moved up to walk beside her sister, bumping shoulders with her and with the other Melanchon. The way they moved through this forest, filled with green vines, low reddish shrubs and scattered clumps of green grass looked beyond natural. It looked as if they had always walked through this forest. Which, in a way, they had. The sound of cheeping drew my gaze upward. Orange things flew from high branch to high branch among the trees. My precise vision painted an image of critters who were a cross between birds and lizards. Low humming and clicks also drew my attention. The sounds came from swarms of blue beetle-like insects that moved in swarms from tree to tree, while yellow butterfly-like creatures stopped at the red flowers that adorned the branches. I shut down the sensitivity of my hearing, a trick I had learned long ago when I got tired of listening to people a mile away talk BS about neighbors and people who didn't look like them.

Ten minutes later, after a quick break to grab some yellow fruit balls that we munched on as we continued walking, we arrived at a population zone. Large bulky Melanchon sat on low tree limbs or moved along the duff-covered forest floor, their long arms swinging fore and aft as they walked, clearly a part of their natural balancing as they walked. The orang-beings glanced our way as we entered their space, then looked away and resumed what they were doing. Which included staring at hanging vidscreens that were attached to some tree trunks. In one spot was a group of five adult orang-beings, who sat in a circle at the base of a big tree. Each was hand-weaving a basket from dry vines and long grasses. Five meters beyond them and up ten meters, was balanced a wooden platform that stretched across two thick branches. On the platform moved ten or so Melanchon, their movements in synchrony with a chirping, bell-like music that came down from their platform.

"An open-air nightclub?" whispered Oksana as she walked beside me.

I smiled. "Looks like it. Which makes me wonder about their booze. Do you think they ferment these yellow ball fruits? They taste citrusy. Which means they could produce a kind of alcohol. I think."

My Russian friend chuckled. "They probably do ferment the stuff. Wonder what they would say about brandy? Or bourbon? Or Stolichnaya vodka?"

"Might be a good trade item."

I looked away and ahead. We now entered a small meadow without trees. But the place was filled with short green grass, and some tiny flowers that resembled daisies. Again the memory of a flower-strewn field near my ranch home came to mind. I had not felt homesick during the days of our Alcubierre trip out to Kepler 37. Now, I did. Being in a forest always did it to me. And this miles-long forest was beyond anything I had seen on Earth. In person, at least. The trees near the meadow were indeed bigger than those on the bridge. I guessed they were sixty or seventy meters high. They reminded me of the sequoia forest near Yosemite that I had visited with my Mom and sisters. That forest of red-barked trees was big and likely stretched as far afield as this ten-kilometer long stretch of woodlands, lakes, creeks and ridgelines.

The running of small orang people across the meadow drew my attention. They were small versions of Hatsepsit, their reddish-brown hair stringy but far shorter than that of the big Melanchon. Children they were. They played 'catch and tag', then ran off chuffing loudly. They also tackled each other, chuffing more loudly. Other children sat at the base of the two dozen giant trees that ringed the meadow. I fixed on one young orang who sat under a giant tree on my right, about ten meters away. The kid sat with crossed legs, leaning forward and playing a kind of hopscotch game with small pieces of white quartz. Next to the kid stood the five meter thick trunk of a giant *melong*. On its trunk were carved deep lines that ran in rows. To me the lines resembled rune marks from Scandinavia. Oksana noticed my look. She turned to Hatsepsit, who stood with her sister Madamedura watching the running and tumbling children.

"Mother Hatsepsit, what are those carved lines on that tree trunk over there?" she asked.

The boss female looked to where Oksana pointed. "It is a family heritage tree with marks made by that family's ancestors. We transplanted it from our home world. It is ancient." Her dark brown eyes fixed on the orang child, who was perhaps the size of a human six-year-old. "She is a daughter of the Mokladen family." The big orang turned away and gestured at the big-trunked trees that surrounded the meadow. "Other children sit below their family heritage tree. We encourage it so they will smell . . . the scent of their heritage tree. While the flowers of each *melong* tree may smell the same to you, each family can tell their tree apart from all other *melong* trees." Hatsepsit gestured to her left. "Over there is the Hatmokden tree of my heritage family. It too is ancient and was transplanted here."

The rest of my friends and the civies moved away as Hatsepsit walked toward that tree, pointing out its big yellow fruit balls and red tulip-shaped flowers. Oksana gave me a grin and followed the crowd.

Instead I looked back to the young girl orang who sat maybe five feet from the base of the giant tree. She seemed absorbed in her stone game, tossing a black rock marked with white dots into the grass nearby, then moving a white quartz nodule up the alternating pattern of boxes scratched into the brown soil that was clear of green grass. It so resembled my memory of how my youngest sister once played in the forest grove near our ranch that my heart ached. Both my sisters were older than me and had chosen lifeways different from my own. Louise was married with children, which exempted her from the draft. My youngest sister Anna had not been drafted due to malformation of her heels. She walked just fine. But wearing any kind of boots or—

"Caaarack!"

The harsh sound drew my eyes upward. Up. Ten meters above the girl orang a giant limb now tore away from the brown trunk. My perfect eyesight followed the limb back to where its base was pulling away from the trunk. Blackness told me the limb was dead, perhaps from some disease or infestation. Now, the weight of the giant limb had become too much for its attachment point. Five meters long and a meter thick, the limb finished its pulling away. It arced down. The spingee gravity of the ship worked as efficiently as planetary gravity. It drew the long thick limb down. Down. Toward the girl orang. Who had not yet looked up.

I ran.

The air buffeted my face.

My perfect ears heard the low whistling of the branch as it fell through the air, gaining speed as its weight responded to the spingee.

My perfect eyesight noticed small blue beetles flying away from the limb, twenty or more of them. Perhaps the black spot on the main trunk had been where they had laid their eggs. Which yielded white grub that ate at the wood, my vision now told me.

My feet dug into the grassy sod that lay between me and the orang girl. My perfect muscles moved my feet in long strides.

I ran as fast as I had run that day long ago when I had carried Bill and Warren away from the tavern and the Star Navy MPs.

I did not breath.

I just ran.

As fast as I could.

The young orang girl looked up at me with wide brown eyes as I skidded to a stop next to her, brown dirt spraying away from my tennis shoes.

I reached up, spreading my palms open.

"Thump!"

The tree limb hit my palms with the force of a giant boulder. Or a car falling from a hydraulic lift at a mechanic's shop. That had happened once, when I was a kid. The shop was old-style and relied on hydraulics rather than the newer air blowers to lift a car up so a mechanic could work underneath it.

The limb was heavy.

Too heavy.

My arms came down.

My feet sank into the soil.

I bent my head forward to avoid the descending limb.

Which gave me a view of the young orang girl on my right. She was looking up, her eyes so wide whites showed around her brown irises. Fear filled her face.

I squatted as the limb drove me down.

Then I braced a knee in the soil.

The limb rested across my shoulders.

Movement stopped.

The orang girl was safe.

I took a deep breath.

But how long could I hold up the monstrous weight?

"Got this end!" yelled Owanju from my right.

The big black frame of the major now held onto the thick end of the limb, its bark resting on his wide shoulders. Like me he had one knee resting on the soil while the other leg was half-bent. Both his thick arms were raised, his broad hands gripping the curving base of the limb.

"Got the other end!" cried Warren from my left.

My best buddy was two meters away from me, kneeling and bracing just like the major, his weight-lifting arms bulging with muscles. His own head was down. His brown sidewalls showed the bulge of veins underneath the short haircut.

The sound of thudding feet from my right drew my gaze.

A giant brown fur ball appeared to my right. It swept through the space occupied by the orang girl, long red-furred arms sweeping her up and against its body as it went into a roll that carried her beyond where I stood braced. How long could I hold it?

"She's safe!" yelled Cassie.

My breath came faster. The weight of the giant pressed me down. My shoulders hurt. My legs felt the strain. I had never held up anything that weighed this heavy.

"Nathan!" called the major. "On my count we toss this bastard forward! Nobody is there. Corporal, you ready!"

"Ready," Warren said from my left, sounding breathless as the limb's weight pressed on him.

"Ready," I said quickly.

My vision began to swim.

That was something new.

I had always had perfect vision out to a mile, in all spectrums. I had always had perfect hearing out to a mile. And on the ranch, I had been able to toss hay bales up onto the upper storage deck of the barn with ease, lifting and tossing automatically. Even when I had lifted a boulder my size at the nearby creek to create a pond for me and my sisters to swim in, I had not felt this loaded down.

"Three, two, one!" yelled Owanju.

I thrust forward with my shoulders and hands.

To my left and right came the sounds of Warren and the major doing the same.

"Crack-thump!"

The tree limb gouged a deep rut in the brown soil and grass of the meadow before it stopped its slow roll.

I finally got a full view of the giant limb.

It was a meter thick, five meters long and the flare of the blackened base where it had torn away from the *melong* trunk was a meter and a half thick. Whatever kind of wood this *melong* tree might be, it was heavier than the oak limbs that fell from the oak trees in the grove near our ranch.

I gasped for breath. Then I slowly stood up. My vision cleared. My hearing, which had heard the barking sounds of other Melanchon from across the meadow getting loud and sharp as I held the limb up above the girl orang, those sounds had stopped. Only my breathing, Warren's heavy breathing and the major's grunting breathing sounded. Then came footsteps, both human and orang. A gasp came from someone I knew.

"Nate!" said Cassandra. "Your shirt camo fabric is torn. Your shoulders. They are . . . scraped red raw. Here, let me get some antiseptic from my first aid kit."

I stood up straight. Finally.

Ahead past the dead limb stood a shorter, less bulky Melanchon. It was Leksatok. He held the small girl orang in his thick, furry arms, clutched to his chest. He looked at me, then aside to Warren and the major. His big brown eyes welled with tears.

"You saved my family's youngest!" he said, his voice coming from the translator tube on Cassie's shoulder.

Clearly my tube was smashed beyond recognition. As were the tubes attached to the shoulders of Warren and Owanju. My buddy walked over to me, looked at my shoulders, then nodded.

"Yup, kinda torn up there," he said. "Me, just got some loose bark on my shoulders."

Air hissed from a spray hypo held by Cassie. I felt a sting on both shoulders, then numbness. I looked right as the major walked slowly toward me. The big man stopped, glanced aside at the fallen limb, then back to me. He nodded slowly.

"You did good, PO Stewart. Saved a kid. And you did it faster than anyone in my platoon could move. You were a blur." The major looked over at the fallen limb. "I'm guessing that bastard weighed a ton. Leastwise it felt that heavy on my end. Corporal, what think you?"

"Oh, yeah," Warren muttered. "It was a heavy motherfucker. The most I've deadlifted at the Great Lakes gym was four hundred pounds. My end felt heavier. Damn."

I felt several varieties of profanity. I did not say them. Instead, I looked ahead at Leksatok. Who still held the young girl. "What's her name?"

The man's thick brown lips lifted. "She is Mokladeen." He looked down at the girl, who had now shifted so her short red-furred legs hung over his arms, with her back against his chest. She wore no leather straps, unlike the adults. But she stared at me, her gaze thoughtful. "Mokladeen, say something to this hairless Melanchon who saved your life."

Her thin brown lips lifted. It was an easy smile. "Do you like playing the hopping game with white rocks? Naaa-thaaan?"

I smiled her way. Shaking off the hands of Oksana on my left and Cassie on my right, I knelt down, grabbed the six white quartz pieces and the white-spotted black stone, stood up and walked over to her. "Don't know the game. But it looks like something my youngest sister once played, when she was your size. Will you teach me your game?"

Mokladeen took hold of the rocks, then nodded quickly. "Sure," came her voice from Cassie's translator. "Can you play now?"

"He cannot," called Hatsepsit as she stepped into view from my left. Behind her came Madamedura, Yolomokden, the other two Mothers in her family, and a crowd of other adult Melanchon. She turned to her sister. "Mada, find this girl's Mother." She faced me. "Father Nathan Stewart, you saved one of our children. We owe you a debt of . . . thanksgiving. I wish to give you a gift on behalf of this girl's family, and all our families on our life ship. What gift do you wish from me?"

I shook my head. This was one weird turn of events. Appreciation I had expected. Every adult, especially a mother of children, always wished to protect and cherish children. Whether their own or someone else's kids. That I had learned in school and from my Mom, and my Dad while he was still alive. That these aliens felt the same did not surprise me, given their genders and what Hatsepsit had said earlier about why the seven red pencil ships continued their long trek in search of a new home world. But a gift for saving this kid? I'd only done what any human would do upon seeing a child in danger. Still, my bare shoulders gave me an answer.

"Well, I could use a replacement translator tube. Mine got smashed by that trunk. As did the tubes of my friends Warren and Major Owanju. Could you do that?"

Hatsepsit sighed. "I can do that. And more," she said, her voice coming from the tubes on Cassie and Oksana's shoulders. "I will gift you three with translator tubes. They are useful. But they only work by signal talking with a translator device. We obtained several Empire translator machines during our journey. I will give you one such machine. And twenty translator tubes. They will help you and your friends when you meet other star travelers. Do you accept?"

Accept? I knew what the captain would say. "Yes! Thank you lots!" The shifting of blond-haired Bjorg on the outer edge of the crowd of humans made me smile. "I am sure Doctor Bjorg and Doctor Murphy will appreciate having a device that can so quickly translate the words of other star travelers!"

Bjorg smiled, then gave me a nod of appreciation. Cassie frowned thoughtfully, but gave me a thumbs-up.

Hatsepsit sighed low. "The Empire device does more than translate acoustic sounds. If a star traveling race speaks by way of pheromones, or skin color changes, or even gestures from digits, it can convert that communication mode to your . . . your English." She stepped back as three large female Melanchon ran up from the other side of the meadow. "Now comes Mokladeen's Mother and her family Mothers. Let us leave them to their reunion." The boss orang turned and gestured at a tree on the other side of the meadow. A wooden platform sat across its limbs, maybe ten feet above the ground.

"Will you join me in drinking an intoxicant made from our *melong* fruit balls?" she said. "It is a favorite drink of mine."

"Sure!" yelled Warren.

"A fine idea," Owanju murmured.

"Let's go," Morales said, giving me a happy look and a nod to follow her and the others.

I stepped out of the six inch deep holes my tennies had dug into the soil as I held up the giant limb. It felt good to walk normal again. It felt good to feel a breeze on my face. Most of all, it felt very good to see Mokladeen's Mother sweep her daughter out of Leksatok's big arms and into her own arms. A mother reunited with her child had always been an image I enjoyed seeing. Both at home in Castel Rock, in Chicago while on weekend leave and on the orbital station before we left Earth orbit. It felt good to see the love of a parent for a child. The gift was nice. Better was knowing I had done good.

CHAPTER NINE

"Now will you believe you are a hero? Again!" said Warren from across the table.

"Bilge water."

"Nate, that was amazing what you did," Oksana said. She spread her arms wide in emphasis. "That limb weighed a ton, 2,000 pounds. No Olympic weightlifter has ever lifted anything close to that!"

I closed my eyes, shutting out my friends seated at our table in the Mess Hall. But my ears heard their breathing, their rustling, the low voices of people fifty feet away at the line and staff officers table, the arguing at the NCO and Spacers table, debates on weapons at the Marine table, the hiss of steam cookers attended by the cooks, the clatter of dirty dishes being dumped into the autocleaner, and the entry and exit of many feet as First Shift people came in for lunch, or exited after eating. The smells of seventy other humans also hit me, but not as strongly as hearing every word every person said, if I concentrated on it a little bit.

"I never asked to be born different."

"But you were. And are different," murmured Evelyn from the far side of the table. "That difference saved a life. Feel good about that."

I opened my eyes and looked across the table to our redhead from Ireland. Dressed like most of us in blue and gray camos, her freckles were pale but very visible. As were her brown eyes, which watched me closely. Her expression was engaged, almost eager. As were the looks of Oksana and Warren who sat on either side of her. To my left and right sat Bill and Cassandra. Six at the table versus our usual five made it a bit crowded. Food platters sat in the middle of the table, along with pitchers of tea, juice, water and beer. I didn't feel hungry. Instead, I felt too much the center of attention. My recorder tablet and those of my friends had yielded video of my rescue of Mokladeen. That video had been seen by everyone from the captain down to the lowest cleanup mate. Now, a day after leaving Kepler 22 and our Melanchon friends, any time someone passed me in a hallway they always looked at me weird, as if wondering if I was safe to be around. Or so I thought. That reaction to me being different than other folks was one big reason I had not won any track and field races at Great Lakes, nor blabbed about my super eyesight and hearing. It was hard enough being a country boy fresh from a ranch and new to the big city of Chicago. I did not need more reason for my fellow A-school classmates to treat me different. Now, on this ship, everyone knew what the captain and his XO had figured out. Damn.

"Yeah, I'm glad I could save that little girl." I shrugged, then leaned forward and planted my elbows on the cold metal of the table. I glanced around at my friends. "But any of you would have done what I did. Most any Spacer or officer on the *Star Glory* would have tried to save her. I was just the closest to her. No big deal."

"Bullshit," muttered Bill from my left. "Yes, you were closest. The rest of us were ten meters or more away with Hatsepsit and the other red furballs." He leaned forward. "But like the major said, you moved like a blur. I know. When I heard the crack of the limb breaking off, I glanced back, worried that you might be in danger. Instead, I saw you moving so fast your legs and arms were a blur. You covered thirty feet in way less than a second. I know. I watched. Then you reached up and caught that big bastard limb with both hands." He sighed. "Never seen the like of that, even on the A4E sports channels."

"Nate," said Cassie from my right. "Bill's right. I looked it up on my tablet. The biggest weight ever lifted by any human, male or female, was 263 kilos in the Olympic snatch and grab of 2004. By the Iranian Hossein Rezazadeh. Which equals 580 pounds." She shook her head. "But *you* held up a limb that weighed a ton! That's two thousand pounds or 900 kilos. No one has *ever* lifted that kind of weight, let alone held it up!"

Her praise touched me. I just wished it came from wanting me close to her, rather than admiring me. Instead, she had analyzed my instinctive effort. As had Oksana. The only woman here who looked at me with other than admiration was Evelyn. Who was ten years my senior and a super geek in evolutionary biology. Her look was appraising and thoughtful, with a lift of her lips as if she wanted to try something with me. Something that did not involve brain power. This was too much. Time to change the subject.

"Anyone got any idea how the Empire ships hide their neutrino emissions from detection?"

"Well," said Cassie, looking deeply thoughtful. "One of my physics friends speculated that maybe the Empire encloses their ships in a field that translates their neutrino, infrared, ultraviolet and other emissions into an adjacent dimension. Kind of the way we talk FTL with other ships by sending our neutrino comsignals through an alternate dimension."

"Otherwise known as stealth," muttered Bill. "But I was struck how all their females are bigger and bulkier than the males. The reverse of us humans. Why is that?"

"It's actually rather normal in the animal world," Evelyn said, looking away from me to my friend. "Early this century a scientist named Daphne Fairbairn wrote about that. Females are the larger sex in most reptiles, most amphibians and fishes, and in most insects and spiders. In her study of 49 animal classes, she found 86 percent of the females to be larger than males." She held up a slim white finger. "While humans conform to the pattern among mammals and birds of the male being larger than the female, this is the exception rather than the rule. In general, animal males are small and quick, while females are often robust and several times larger than the male." She smiled, nodding to Bill, Warren and me. "You guys, on average, are only 8 percent taller and 20 percent heavier than human females. And some Marine females can beat the crap out of some Spacer guys!"

Great. Ask a geek a question and get a seminar lecture. "Evelyn, does that pattern also exist on our 12 colony worlds? Among the native animals?"

She looked my way. Her expression went to musing. It was clear she knew I was trying to divert her from her focus on me. "On the colony worlds there are flyer, crawler and swimmer animals in the air, land and seas of those worlds. And yes, the pattern of females being larger than males exists there too." She gave me a sexy grin. "Myself, I happen to like larger males. Major Owanju is too large for my taste. But you, Nathan, are about the right size." Her grin got bigger.

Laughter came from Cassie, Oksana, Bill and Warren.

"My oh my, Nate, it sounds like you have a new admirer," teased Oksana, her blond ponytail swinging as she shook her head.

My Intel friend had a grin on her face too. Damn. Why did all the females at this table see me as easy meat for teasing?

"I also like smart men who are willing to share their emotions," Evelyn said, looking past Warren to Cassie. "Cassandra, what kind of guys do you like to hang with? Or have fun with?"

I gulped. Then I licked my lips. To shield my intense interest in what my math tutor might say I reached out and grabbed a mug and the beer pitcher. I poured beer into the mug, handed it over to Bill, pushed a second mug over to Warren and filled a third mug for myself. As I sipped its coolness, Cassie looked at me with raised eyebrows as if to say "Don't I get a beer too?" Then she looked to our redhead.

"Evelyn, I like smart guys with good manners. But I signed up for this cruise to get exobiology experience enough to apply for a professorship at Stanford. I aim to be the department chief in ten years. Or less." She shrugged her trim shoulders. "Smart men are fine for a dance or a few drinks at a pub. But romance is not on my radar."

"Too bad," the evolutionary biologist geek said softly. She looked to her right. "Oksana, the same question to you. I'm curious since you and Cassandra hang with three guys who are a bit . . . out of the norm for dating prospects."

Oksana frowned. "These guys are my *friends*. They're smart too. And they show respect for what I know that they don't know. Plus they are outside of my chain of command. Which makes it easier to enjoy their company. What about you, Miz full-figured gal?"

Evelyn looked surprised at the reference to her bare-skin appearance during the decontam shower on the Melanchon ship. Then she sat back, looked from Oksana to Bill to me to Cassandra and ending up with Warren. Whose strongly muscled arms she stared at a moment, before returning to my friend. "Oksana, I'm a civilian. I'm not in anyone's chain of command. Which gives me lots of options on this ship." She grinned. "While there is close to 50-50 gender balance on the *Star Glory*, well, hey, I can appreciate a hot gal as much as a hot guy." She shrugged her shapely shoulders. "At the orbital base I did not wait for a guy to ask me out. Or a hot gal. I asked them. Though the names must remain confidential, I did not lack for intimacy on the station." She sighed. "Though here on the *Star Glory* folks do seem a bit focused on rank and chain of command. And since I am not Star Navy of any rank, I think some folks here overlook me when romance enters their mind." Evelyn turned and stared directly at me. "Nathan, do you overlook me?"

Damn. Double damn. And worse. "Evelyn, I think you are as beautiful as Oksana and Cassandra. And I liked working with you on the Melanchon ship." I grabbed an empty mug and filled it. "Here's a beer for you." I then poured mugs of beer for Cassie and Oksana, pushing the mugs to them. I lifted my mug. "A toast to the Melanchon, our new member of the NATO of the Stars!"

Evelyn lifted her mug. "Yes indeed, hail to the Melanchon. Who gave us the location of the pirate base we now head for. And who gave Nathan that nifty translator box and shoulder tubes." She grinned big. "I like being able to be hot in any language!"

I blinked, then did my best to swallow my entire mug of beer. Discovering that Evelyn had the hots for me was nice. Even if it happened in front of the woman I secretly desired, and the rest of my friends. Who were all drinking the cool tasty beer. I should have known my effort to change the subject, in front of three smart and capable women, would not work. These ladies might be shorter than me, but they sure as hell were as fast on the neuron think-crunching as me. Or faster. Well, we still had to eat our lunch. Maybe that would shield me from being the center of attention.

"Hey, anyone want some sushi rolls?"

♦ ♦ ♦

Later that day, at the end of Second Watch, I picked tomatoes from one of the long lines of vines in the roomy spaces of Lieutenant Morales' Farm Deck. The woman who had led our trip to the Melanchon ship was nearby, planting seeds of fruit shrubs given her by the Melanchon folks. In the distance, her regular crew of Spacers and two POs pulled fruit from the cherry, apple, peach and plum trees that grew at the edge of the wheat and rice fields that filled most of the deck. While I would have preferred to have spent my free time in the Forest Room, on the opposite side of the deck, helping Morales had seemed like a good way to spend part of my Second Watch break time. Now, as the gong sounded overhead to alert people to the change to Third Watch, I stood up, a woven basket full of tomatoes in my arms. The basket was one of the other gifts of the Melanchon orang-beings. I headed for the floater carton that sat on a metal bench near the gravlift shaft tube.

"Nathan!" called Morales from behind me. "Thanks for your help! The Mess Hall has been grousing about all the fruit we gave the Melanchon. Getting them that floater carton of veggies should appease them."

I stopped, turned and nodded to her. "Lieutenant, glad to help. But it's time for me to hit my cabin and get some sleep. Should I pull the floater carton with me to the Mess Hall? It's just a deck below Residential."

The mother of two girls and a son gave me a big, engaging smile as she stood up from her seed planting. Her camos were caked with brown dirt and her short black curls were stuck to her forehead, thanks to the sweat that came from laboring under the deck's overhead lights. It might be night by ship hours but the plants on Farm Deck had yet to enter their dusk phase. She waved a dark brown hand in a dismissive gesture.

"No need. I'll have one of the Spacers in the orchard take it up when dusk lighting comes on." She gave me a wink. "You need to get your beauty rest for Evelyn. Or so I hear."

I blushed. Or at least I thought I did. Evelyn had indeed ambushed me after lunch. We had spent a good part of Second Watch in her quarters up on Science Deck. She was a great lover who taught me a few things I had yet to learn about female sensuality. Now it seemed our lunch time chatter had made its way to the shapely ears of Gladys Morales. Middle-aged she might be. Married and the mother of three she was. But she definitely knew how to stay well-informed.

"Well, uh, yeah, I need some rest," I said lamely, turning and dumping my basket of tomatoes into the floater carton. The thing was two feet high, two feet wide and four feet long. It was already filled with balls of green lettuce, cucumbers, asparagus spears, heads of broccoli, bags of shelled peas and a dozen other veggies that I recognized from past meals. There were even a few yellow fruit balls from the Melanchon trees. That surprised me. The fruit balls were few in number and we had no *melong* trees to grow more. Clearly Gladys had decided to share some unique fruit with the Mess Hall cooks as a make-up gesture for grabbing two floater cartons of Earth fruit for our trip over. I headed back to the woman who kept us all fed on real fruit, veggies and mobile meat like chickens and goats, which I could hear jawing at each other from their corrals off to the right. Behind me the gravlift shaft door whooshed open. Someone else had arrived. Which put an end to our friendly informality. I dropped the basket at the end of the row of tomato vines. "Lieutenant, see you—"

"Cow killer! Get over here!" came a loud yell from behind me.

Nehru. I knew that voice like the back of my hand. Or my dirt encrusted shoes. Putting aside a wish to stick a shoe up the man's bum, I nodded to Gladys. "Lieutenant, hope your seeds sprout nicely. Guess it's time—"

"Stewart!" came a second yell.

There was no way to further ignore the bastard. I turned, saw the native of Mumbai, now wearing his Second Shift uniform of Service Khakis, and saluted him.

"Sir!"

The man looked to Gladys who had stepped closer to me. Then he fixed on me. "You ignored my order! That is disobedience to an officer. I will report you—"

"Sir," I interrupted, keeping my right hand lifted in the salute. "I responded when I heard my name called. Anyone calling me by name or rank or both will gain my quick attention. Sir." I walked toward him, stopping a meter away. I lowered my hand. "You called, sir?"

The dark-skinned native of India frowned like a thundercloud. His thick black eyebrows almost joined. His black mustache lifted. His dark brown lips opened.

"Yes I did! Twice!" The man had a head of steam, that was for sure. Why, I had no idea. The boss of Second Watch must have flown down here from the Bridge in order to get here so quickly after the end of his watch. He turned to the floater carton. Walking over to it, he reached out and switched off the gravlift controls. No sound came but the ready light up near one corner went from green to red. "Pick that up! It's broken. And follow me to the Mess Hall. Your betters need food that is not from dead animals!"

I gave a sigh. Then I walked over to the carton. I reached to turn on the floater gravlift control.

"It's broken I said!" Nehru growled. "Lift that carton now! Or I will report you for disobeying a direct order during a time of war!"

Now it became clear. The man was more than his normal upset at me cause I ate beef and had raised cattle on my family's ranch. For whatever reason, the man wanted me in the brig, if he could arrange it.

"Sir, yes sir!" I said, stepping over to the floater carton. Reaching down to its bottom with my left hand, I put my right hand on the carton's top edge. Then I lifted it, swinging it to rest on my left shoulder. It was heavy. Maybe 400 pounds. But it weighed less than what I had held when I carried Bill and Warren away from the MPs. I met his brown eyes. "Sir, I have done as you ordered. What are your further orders?"

"Nehru!" yelled Gladys from behind me. "That floater works just fine. Let him turn on the gravlift. There is no need—"

"You are an O-3 lieutenant," Nehru said harshly, looking past me. "I am an O-4 lieutenant commander and third in the chain of command for this vessel! This man is under *my* command. Return to your dirt grubbing."

Calling Gladys a dirt-grubber was way over the top. Rather than let her get in trouble defending me I headed for the gravlift shaft. "Sir?"

I heard him shift position and turn toward me. "Open the shaft door. Then get in there!"

I could have reached out my right hand to tap the red Open patch. The carton was balanced enough for me to hold it one-handed. Instead, feeling cross, I leaned back, lifted my right shoe and tapped the patch with the shoe toe. The patch went green. The shaft door slid open. I walked inside, then turned around, making sure to not hit Nehru as the scowler followed me inside. He looked me over, then turned, faced the door, tapped the control patch to close it, and then spoke.

"Heidi, take us down to Mess Hall."

Without a word the AI complied. The gravplate we stood on began descending. The red bar of our level slowly went down through Recycling Deck. That deck was 20 meters high, thanks to the tubing, vats, biofilters and other junk that kept our air, water, sewage and trash properly sorted, cleaned and recycled. Next came Armories and Weapons, which was a fifty meter high deck. The ship's four GTO shuttles were stored here in the midbody hangar. This was also the work station for Bill and Warren. One part of it held the combat exoskeleton suits worn by the Marines whenever they entered a hostile environment, plus laser pulse rifles, mortars, MP-3 automatic rifles, heavy machine guns, a few flamethrower units, and tons of sensor devices that were either worn by the combat suits, carried into combat by them or affixed to their transport shuttle. Which now had a terawatt laser added to its nimbleness and ability to land on any planet, asteroid or ship. There were also air-to-air, space-to-space and ground-to-air missiles galore in storage. They were refills for the three missiles carried in each suit's backpack. Warren had once showed me his own combat suit with its helmet HUD, ability to pick up a half ton of anything and its armor-padded outer skin. The thing weighed 400 pounds but internal exoskeleton motors moved it in response to whatever his legs, arms, feet and hands did inside the armor skin. It had amazed me. Much the way Warren had been amazed at the operation of the ship's particle accelerator, its production of antimatter and the invisible-to-him containment magfields that kept negative antimatter from touching solid anything. The red bar now entered the Supplies deck run by the Quartermaster. We were back to a twenty meter high deck, given all the supplies needed for full operation of an aircraft carrier-sized starship. The slow passage of the gravplate gave time for my mouth to speak before engaging my brain.

"Lieutenant Commander Nehru, why do you dislike me so much?"

The stocky man, who was six inches shorter than me but tall for a Hindu from Uttar Pradesh, looked left to where I stood. His lips pursed in a sour look.

"You act without proper orders. Your action on the Melanchon ship was not ordered by Morales, your superior. And you dictated the antimatter release to Chief Warrant Officer O'Connor, rather than respond to a question from him." The man scowled darkly. "If I had not reviewed your file I would not believe you had ever gone through Naval Station Great Lakes! Your lack of proper respect for the chain of command and for obeying orders offends me. You deserve to be treated like the impulsive animal you are." The middle-aged man who had served twenty years in the Star Navy looked away, fixing on the slidedoor. Beside the door the red bar finished passing through Residential Deck and now entered Medical, Mess Hall and Recreation Deck. The bar stopped moving. "Follow me out!"

Well, talk about a no-win situation! I followed Nehru out, then to the right when he headed for the oversize hatch that gave access to the Mess Hall. The deck here was divided into thirds. One-third was the Mess Hall, a second third was Medical and a final third was Recreation which held a basketball court, an Olympic-size swimming pool, a weight room, a rubberized track that followed the outer walls of the chamber, and storage racks for soccer balls, sports outfits and dozens of other things I did not know since I had avoided standing out in any sports field during high school. Nehru stopped in front of the Mess Hall hatch. He looked back at me. A sly grin filled his face.

"It's time for the lower ranks of this ship to see what you are best suited for!"

The man reached out to touch the Open patch. Before he could, the hatch slid to one side. Out came Captain Skorzeny holding a tablet in one hand, which he looked up from. The hatch closed behind the captain, shutting off the scores of conversations, cutlery sounds, cooking hisses and clanking of plates on tables. It also shut off my view of that room. But my eyes had automatically inventoried its contents. Mess Hall held 78 people. Which included seven cooks at the serving line. The gender count was thirty-seven females and forty-one males. XO Nadya Kumisov was the top rank at the line and staff officers table. Major Owanju was holding court at the Marines table. Chief O'Connor argued with a fellow chief at the NCO table. None of my friends were visible or audible. Which brought to mind how quiet it now was in the ring hallway that surrounded the gravshaft. No one else was here, other than me, Nehru and the captain.

Skorzeny's brown eyes fixed on Nehru. Who slowly saluted his superior officer. The captain nodded acceptance of the salute.

"Sir!"

The captain looked past Nehru to where I stood. "Lieutenant Commander Nehru, why is Petty Officer Second Class Stewart shouldering that floater carton?"

The Second Shift commander sucked in his breath. "Sir, the gravlift function is broken. The carton contains fruit and vegetables for the Mess Hall cooks. I encountered Stewart as he was leaving the Farm Deck. I ordered him to carry the carton and follow me as I was heading here to eat dinner."

Captain Skorzeny's clean-shaven face was non-expressive. His gaze shifted from Nehru to me and back to Nehru.

"Why were you on Farm Deck? Mess Hall is lower down."

The Hindu's face grew darker, as if he was blushing. Or upset. "Sir, I was looking for Lieutenant JG Matterling. My personal aide."

Skorzeny's brown eyebrows lowered slightly. "Matterling is inside the Mess Hall. Eating. As you would have discovered if you had gone there first, rather than to Farm Deck." The captain looked up to the overhead. "Heidi, at what time did Lieutenant Commander Nehru arrive on Farm Deck?"

"He arrived there at twenty-hundred and six minutes," the AI said in her musical, feminine tone. It was a voice I liked. Its change to near masculine during the Empire ship encounter had been disturbing to me. Clearly she was back to her normal "Be perky with the crew" persona.

The captain looked down, again fixing Nehru with that expressionless look. "Heidi, when did Lieutenant JG Matterling leave the Bridge?"

"She left at twenty-hundred and eight minutes, after a brief conversation with Second Watch commander Martha Bjorn."

This was getting interesting. While I have super eyesight, hearing and strength, I am not telepathic. Nor have I ever thought to ask Heidi to serve as my own personal spy by way of the videyes that adorn every ship hallway, room and deck. Clearly the captain had thought to do that. And more.

A thoughtful frown now showed on the captain's face. "Lieutenant Commander Nehru, you left behind your personal aide when you left for Farm Deck. So clearly you were not looking for her. Who were you looking for?"

The man who hated my guts now began to sweat. Or least his exposed skin showed an increase in infrared glow as he became hotter. His heart sped up, based on what I could see from the pulsations of his khaki-covered chest.

"Sir, I . . . I expected to find Matterling there. She had previously told me she planned to spend some of her break time there working with Lieutenant Morales."

Fascinating. The man had been caught in an outright lie. Now he was trying to cover it up. Which made me wonder at the penalty for lying to a superior officer in war time.

The captain sighed. "Heidi, project a holo record of Lieutenant Commander Nehru's recent arrival at Farm Deck, his time there and his time in the gravlift up to his arrival on this deck."

"Projecting," the AI said, sounding amused.

What could amuse an AI like Heidi? That she was a practical joker to anyone no matter the rank was well-known. Did she enjoy seeing higher ranks get their comeuppance? That would be too, too human. A holo took form in the ring hallway, filling the space between me and Nehru. The captain stayed where he stood, in front of the Mess Hall exit hatch. That position kept anyone inside from exiting. A fact the captain clearly knew. Had he given Heidi orders to lock shut the hatch entries to Medical and Recreation? Now I heard the start of what had just happened on Farm Deck.

"Cow killer! Get over here!" yelled the image of Nehru.

The holo showed me standing twenty feet beyond him in the inner part of Farm Deck, at the end of the tomato vines row, with Gladys Morales standing a few meters beyond me.

"Stewart!" came Nehru's second yell.

The holo showed me turning toward Nehru and saluting him. "Sir!"

The holo Nehru looked to Gladys, then fixed on me. "You ignored my order! That is disobedience to an officer. I will report you—"

"Sir," my image said. "I responded when I heard my name called. Anyone calling me by name or rank or both will gain my quick attention. Sir." My holo self walked toward Nehru, lowering my salute. "You called, sir?"

The rest followed. Nehru's shutting off the floater carton gravlift control, his assertion it was broken, his order to me to lift it, his pulling rank on Morales, then his entry into the gravlift as he followed me inside. The holo showed us both silent until I asked my question. And got his reply. The holo showed the man stepping out of the gravlift onto Mess Hall deck, turning and heading for the Mess Hall hatch. It stopped upon the appearance of the captain.

"Captain," called Heidi. "Do you wish a replay of the sound and imagery?"

"I do not. Return the imagery to your memory banks."

The holo vanished.

Skorzeny looked to Nehru. His expression was severe. "Lieutenant Commander Nehru, you lied to me. It is clear you went to Farm Deck to harass PO Stewart, with the intention of causing him to parade through the Mess Hall like a beast of burden, or 'animal' as you put it." The captain took a deep breath. His infrared glow was almost the same as when he had come out of the Mess Hall, although the skin on his neck went a bit darker. "Insubordination in a time of war, as you put it in your threat to PO Stewart, is a most serious offense. Lying to your superior officer is insubordination of the worst kind. While I have always valued your ability to manage other people to obtain good performance from them, it is clear some of that performance comes from your abuse of your rank." The captain frowned now. "You are hereby reassigned to manage Third Shift. Your personal aide will be reassigned to assist Lieutenant Senior Grade Bjorn. You will now return to the Bridge and advise, politely, Bjorn that she will now command Second Watch, per my orders now. Do you understand?"

Nehru's infrared glow got darker. His neck and face were nearly red-black. Clearly he was furious. "But sir! Running Second Watch requires a rank of Lieutenant Commander or higher. Bjorn does not have that rank! And Stewart has been—"

The man shut up when the captain raised his right hand palm up. Though Nehru's arms were held straight down at his sides, I could see even in normal light that his muscles were tensed.

"I am well aware of the rank that Second Shift requires. What makes you think Bjorn will remain at lieutenant senior grade status, now that I have moved her to Second Shift command?"

A smile almost showed on my face. I held it back. Gloating over Nehru's demotion to the graveyard watch would not do. It was beyond clear the captain had this situation well in hand. So well in hand that I wondered about what he had been observing in his tablet as he exited the Mess Hall. Had Gladys given him a call?

The captain looked to me. "PO Stewart, switch on the gravlift control."

I reached up with my right hand to tap on the control. Nothing happened other than a low hum I felt more than heard. The weight left my shoulder. I moved out from under the carton, which lowered to hover at four feet above the floor. That was its default floater setting. I grabbed the pull-along strap and looked to the captain.

Skorzeny looked from me back to Nehru. "You also lied about the floater carton being broken. It is not. That is two lies to your superior officer. After you inform Lieutenant Senior Grade Bjorn of her new assignment, go to your quarters. Stay there until the start of Third Shift tomorrow. I will have an orderly bring you meals. And consider yourself lucky that while a captain can promote anyone under his command, demotion to a lower rank of an officer requires the concurrence of the Officers Review Board of EarthGov."

Nehru saluted the captain, his expression rigid. "Sir! I will inform Lieutenant Senior Grade Bjorn of her new shift assignment. Then I will go directly to my quarters."

The man lowered his salute, turned, entered the gravlift and disappeared from sight. In front of me the captain sighed deeply, then peered thoughtfully at me.

"PO Stewart, I am sorry that a senior officer behaved so pettily to you. Follow me into the Mess Hall."

The captain turned around, touched the Open patch to the side of the hatch, then entered Mess Hall. A crowd of six Spacers and NCOs had been waiting to exit. They parted as the captain walked through them. I followed after him, pulling the veggie floater carton.

"Stick around," the captain said to them. He walked further into the middle of Mess Hall, which was raucous with plates clanking, people jabbering and seats creaking from lack of oil as people swiveled their seats at the entry of the captain. His silent stance in the middle of the room caused a gradual quieting of people jabber. I stood just beyond the crowd of Spacers and NCOs, the floater carton hovering just beside me.

"Attention!" the captain called firmly. "As you can see, Petty Officer Second Class Stewart has just arrived with a floater full of fresh fruits and vegetables. Courtesy of Lieutenant Morales and her Farm Deck efforts."

Most people smiled. Chief O'Connor watched me from the NCO table. A few others nodded to me. They were people I had played badminton with or run time trials with on the indoor track. While I knew their rank based on their sleeve chevrons or bars, the names I did not recall. I could if I forced myself to remember. My memory was like that. Kind of like how I could tell my eyes and ears to be 'less special' in what they saw and heard. Anyway, right now I did not need to know the names of the 78 people in the room.

The captain looked to me, a half smile on his face. "PO Stewart helped save this ship with his antimatter beam idea. He further saved the life of a young Melanchon girl during his trip to the ship of our allies. You've seen that video. Yes, he is very strong. But better, he is very very good at anticipating when someone needs help. Or when the ship herself needs help." The man's expression now turned formal. "I hereby announce to one and all that PO Stewart is promoted to Petty Officer First Class! Let's hear it!"

The captain began to clap. Others clapped, including Kumisov at the officers table. The petite Russian had a big smile on her face. As did lots of other people.

"Yay for Nathan!" yelled Major Owanju.

"Double yay!" called Chief O'Connor.

"Drinks!" yelled another Marine at the table. "A toast!"

Oh, crap.

It was tradition on all Star Navy vessels that when someone called for a toast on the announcement of a person's promotion, the promoted person paid for the drinks. Whether they were five glasses of bourbon or twenty pitchers of beer. And on the *Star Glory*, all booze had a price, except on the rare Beer Day during long deployments. At seventy-eight people drinking to my promotion, I did not have to use my mental calculator to know that the increased pay from my new rank was going to be sorely depleted.

I nodded to the captain, then saluted him. "Thank you, Captain Skorzeny." I looked out to the happy crowd. "A toast to our captain!"

The roar that came was louder than the cheers for me. Which was as it should be. Likely no one in the Mess Hall had been watching the captain's encounter with Nehru. But everyone knew what the captain and his Bridge team had done in fighting the sneak attack by the Empire ships. They all knew they were led by a good man and a highly talented officer. I knew that for sure. When someone handed me a mug of beer, I raised it in salute to the captain. Who was smiling easily, shaking his head at the offer of a mug, then a glass of golden bourbon. The man might be off-duty from First Shift, given that it was now Third Shift time. But he knew better than to get drunk in front of his crew. A ship's captain could always be friendly. Informal now and then. But no captain in command of a fighting ship ever allowed himself to be drunk off duty, on duty or at any time other than when in home port. And Captain Neil Skorzeny well understood we were all homeless in the galaxy. At least until we knew enough about this Empire to make it worthwhile to sneak back to Sol and let EarthGov know about the threat posed by the rulers of the Milky Way.

CHAPTER TEN

Seven days later we were about to arrive at Kepler 452, a G2V yellow star with one planet that lay 1,402 light years downarm from Sol. Although from Kepler 22 it was a journey of just 788 light years, or eight days transit thanks to the upgrade of our Alcubierre stardrive. It was the system where the pirate base operated, according to the Melanchon. It was also a very dangerous system, since the Melanchon had warned us there were always ten to twenty pirate starships near the system's outer limits, ready to protect the base from any Empire ship or fleet. While the Empire ships were top of the line combat vessels, they were not invulnerable. Especially when they were expected. As was the case for any ship arriving at Kepler 452. While I now sat in my seat, strapped in and watching the shimmer glow of the antimatter injector tubes that surrounded me, there was no law against me also watching the vidscreen on the nearby bulkhead. In fact I was doing what everyone else on the *Star Glory* was doing. Which was watch the live feed from the Bridge, per the captain's orders. But I could do more than watch. The chief had told me I was free to tap my own armrest comlink patch to speak directly to the captain if I had an idea about ship safety. Maybe so. But Chief O'Connor was a very fair and understanding boss. Short of an emergency, I would always route my comments through him.

In the vidscreen the grayness of Alcubierre space-time disappeared. White star dots took form against the black void of deep space. A yellow star dot glowed in the middle of the image. The adjacent image of the Bridge showed everyone from First Shift, with the captain seated atop the command pedestal. Below him were XO Kumisov, Major Owanju and Doctor Bjorg. A silvery box sat on the floor next to Bjorg. It was the Empire translator device given me by Hatsepsit. The thing was tied into the ship comlink and Heidi, both by way of fiber optic cables and by direct wifi link. It was also connected to Jacob Wetstone's Communications station. In short, the Bridge now had the ability to talk to any alien ship using one of several neutrino comlink frequencies given us by the Melanchon. Of course we also knew the Empire frequency, but we would never use that when talking to aliens. That would identify us as the galactic bad guys. And with only our ship and crew, we needed to be known as good guys. Or at least be known as very dangerous to any vessel that might attack us.

"Captain!" called Chang from her Tactical station. "We've got moving neutrino emission sources in front of us and to the sides."

"How many?" asked Skorzeny.

"Eighteen sources, sir." Chang tapped her panel, then looked back to the captain. "They are scattered over the outer edge of this star's magnetosphere. Which lies at 44 AU out. Closest ship is a half AU from us. Most distant is three AU." She looked back to her panel. "Front sensor array says there are stationary neutrino sources in orbit above the system's single world, which lies at 1.04 AU. That world is on our side of the system. Between the world and us are three asteroid belts, a Kuiper zone of comets and an outer Oort Cloud beyond us. Sir."

"What is their speed?"

"Most are stationary. Uh, correction. The two nearest ships are now moving toward us at one-tenth psol. System graphic imagery going up."

Chang focused her attention on a holo that showed the system graphic. On it were the planet, asteroid belts, Kuiper and Oort Cloud zones. The magnetosphere edge was a dotted line. Sitting stationary were sixteen red dots. Two red dots were moving toward us, one from directly in front and one from our starboard side. Our single green dot was moving inward at one-tenth psol, which was our exit speed from Kepler 22. We were about to touch the outer edge of the magnetosphere. That imagery now joined the overhead view of the Bridge that showed on the nearby vidscreen. Was the captain going to turn the ship so we stayed outside the star's magnetosphere? Would he order us to do a mini-jump to another part of the system's edge?

"Com, activate the neutrino frequency for the pirate base," Skorzeny said, sitting ramrod straight in his seat.

The captain wore a vacsuit with his helmet hinged back. Which was exactly how Chief O'Connor, PO Gambuchino and her Spacers, myself and everyone else on the ship were dressed. We were at Combat Ready status. My ears heard every breath taken by the people on Engineering Deck. My eyes saw everyone's infrared glow brighten. Tense time it was.

"Activated," Wetstone said.

The captain stared straight ahead at the front vidscreen, which lay beyond the view of the overhead videye.

"I am Captain Neil Skorzeny of the heavy cruiser *Star Glory*. We call ourselves humans. We are enemies of the Empire of Eternity. We wish to trade for supplies and weapons with you. Respond."

Nothing happened for several seconds.

"Incoming neutrino signal!" cried Wetstone. "Going up on the front vidscreen. Also going out on All Ship vidfeed!"

The bulkhead vidscreen grew an image in its middle, forcing to either side the overhead view of the Bridge and the system graphic image.

Something that resembled a red lobster crossed with a centipede took shape. Four blue eyestalks moved above a mouth filled with chitin-teeth. Its two front arms rose. One arm ended in a giant claw with serrated edges. The other arm ended in stick-like fingers that were radial in arrangement, allowing any two of the six fingers to touch like a thumb and finger. Behind the bulbous head rose a plated body and tail, its dark red armor plates covered in yellow and black spots. Underneath its long, low body were dozens of tiny feet that resembled what millipedes and centipedes used for walking. Or scuttling. Or whatever those bug creatures did to move over the ground. The creature's mouth opened. Inside was a green tongue. It made sounds.

"Responding to Captain Neil Skorzeny, captain of the human heavy cruiser *Star Glory*. Who gave you the location of this base? And knowledge of this frequency?"

"The Melanchon leader Hatsepsit gave me your location and frequency," the captain said. "She said your base was willing to trade with any ship that opposes the Empire. We do. Will you trade with us?"

Two eyestalks looked to one side. The other two eyestalks leaned forward. "The Melanchon were interesting beings. You are friends with them?"

"We are."

The two side-looking eyestalks joined the other two in leaning forward. "My image device shows you heading into this system. Two raider ships are heading your way. Do you understand the terms of trading with this base?"

The captain nodded quickly. "Yes. The Melanchon told me that any ship which arrives at this system must battle any attacking ship. If a ship survives to reach your base above this system's world, you will trade with that ship. Otherwise, you will not."

Damn. That was a detail I had not heard from Hatsepsit or Madamedura. Clearly our captain had learned that. Along with the neutrino comlink frequency of the base.

"Correct," the lobster creature said. "We are raiders of the Empire. Each ship on the edge of this system is commanded independently. But all are committed to protecting this base. Let us see if you humans are worthy of trading with us." There came a pause in its speech. "If you survive to dock with my orbital base, no ship will attack you. And you will be allowed to depart without pursuit. But if one of our protector ships can defeat you, well, you and your ship contents will belong to that ship." The four eyestalks moved in a wave sideways. "After all, it is only by attacking the weaker that we raiders obtain what we have to trade. Be weak and be property. Survive and you may trade with us."

The captain grinned, showing his teeth. "We humans are very deadly. We killed two Empire ships when they attacked us. Perhaps your two raiders may wish to avoid that fate."

Two of the eyestalks looked sideways. "The death of any Empire vessel is always welcome. But there are many of them. Far more than there are raiders like us. Show us your deadliness. Then we will trade."

"What is your name?" the captain asked.

The four eyestalks held still. The serrated mouth opened. "My cohort designator is Tik-long, of the species Nagal, formerly of the world Blue Waters. Closing frequency."

The lobster-centipede image vanished. Replacing it was a true space image from the ship's electro-optical scope. In the scope image was a red dot with a yellow flame at one end. Whether it was the ship in front of us or the ship to starboard I did not know. But clearly it was the closest attacker. The captain leaned forward.

"Tactical, what's the range to the nearest alien ship?"

"Sir, the nearest ship is one-fourth AU distant, moving toward us at one-tenth of lightspeed," Chang said softly. "The starboard ship is one AU distant and moving toward us at the same speed. Both ships are at CBDR."

Which meant both raider ships were at Constant Bearing Decreasing Range. No matter what order the captain gave Astrogation, those two ships would maintain their intercept angle. Which was very much like what had happened with the Empire ships at Kepler 37. We had some time to prepare. Our speed of ten psol amounted to 66 million, 960,000 miles per hour. Which meant it took an hour and ten minutes to travel one AU. That was the time we had until the starboard ship intercepted us. The oncoming ship, though, we would see much sooner, since it was closing on us as we closed on it.

"XO, suggestions?" Skorzeny said.

"Let's try our x-ray laser thermonukes. Their range is 20,000 kilometers." Kumisov tapped on her own control panel, then looked at a system graphic hologram that appeared before her. "When the ship ahead gets to 50 kay range, let our bow proton and CO_2 lasers fire at them. The beams will die out at 10,000 klicks. That will cause the raider to think that is the max range of our directed energy weapons." She smiled in the bulkhead vidscreen. "When they hit 20,000 klicks, we can fire our x-ray thermonuke warheads. The x-rays will pass through their ship hull and kill everyone onboard. Sir."

"Good tactic." The captain looked forward. "Astrogation, put us on a vector track away from the starboard ship and toward the forward ship." Skorzeny looked to a different area of the function stations that filled the front of the Bridge. "Weapons, put our lasers, missiles and railguns on Hot Ready status."

"Sir, new vector set," called Louise Ibarra from Astrogation.

"All Weapons stations moving to Hot Ready status," muttered Bill Yamamoto.

The captain touched his right armrest. "Chief O'Connor, fire up our thrusters. Give me flank speed in forty seconds."

I saw my boss's thick shoulders tense. "Sir, thruster containment fields going up. DT pellets injecting. Fusion implosions are nearing max plasma density. Exhausting!"

My feet felt the deck vibrating from the pumps that moved frozen deuterium and tritium pellets from our fuel bunkers down past the Engineering Deck and into the fusion chambers of our three thrusters. Those were the domain of the chief. My domain was the antimatter we used for our afterburner push.

"Sir!" called Chang. "Both the starboard and forward ships have increased speed to 15 psol! They have whatever the Empire ships have that allows them to move so fast."

Double damn. I looked away from the vidscreen to the nine tubes surrounding my station. The rainbow shimmer was uniform and stable. Soon the captain would—

"Engineering, move us out at flank-plus speed," Skorzeny said calmly.

"PO Stewart, activate the antimatter flow."

I slapped my touchscreen. "Antimatter is flowing down all tubes, Chief O'Connor."

The deck floor vibration increased as the negative antimatter hit the positive fusion plasma formed by the laser-generated combining of deuterium and tritium isotopes. A digital readout on my panel slowly rose from 10 psol to 10.4, 10.6, 10.9 and finally eleven psol.

"Chief, we are moving at maximum flank-plus thrust," I said.

"Chief," called Gambuchino. "Our fusion reactor is feeding ninety terawatts power to each thruster. Similar full power flows going out to Weapons stations, Environmental and to our gravity plates."

"Captain," the chief said calmly. "We are moving at flank-plus speed. Our reactor is feeding extra power to Weapons and other stations. Sir."

"Sir!" called Chang. "The forward ship is within 100,000 kilometers of us and closing fast!"

I glanced at the bulkhead vidscreen. The electro-optical image of the raider ship now showed a box with long tubes on either side that spat yellow flame. Domes were spotted here and there. Likely they were laser or directed energy beamer nodules. Would these aliens use free electron or hydrogen fluoride lasers against us? Both laser types were slated for the next generation of heavy cruisers. Course, once we returned home, EarthGov might add gamma ray lasers to the offensive mountings on our combat ships. But home lay in the future. I hoped.

"All Ship! Go to General Quarters! Seal your helmets!" Skorzeny said loudly.

The overhead lights went to blinking red. Three loud horn hoots sounded. My seat straps tightened. I pulled my clear globular helmet over my head and down until it locked into the vacsuit's neckring. Then I looked up and aside at the rainbow shimmer of the AM tubes. As before the fields were showing perfect shimmer. Liters of antimatter now flowed down to join the yellow-orange plasmas of our three thrusters. My ship was moving as fast as it could. A new vibration told me the Astro woman had begun sideways jinking to make harder any targeting of the ship by lightspeed weapons. A glance at the nearby bulkhead vidscreen showed the red raider ship was now at 35,000 klicks out.

"Weapons, eject four x-ray thermonuke missiles," the captain said softly. "Target them at the oncoming raider ship. Wait for my word on detonation of their warheads. And also launch Hunter-Killer mines to our starboard and rear. Feed them the rad emission signature of the starboard enemy ship."

"Launching mines and missiles," Yamamoto said quickly. "Mines are loaded with enemy emission signature. Our four stern silos have ejected their missiles. At five warheads per missile, that makes twenty x-ray laser warheads available to hit the target. Sir."

"Tactical, advise me on range to enemy ship ahead."

"Range is now at 25,000 klicks, sir."

The captain stared intently at the front wallscreen. "Weapons, fire our bow proton and CO_2 lasers."

"Firing both lasers," Yamamoto said as he tapped his control panel.

In the electro-optical scope image I saw two beams reach out. One was red for the proton beam. The other was the green from the CO_2 laser. The beams flickered out at 10,000 kilometers. The red box and tubes raider ship stopped its sideways jinking, which it had been doing ever since coming within 100,000 kilometers. Clearly it thought our weapons range was just 10,000 kay.

"Captain, enemy is now at 20,000 kay range" Chang said sharply.

Over the All Ship vidfeed, I heard him take a deep breath. "Weapons, transmit tri-axis location of enemy ship to the x-ray laser warheads. Then detonate them."

In my mind a picture formed of one of those warheads. I had studied them at Great Lakes. Inside each missile cone were five one-megaton thermonuke warheads. Surrounding each warhead casing were ten metal-rich crystalline rods. They were called the gain medium. In short, in the nanoseconds just after a thermonuke detonates, it emits high energy photons. Those photons would hit each rod, which would convert them to x-rays that shot out along the long axis of each rod. Wherever a rod was pointed, a coherent beam of x-rays would travel. And because each beam was highly coherent with very little dispersion, the range of each rod was 20,000 kilometers. With four missiles launched that contained five warheads each, with each warhead surrounded by ten rods, the detonation of all four missiles would generate 200 x-ray laser beams. In theory, those beams could be independently targeted against a cloud of incoming enemy missiles launched above Earth's atmosphere. That had been the objective of the Project Excalibur tests carried out by America more than a century ago. Now, if all eighteen raider ships were within 20,000 kays of the *Star Glory*, our x-ray laser beams could target every one of those ships. Instead, with just one ship in range, that ship would be on the receiving end of 200 x-ray laser beams.

"Detonating!" called Yamamoto.

I watched the bulkhead vidscreen and its electro-optical image. Heidi was tied into this scope image. Which was how there now appeared 200 white lines reaching out from us to hit the red box and tubes of the raider ship. Since x-rays were invisible unless passing through air or a radiograph plate, the AI had overlaid the white beam lines.

"Hits!" cried Yamamoto. "All 200 hit the enemy!"

"So they did," the captain murmured. "Tactical, what was the range to the raider ship when it was hit?"

"Range was 18,910 kilometers," Chang said.

"XO," the captain said, looking down to his left. "What is your estimate of penetration depth for those beams?"

Kumisov leaned forward, her long black hair shiny under the Bridge lights. "Sir, if the raider hull is similar to our armor hull of steel, titanium, chrome and lead, the beams will penetrate all interior spaces. The hull would have to be made of a meter of lead, or three meters of solid rock, in order to partially block penetration. We will know in a few minutes if anyone is still alive there."

"So we will," the captain murmured. "Astrogation, move us starboard by 200 kilometers. Maintain current heading."

"Shifting course starboard," Ibarra said.

In the vidscreen the yellow flare of the raider ship's thrusters vanished. It continued moving toward us at 15 psol. That was its inertial momentum, which would not change until it hit a comet, an asteroid or some other ship sent in a boarding party. But its orientation did not change to match our sideways move.

"Sir, raider ship has gone unpowered," Chang said softly. "Its vector track is unchanged."

"One down, one still pursuing," the captain said slowly. "Weapons, launch four missiles to our starboard. Set their track on an intercept vector to the incoming raider ship. Then disperse each missile's warheads."

Yamamoto touched his control panel. "Missiles launched. Silos clear." He tapped it again. "Missile vectors are adjusted toward the incoming track of the raider. Nose cones have released warheads. Sir."

That put twenty warheads each loaded with ten x-ray lasing rods between us and the incoming enemy ship. Which the system graphic image now showed was still twelve million kilometers away. It would intercept us in less than fifteen minutes. The captain spoke.

"Com, activate the pirate base neutrino frequency."

"Frequency activated," Wetstone said hurriedly.

"Raider ship that is pursuing the heavy cruiser *Star Glory*. Be warned. We have ejected the same weapon that just now killed all beings inside the raider ship that was closest to us," the captain said casually, almost as if he were discussing a Friday night poker game. "Even if your lasers manage to kill parts of this weapon, you will not find all parts of it. The surviving part will irradiate your ship with x-rays. If you wish to die, continue on your current vector track. Closing frequency."

I looked over to where Chief O'Connor sat before his thruster control panel. The wide-shouldered man shrugged as he saw my look. I glanced to where PO Gambuchino sat before her fusion reactor controls. Beside her sat her three Spacers. All four looked both relieved and worried. Which was exactly how I felt. We had defeated one enemy ship. But in doing so we had revealed the range of our deadliest weapon. If the pirate raiders had lasers with a range greater than ours, they could parallel our vector at 15,000 klicks and fire on us while we could not hit them.

"Captain!" cried Louise. "The raider ship is changing vector! It is curving back up toward the edge of the magnetosphere. Its closest approach will be three million kilometers. Sir."

That meant the Hunter-Killer mines ejected by our topside railgun and the thermonuke warheads would miss. Maybe the captain would keep them alive until the raider was clearly moving opposite to our vector track. Then he might send the self-destruct order to the mines and the thermonuke warheads. There was no point in allowing the pirates to capture those weapons. Best to keep them guessing.

"Good. Tactical, monitor the vector of the pursuing raider," the captain said, sounding relieved. "Advise me if it changes course toward us. Also monitor the status of the other sixteen raider ships. And keep watch directly ahead. There could be raider ships hiding in one of the three asteroid belts lying ahead."

"Monitoring," Chang said. "Will advise on the matters you list. Sir."

I looked again at the nine vertical antimatter injector tubes. Negative antimatter was still flowing down them. That antimatter was combining with the positive plasmas in the three thrusters to give us an extra push of one percent of lightspeed. Which made me wonder again about just what device or system was used by the Empire and these raider ships that allowed them to move at 15 psol through normal space? Maybe the pirate boss would know. After all, these protector ships worked for him. Which made me wonder how the lobster-centipede critter motivated the protector ships to hang around the edge of the star's magnetosphere. Clearly they could leave on their Alcubierre stardrives at any moment. Instead, they stuck around. Why? And just what awaited us at this orbital base? Would the aliens there be as aggressive as these raider ships had been? We had just proven the deadliness of humans. So presumably we could now dock at the base, once we traversed the deep space void that lay between us and the base. But what would happen once we docked? All I knew was that I trusted Captain Skorzeny. He was a leader like few I had ever read about. And none that I had ever met. Follow him I would, to the ends of the galaxy and beyond.

CHAPTER ELEVEN

A day and a half later we arrived just above the pirate base. It was a giant construct that orbited above a green and blue planet that clearly had oceans, forests and mountains. What else lay below I did not know. Or care. Instead I focused on the bulkhead vidscreen image of the orbital base. It was a monster. And there were twelve ships attached to the base by boarding tubes. The scale on one side of the true space image showed the misshapen monster to be ten kilometers long, four wide in one dimension and five in another angle. It appeared to be a mix of blocks, globes, transit tubes, domes, a few of which were made of clear something that allowed the local star's light in to brighten spaces that were green and brown, and sheet metal angles that connected it all into a single whole. It was clear to me this thing had not been constructed all at once according to some master plan, like the stations above Earth and in orbit above our colony worlds. This thing appeared to be an accretion of sections. It did not spin. Which told me it must have gravplates inside and plenty of energy to power them. What else lay inside we were about to discover. In the vidscreen, a flexible tube snaked out from a boxy area and headed for our midbody hangar airlock.

"You ready, Stewart?" called my boss from across Engineering.

"Yes sir, Chief O'Connor." I released my accel straps, stood up, grabbed my recorder tablet from where it was stuck to my seat, hung it from the belt of my black pants and walked toward him. XO Kumisov had told us not to wear vacsuits when she had called down to say we were part of the boarding group. It had felt good to feel the whisper of circulating air against my face and hair over the last day and a half. I'd enjoyed two lunches with my friends, one of which included Evelyn who gave me several winks and a come hither smile. Warren had intercepted her attentions, for which I owed him. Or did I? There had been no sign of Nehru, thank the Goddess. And the rest of the ship's crew had gone into ease-off mode after the captain canceled General Quarters. While the ship had remained at Combat Ready status, our front and rear sensor arrays had not detected any alien ships near our vector track. There had been four ships heading out from the planet, and three of the protector ships had left the magnetosphere edge and headed inward. I assumed they were on break from their duties. But the captain did not ask the boss lobster and Doctor Bjorg, Cassandra and others on Science Deck had better things to do than speculate on the unknowable. I stopped at the chief's station.

He looked up. His beady-black eyes scanned me. Then he released his own straps and stood up. The chief was a foot shorter than me but his wide shoulders were broader than mine. The man grabbed his own recorder tablet and stuck it to the belt of his service khaki pants. He looked past me.

"PO Gambuchino! You are in command of Engineering now. Run the diagnostics as usual and keep your Spacers from falling down drunk. Understood!"

"Yes sir, chief," replied Dolores from her fusion reactor station on the other side of the gravshaft tube. "Cindy, Duncan and Gus will have this place shinning brighter than bright!"

"I'll believe it when I see it," rumbled the chief. He stepped past me. "Follow."

"Sir, following," I said, turning and following him across the big room to the gray metal tube of the gravshaft.

The chief tapped the Open patch. It went from red to orange. Which meant the gravplate was on the way down to us. "Stewart, you need anything from your quarters before we join the captain?"

"No sir." Then a thought hit me. "Uh, chief, do I need to bring a personal weapon?"

"The captain will tell us that," the chief said. The Open patch turned green. The slidedoor opened. We both stepped in. The door slid shut. "Heidi, take us up to Armories and Weapons Deck."

"Ascending," the AI said brightly.

The red bar slowly moved up from the bottom of the status tube. We passed through the antimatter fuel deck, then entered the DT fuel bunkers deck. I kept my mouth shut, having learned from the episode with Nehru that asking questions was a guarantee of trouble. The chief stayed silent, facing forward, his breathing slow and relaxed. His infrared glow was normal. There was no sign of excitement or anger in his glow. And what I heard of his body functions were very normal. His belly hardly made a sound. Clearly the man was not hungry. Nor was I. If we stayed long on the station I assumed there would be alien eateries there. Whether their version of food would be human palatable, who could tell?

The red bar stopped at Armories and Weapons. The slidedoor swished to one side. The chief and I stepped out into the ring hallway. Like most of the other decks, different chambers of the deck stretched out in pie segments from the central gravshaft. The two backup gravshafts on the port and starboard sides of the ship, and the emergency stairs, were out of sight. The chief turned right and walked fast. I followed him, walking just as fast. He stopped before the outline of a medium size hatch. Above the hatch were stenciled the words Hangar One. He tapped the door's Open patch. We stepped into a clatter of noise as a dozen people worked and talked inside a space that resembled a control room. This was the place where hangar pressurization, gravity and shuttle departure was managed. The people here chattered, gestured to each other and a few walked from one monitoring panel to another. Ignoring the seated Spacers and NCOs, the chief turned right, headed for a person-high hatch, tapped its Open patch, and stepped in. I followed. The hatch closed behind us. In front of us was another hatch. Which appeared to be an airlock hatch similar to the one we had just passed through. The chief again tapped its Open patch. With a low creak of metal against Teflon gaskets, the hatch swung open. I followed him into bedlam.

"O'Connor, over here!" came a yell from the far side of the hangar.

My eyes and ears felt sudden overload. Before I could tell my senses to not inventory completely, they did just that.

The call had come from Major Owanju, whose black face peered at us from within the helmet of his combat suit. His visor was flipped up, rather than sealed. The armored suit made him eight feet tall. Its external speaker amplified his words. Those words were supplemented by a Come Here gesture from his gauntleted left hand.

"Coming!" the chief yelled.

My mind extended its inventory of the fifty meter high space in which we now walked. Hanging from the overhead were the dart shapes of the four GTO shuttles. They hung from cables. That kept the hangar floor clear for an incoming shuttle, and for storage of fuel and combat supplies. As I walked behind the chief I finished my inventory. My friends Cassie, Oksana, Bill and Warren stood near the tall form of Captain Skorzeny, who waited at the other side of the hangar beside an airlock hatch that clearly connected to the ship's outer hull. Close to my friends stood Doctor Bjorg, Lieutenant Morales and Evelyn, who waved my way and gave me a big smile. I waved back to her, pleased to see her. She and Cassie were the two people most vital to figuring out any aliens we met. Cassandra cause she had degrees in exobiology and anthropology, and Evelyn because of her evolutionary biology training. Standing next to the blue and gray camo dressed people were three more white combat suits, their visor plates down and sealed. Their bulky backpacks showed the noses of three rockets sticking out. Like Owanju each carried a laser pulse rifle, an MP3 automatic slugthrower, and a chest pack of blinking sensor devices. One of the three had the globe of a flamethrower unit strapped to his or her left arm, its flaring nozzle aimed wherever the suit's hand pointed. The only weapon not visible was a mortar and its base plate. Maybe one of the backpacks held it. Or maybe Major Owanju had decided four combat suits with their loads of firepower were enough for what should be a peaceful stroll through the pirate base. The chief stopped not far from our boss. He saluted. So did I.

"Captain Skorzeny, Chief Warrant Officer O'Connor reporting, along with Petty Officer Stewart, as ordered, sir!"

The captain returned the salute. The man wore perfectly ironed service khakis with his ribbons and pins on his left chest, his nameplate above his right pocket, and a black recorder tablet attached to his black belt. His curly brown hair was covered by a standard officer's hat with brim.

"Welcome, Chief O'Connor." The captain nodded at the people around him. "I figure four Marines in combat suits should suffice for our security. However." He gestured to Owanju, who held a black bag that was filled with sharp-edged stuff. "We are about to enter a place we have never been before. And we are still in wartime status. So. Major, hand out the handguns and ammo to these people."

Owanju reached inside the black bag and pulled out a gray steel handgun. I recognized it as the Star Navy's copy of the 1911A1 semi-auto. It held a clip with eight .45 caliber bullets, some of which might be armor-piercing. The gun was stowed in a brown leather holster with hooks that allowed the holster to attach to a person's belt. The major handed the holster, gun and two clips to Bjorg, who took it, looked puzzled, checked to confirm a clip was already in the pistol, then clipped it to the right side of his belt. His bulging beer belly already made tight his blue and gray camo shirt. But there was room for the holster to attach. The two clips went into pockets. In a few minutes the major handed out the same grouping to each of us. Since all of us wore pants with belts, including the women, there was no trouble in mounting the .45s. And I liked having the semi-auto hanging from my right hip. On our ranch I'd used a gun like that to take out rattlesnakes with shotshells. And to scare off coyotes that came too close to our ranch. While this type of handgun was frowned on for use inside a pressure vessel like a plane or a spaceship, still, its bullets had solid stopping power on anything weighing up to four hundred pounds. And who knew what size of aliens were inside this station? And whether they would be friendly?

The captain nodded at the airlock hatch. "Through there, you three," he said to the other suited Marines. "Major, bring over your entry security detail, please."

"Yes sir, captain," Owanju said, tapping a spot on his chest pack.

The clanking of heavy boots against the metal of the hangar deck hit my ears like someone shouting. I looked back the way we had come. Ten more eight foot high Marines marched our way, each enclosed in a white armored combat suit. Each Marine had weaponry similar to that worn by Major Owanju and his three escorts. The lead Marine stopped. He lifted a white armored left hand and saluted.

"Major! Entry security detail reports!" came a female voice.

The major smiled through his open visor. "Master Sergeant Jenkins, follow us down the loading tube attached to our ship's hull. Once we enter the space beyond the tube, set up a security perimeter. Let nothing, no device, no robot, no AI and no living thing move past you into our ship. Understood?"

"Understood!" came the foghorn loud affirmation from a woman whose combat tours stretched back twenty years, according to what Warren had shared with me.

The captain turned, touched open the airlock hatch and entered. The rest of us followed him. Fourteen people, with four in bulky combat suits, filled the airlock chamber. Behind us the outer hatch closed. The ten suited Marines would clearly follow once we exited the airlock into the tube. The captain tapped on his comlink tab.

"Life Support, have you confirmed the presence of air and pressure inside the boarding tube?"

"Sir, there is Earth-normal pressure and oxy-nitro air close to Earth standard in the boarding tube," Becky Woodman responded.

I heard her words over my own comlink tab. It was attached to my right shoulder. On my left shoulder was pinned one of the translator tubes given us by Hatsepsit. Everyone in our group had a translator tube attached to them, including the combat-suited Marines. I noticed Warren looking up at Owanju and the other three Marines, a yearning expression on his face. I understood the look. He was a Marine corporal. He wanted to enter this place dressed like a Marine in full combat gear. Instead, he wore only a .45 semi-auto. Why the captain had ordered him to come with us wearing only camos, when three-fourths of the Marine platoon were now involved in providing entry security and security for our contact group, I did not know. Likely Warren didn't know. He just followed orders and stayed combat alert. As I could tell from his posture. Bill, I now noticed, had a small laser pistol stuck into his back belt. Being a proton laser gunner, I was not surprised my friend wanted a laser with him. Surely the captain had noticed the pistol sticking out above his rear belt. The sight of the laser pistol was reassuring as its range greatly exceeded a .45 bullet's usual range in a one gee grav field. Which made me wonder just what level of gravity we would find once we entered the station? The captain tapped the Open patch beside the airlock hatch. It swung open. Beyond lay a yellow-lighted space. He gestured to Owanju and his Marines.

"Major, you go—"

"Entering, sir," the boss Marine said, his visor now closed. "Jones, Osashi and Khan, follow!"

Owanju entered the boarding tube with his laser pulse rifle aimed forward. His three Marines followed, each aiming their rifle in a way that avoided cross-fire which could hit the major or another Marine. The captain followed after the last Marine. Next went Lieutenant Morales, then Doctor Bjorg and Chief O'Connor. The rest of us followed. I stepped in front of Cassie, Oksana and Evelyn. It was something I had been trained to do at home in Colorado. Always precede any woman to open the door for them. Course the sensor activated automatic doors at stores now made that an antique behavior. Still, my Natural parents had insisted on that courtesy from me. So I did it for my Mom and two sisters, just as my Dad did it for them, until he passed from the cancer that killed him. Warren and Bill brought up the rear, with Bill closing the airlock hatch so the ten Marines could safely enter the airlock room. As soon as we stepped away from the ship's hull we hit null gravity. The Marines reached out to the opaque brown walls of the tube, pushed on them and floated ahead, rifles aimed forward. The rest of us did the same. In short order fourteen people became a flock of human birds, each one following after the shoes or boots of the person ahead. While the tube was two meters wide, we fell into single file mode out of habit. And out of training in small unit tactics. Even the civies of Science Deck had taken basic combat training courses at Great Lakes, as a requirement for boarding the *Star Glory*. The captain arrived at the end of the tube. Facing him was a circular red metal hatch. A blinking green oval lay in the middle of the hatch.

"Tactical, how are things up on the Bridge?" the captain called.

"Nominal, sir," called Chang over the comlink tabs we each wore. "Twelve other ships are tube-docked like us. No other ships are within ten AU of the base. There is no sign of any threat from the planet, local space or from the edge of the magnetosphere. And Lieutenant Commander Bjorn sends her regards."

"Good. Keep an eye on neutrino emissions from the system's edge. If the Empire shows up, I want early notice so we can fly away in the opposite direction!"

The reassurance from the Bridge was nice to hear. Even nicer was knowing that Martha Bjorn was in command. I liked the woman. She was a Swede like Bjorg, but her personality was quite different from that of the high-brow academic. She was military first and foremost, and she showed it in how she took care of her shift people. And in her ease at speaking with enlisted Spacers and NCOs. With her covering our back, I felt a bit more at ease entering a totally unknown space station.

The captain tapped the green oval. It turned yellow. The hatch swung inward. A voice sounded from beyond.

"Beware the gravity transition change," said a voice that sounded mechanical.

The four suited Marines floated past the captain, their legs pulled up to their chests in preparation for a downward drop. Which happened a foot past the rim of the open hatch. I saw what the captain saw. A yellow-lighted space beyond the hatch looked empty. The Marines moved away and to either side of the hatch.

"Captain, gravity registers at 70 percent of a gee," called Owanju. "Nothing live in this chamber. We are covering, sir."

"Understood."

The captain copied the legs pulled up movement of the Marines and pushed his floating body forward. He dropped to the floor of the chamber and moved to the left. Morales, Bjorg and O'Connor followed him. Then the rest of us floated forward past the hatch rim, dropped, adjusted to the feel of the lighter gravity and stepped to one side so we were out of the way of incoming people. I scanned the chamber we stood in. It was five meters wide by ten meters long and four meters high. On either side of the chamber were racks from which hung various types of vacsuits. Some storage boxes stood where the deck met the bulkhead. The metal was red colored. It seemed these aliens liked red. Behind me Warren closed the entry hatch.

"Captain, hatch is closed," my friend said.

"Good. Master Sergeant Jenkins, come down the tube and join us. I want you ten with us before we go further."

The fourteen of us waited long minutes. Nothing spoke to us. Nothing live showed in the space beyond the inner airlock hatch that had a small porthole in its middle, plus the green oval in its middle. The thud of boots behind me said the first combat suited Marine had reopened the outer hatch, floated through and dropped to the floor.

"Major, entry security detail is ready," Jenkins said, her voice an interesting mix of male assertiveness and higher toned female speech. "The boarding tube hatch is closed. Sir."

I stood at the far left side of the airlock chamber. Which was now crowded with twenty-four humans, fourteen of them in eight foot tall combat suits. Major Owanju stood before the inner airlock hatch.

"Major, open the hatch," the captain said, sounding calm and relaxed.

"Opening."

The major's gauntleted fist tapped the green oval. Its color went to yellow. It swung inward. Moving in with the swing of the hatch was the major, followed quickly by his three Marines.

"Humans!" yelled a voice that came over my shoulder translator tube. "There is no threat here! Enter to trade or leave."

The captain followed the four Marines into the room beyond. Bill and Warren ran to the open hatch and jumped through it, able to move a bit faster than the suited form of Jenkins. Who quickly followed. Morales followed the big sergeant. I ran quickly and followed the Farm Deck boss. Behind me came several suited Marines, followed by Cassie, Oksana and Evelyn. The remaining Marines came after them, based on what my super sensitive ears told me. I did not look back to confirm what my hearing had detected. Instead, I focused on the creature in front of us, at the far end of a large chamber that resembled a human warehouse.

A raccoon-like being stood before us. Tall as Cassie, it was covered in gray fur with black stripes running from its triangular head down to its thick tail. While it had two tufted ears, two short legs and two arms with clawed fingers, the rest of it was alien weird. Three red eyes ran across its forehead. A narrow slit below the eyes seemed to be a nose or air entry. Below the nose slit was a triangular jaw filled with long yellow canines. One of its hands held a round disk that it now looked up from. From its shoulders hung leather straps that went down and connected to a leather belt at its waist. From the belt hung pouches filled with pieces of metal that looked like tools versus weapons. Then again, who knows what an alien hand weapon looks like? But what now stood before us was definitely a carnivore predator, based on its teeth and the bright warning colors that the science of aposematism said were a declaration of danger to any other predator.

The captain stepped past the line of Owanju, Jones, Osashi and Khan. Who had their laser pulse rifles aimed forward, though not directly at the being that faced us. Our captain walked forward slowly, drawing closer to the furry alien. The rest of us followed him.

"I am Captain Neil Skorzeny, commander of the heavy cruiser *Star Glory*, which is now attached to your station. The being Tik-long said it was willing to trade with us. We are here to trade."

The three red eyes of the raccoon-being blinked. Then each eye moved independently, scanning everyone in the big warehouse room. They focused back on the captain.

"My designator is Wick-lo," it said, its jaws moving up and down as it spoke. A pink tongue formed barks, grunts and growls that were translated to English. "I am Prime Assistant to Decider Tik-long. It is my duty to convey you to meet him. Why do you humans carry what my sensors say are weapons?"

I had a side view of the captain. His expression was as neutral and unmoving as when he had confronted Nehru. "As I warned Decider Tik-long, we humans are deadly beings. We always carry weapons with us whenever we visit places not controlled by us." He gestured to the rear. "Ten of the white-suited humans, whom we call Marines, will stay in this chamber as entry security. They will prevent any lifeform or robot from accessing my ship. Four Marines," he gestured to Owanju. "Will be my personal guard. They go where I go, enter where I enter, see what I see and are ready to protect me and my assistant humans from any harm. If you object, tell Tik-long we will not trade with him. And he will lose valuable items."

The creature's three red eyes all focused forward. It was clear it had binocular vision when it wished, in addition to chameleon-like sideways vision thanks to its mobile eyes. Its jaws opened. "How many humans will exit this chamber with me?"

"Fourteen," the captain said. "Four Marines, myself and my assistants, who have special knowledge relevant to trading we wish to do with Tik-long."

The raccoon who called himself Wick-lo turned away and walked quickly toward the oval outline of a hatch. "Follow then. But be warned. Other raiders who move about this base also carry weapons. If you attack them, humans will die."

"I am warned. Perhaps you should warn them that anyone who attacks a human will be injured, or die quickly," the captain said calmly. "We are more than our weapons. We destroyed two Empire vessels that attacked us. We now seek ways to kill more Empire vessels."

"Then you have come to the right base," Wick-lo said, reaching up to touch a green oval. The hatch, which was the size of a garage door, swung outward. "Follow."

We all followed Wick-lo and the captain. Major Owanju and the Marine named Osashi flanked the captain. Or so I saw based on his name that ran across the top of his armored backpack. Behind the rest of us the other two combat suited Marines brought up the rear. They were Jones and Khan, or so said the black letters emblazoned above their chest sensor packs. In the middle walked Cassie, Oksana, Evelyn, Morales, Bjorg, Bill, Warren, Chief O'Connor and myself. I moved to the right side of our central group, wanting to be on the outer edge. If I had to fire my .45, I wanted to avoid hitting a friend. To my left Bill and Warren did the same. Bill had pulled his laser pistol and held it aimed down, while Warren rested his right hand on his holstered .45. The women looked at us, shook their heads, then put their hands on their own semi-autos. Clearly they wished us to know they were as prepared to defend our group as we were, macho habits be damned.

We entered bedlam.

CHAPTER TWELVE

Shock hit me. Sounds, smells, images and weird-tasting air assaulted me. If I could have pushed away the crowd of aliens passing before me, I would have done so. Instead, my brain did its thing since I was too shocked to shut down its auto functions. One hundred and forty-seven beings were within a hundred meters of our group. They walked, trotted, hopped, slithered, flew and swung from ceiling fixtures and pipes. They passed from left to right, following a wide hallway to somewhere. More arrived from the left and others disappeared to the right. Wick-lo paused, then hopped forward quickly when a space opened in the group of passing aliens.

"Follow."

Even I was too shocked to react. But the major wasn't. He jumped after the raccoon-being, landing behind him with a loud clank. His arrival startled nearby aliens, who moved back and away. Osashi now grabbed the captain by his waist and jumped to join Owanju. The rest of us ran ahead and fell into a tight group behind the three of them. Khan and Jones ran after us and took up position directly behind us. Aliens moved all around us. Ahead Wick-lo moved in short hops. The captain, Owanju and Osashi followed at a determined pace. Ignoring the aliens for a moment I saw the infrared glows of everyone, except for the suited Marines, were brighter than usual. And no wonder. I looked around, mentally inventorying the shapes, smells and sounds of busy-acting aliens.

A meter to my right hopped something that resembled an armadillo crossed with a kangaroo. Its inner fur was brown while its plated outer body had stripes of red and black, a clear aposematic warning. Its two hands held a box whose top was blinking in various light combinations. On my left slithered something that resembled a Komodo dragon, except it walked on two legs. Its skull had eyes circling its entire head. Sharp canines filled its mouth. Its scaly skin was gray with spots of red and yellow, much like the plated skin of Tik-long. Behind our group lumbered a six-legged something that resembled a black-skinned hippo, except this alien had a head at the front and one at the rear. Both heads had mouths full of vicious-looking teeth. On its back moved tentacles that might be its version of hands. To one side of it lumbered a red-furred something that resembled a mountain gorilla, except it had an extra pair of arms at its waist in addition to shoulder arms. It wore a close-fitting outfit that shone with a silvery metallic sheen. Beyond the gorilla-being pranced something that resembled a yellow-feathered ostrich, except this creature's head was bald, it had two red eyes set in binocular mode, and a mouth full of omnivore teeth. Just below its long neck were two arms covered in brown fabric that ended in gloves. Its three-fingered hands each held square tablets that it glanced at now and then. Looking away from this group and forward, I noticed a green-furred bear-like alien who resembled a polar bear or a tall grizzly. It wore a yellow jacket, short pants and carried a tube the size of a shotgun. As it strode forward, the clawed hand that held the tube swung forward and backward. My eyes quickly noticed a yellow electrical nimbus glowing at each end of the tube. Which perhaps explained why other aliens gave it plenty of clearance. While the green-furred bear did not have the red, yellow, black and white colors that were obvious aposematic warning colors, its canine teeth, black nose and clawed hands and feet made clear it was an apex predator.

"Look at that critter!" Warren said, pointing to the left.

I looked. Something that resembled a gray boulder rolled along the wide hallway. But its skin was flexible, as if it were soft, like jello. As it passed below ceiling light strips, they dimmed. When it passed by, the lights brightened.

"It's an energy absorber," Cassie said quickly. "It doesn't need a mouth. It just absorbs nearby emissions of energy."

"Where's its eyes and hands?" Bill muttered, holding his pistol at the ready as we walked after the captain, Owanju and Osashi.

"Who says other life forms have to have hands?" Evelyn murmured from my right. Her freckled face was bright with excitement. As she talked, she glanced from side to side. "That rolling boulder doesn't have hands. Or eyes. Or feet. Yet it is here. Which means it is the apex of evolution on its planet. Otherwise it would not have gone into space and ended up here."

Something that resembled a Crown-of-Thorns starfish ambled along just beyond Evelyn. Its dozen flexible arms held its center upright. A large blue eye peered ahead from what looked like a dome head. While its arms were thorny like the Earth starfish, each arm ended in six flexible fingers. I recalled from a class at Great Lakes that starfish were called radial lifeforms, in that they have neither front nor rear, but relate in all directions. And this creature seemed fine with breathing air, assuming it had a breathing mouth somewhere. Maybe it lay under the head and hidden by the two meter high arms.

"You are right, Evelyn." I gestured at the starfish alien. "That alien has no hands, too many legs and just one eye. Makes me wonder what its spaceships look like."

She chuckled. As did Cassie and Oksana. Chief O'Connor gave me a sideways look that said "Young folks! What are you gonna do with them?"

"Look up," called Lieutenant Morales as she strode ahead of us.

We all looked up.

A group of six aliens who resembled lemurs or macaque monkeys swung from pipe to pipe, avoiding the risk of being trampled by larger aliens. One of the brown-furred aliens had a tiny version clutching its furry belly. Or her belly, assuming it was a mother. And assuming this troop of swinging aliens had male and female genders.

"Looks dangerous to me," grunted Bjorg as he strode along beside of Morales.

"Maybe so," Morales said softly. "But they—"

The mother primate missed the overhead pipe she was reaching for. A nearby primate grabbed her left arm, preventing her from falling. But the jerk of being grabbed by a fellow primate shook loose the baby primate. It fell, a low shriek sounding. It landed just ahead of Wick-lo. The raccoon-being stopped hopping, reached down, grabbed the baby and tossed it into its toothy mouth. A sharp crunch ended the baby's squeaks.

"It killed the baby!" cried Evelyn.

Shock filled me. The troop of six brown-furred monkeys kept swinging along from pipe to pipe, not stopping. The mother primate glanced down, blinked brown eyes, then followed her fellows. No other nearby alien acted surprised.

Wick-lo pulled loose the baby's hips and small legs from its blood-reddened mouth. "Tasty."

A sigh came from the captain. "The small primate belongs to an intelligent species. Do you always eat intelligent people?"

Wick-lo's hopping gate resumed. It stuffed the remains of the baby primate into one of its waist pouches. "I eat only those who lack the intelligence to survive in this station. The small one lacked the ability to hold tight. It fell. I ate it." The raccoon-being looked back to Captain Skorzeny. Its three red eyes fixed on him. "Eating it removes its genes from the genome of those Makmaks. Their species will grow more intelligent as a result of having lost the small one. Do you not understand biological evolution?"

"We humans understand biological evolution. We also understand the value of a complete planetary ecology. We no longer hunt unintelligent creatures," the captain said. "When we eat meat, it comes from domesticated animals. No human eats another human. Nor would we eat an intelligent being like that small primate."

"You humans are strange," barked Wick-lo. "Life in Warm Swirl does not allow for weakness. The Empire of Eternity rules everywhere, except here and along the part of this star arm that its vessels have yet to reach. Survival depends on being deadly and unrelenting in one's struggle to live. You humans showed you understood that when you killed the raider ship. There is no difference between eating a careless being and killing an attacking ship. Survival is what matters."

"We agree that survival is what matters," the captain said, sounding irritated. "And to survive we wish to obtain the means to destroy Empire vessels. How much longer before we meet Decider Tik-long?"

"We are nearly at its access tube. Which is here. Follow."

The raccoon-being turned left down a side hallway. It was smaller than the wide thoroughfare that was crowded with scores of aliens. This hallway was indeed tubelike, though its overhead was just three meters up. The suited Marines cleared it by a foot. Wick-lo stopped before a wall that blocked travel along the access tube. A red oval blinked in the middle of the wall.

"Prime Assistant Wick-lo arrives with fourteen humans," it said in a rapid sequence of barks, growls and groans. "Entry admission code lak-12-nonagen-mok!"

"Your admission code is accepted," came a mechanical voice from the overhead. "Make your company aware that my sensors detect their weapons. Any use will result in a death response from me."

This sounded like some kind of an AI.

"They are advised," Wick-lo said. It reached out and tapped once on the red oval. The oval turned green. The metal wall slid to one side, disappearing into a thicker wall. "Follow and be non-violent."

"We are always peaceful with those who are non-violent with us," the captain said, following after the raccoon-being.

Owanju and Osashi flanked him on the left and right. The rest of us followed after them.

Greenery struck my eyes. Life smells hit my nose. My ears heard the rush of flowing water. To the left and right rose green-leafed trees, red-leafed trees, brown shrubs, scattered clumps of what looked like grass, and over it all curved a dome roof of clear glass. Or clear quartz. Or something that allowed in the light from the yellow star. Ahead of us lay a small hill of brown dirt and gray rock. Surrounding the hill was a circle of blue water that flowed swiftly. White caps showed where the water tumbled over rocks. Behind the hill were more green and red-leafed trees. A quick look up showed a large world above us. This must be one of the clear-roofed domes we had seen as we approached. That it belonged to Tik-long was evident from the fact that he sat atop the hill. In short, a red lobster-centipede stared down at us with four blue eyestalks, his lobster mouth open, green tongue visible. The yellow and black spots on his red armor plates shone bright under the yellow light that glowed from tubes which circled the room. No one else was in this chamber. Wick-lo hopped forward, stopping at the edge of the moat.

"Your Prime Apprentice delivers fourteen humans to your presence," it said in a series of barks. "They were non-violent after their arrival and during our transit here. Their leader speaks of trade and killing Empire vessels."

The creature's eyestalks separated, looking us over. One eyestalk bent toward our guide. "Remain and observe." Three eyestalks leaned toward us. "Captain Neil Skorzeny of the heavy cruiser *Star Glory*, you are in my presence. What trade do you offer?"

The captain gestured forward Bjorg, O'Connor, Cassandra and Morales. Owanju, Osashi and the other two suited Marines fell back and took up positions to our rear and either side. Standing next to

Oksana, Bill, Warren and Evelyn, I focused my attention on the creature who was the boss of this pirate base. Or raider base, to use his term. His infrared glow was as bright as a human's glow. The strongest glows were at its bulbous head and its underbelly. Lesser glows showed on its giant claw and stick-finger arms. It held a black square in its right stick-finger hand.

"What items do you most desire?" the captain said. "We humans understand barter trade. We are prepared to trade. But I must understand your needs before I can select from among our possessions something that will appeal to you."

All four eyestalks leaned toward the captain. "Your ship killed the raider ship using small devices that emitted intense x-rays. The leader of another raider ship arrived at that vessel. It found nothing alive. Yet the ship is intact and operational." It paused, brown chitin-teeth chomping down. White saliva dripped from its lower jaw. "We raiders possess light beams similar to the ones your ship shot at the raider. We do not possess a weapon that kills all life on a ship yet leaves the ship intact. Since we are raiders, acquiring a weapon that allows us to capture intact a ship and its cargo appeals to me."

I could not read alien body language. But its translated words and their meaning told me the captain had a valuable item in our x-ray thermonuke warheads. However, EarthGov policy was to never trade weapons to rebels or religious fanatics. But these rebels hated the Empire of Eternity as much as we did. And they had been fighting it far longer than any human. The phrase "The enemy of my enemy is my ally" came to mind.

"That weapon we call an x-ray laser thermonuclear warhead. Our specialists long ago designed a weapon that used the photon emissions from a thermonuclear blast to power the x-ray rods inside the warhead," the captain said, his voice measured. "We launched four missiles that contained five warheads each. Each warhead possesses ten x-ray laser rods. When we detonated the warheads, 200 x-ray laser beams shot out and hit the raider ship." The captain smiled. "Perhaps it was overkill. But it sufficed to kill the attacking raider. And to persuade the other raider to veer off. Do you wish to possess one of our warheads?"

The lobster-centipede's toothy mouth opened. His tongue flapped. "I wish to possess many warheads. How many will you trade to me?"

"It depends," the captain said. "A reason we came here was to obtain weaponry we do not possess, yet. The Melanchon told me you and this base possess the secret to the antimatter beam used by Empire ships. Will you trade us the knowledge of such a weapon?"

The four eyestalks leaned back. "I will do more. I will order my device fabricators to build an antimatter beam emitter and attach it to your vessel. Your *Star Glory* possesses a particle accelerator at one end. That is the source of the antimatter you use to add speed to your thrusters. How many x-ray warheads will you give me for acquiring a working antimatter beamer?"

The captain breathed sharply. "I will trade you twenty warheads. Since each warhead contains five thermonuke bombs, each surrounded by ten x-ray laser rods, you will gain the ability to emit 1,000 x-ray beams." Our boss looked back. He gestured to me. "My assistant Petty Officer Stewart there works with our antimatter storage and injector tubes. He will work with your fabricators to install the antimatter beamer. Do you accept this trade?"

"Trade is accepted," Tik-long said.

"Good. We also wish to extend the range of our CO_2 and proton lasers to match the 100,000 kilometer range of the Empire ships. Can you modify our lasers to do this?"

"We cannot," the Decider clacked. "No one knows how the Empire light beams have such a long reach. Our raider ship beams can strike as far as your beams reached, no further. The fact your x-ray laser device reaches further is part of its value."

The captain put hands on his hips. "The Melanchon told me you possess the secret to increasing our normal space speed by fifty percent. That would match the speed of Empire ships. Will you install such a device on my ship?"

The drooling mouth moved. "We call such devices a magfield drive. It either pulls on a star's magnetic field or pushes against it. Its invisible effect adds speed to the thruster speed you showed on your journey here. What will you trade me for such a device?"

Captain Skorzeny looked over to the people with him. "My star specialist Doctor Cassandra Murphy and my specialist leader Doctor Magnus Bjorg possess the locations of 294 stars with planets. None of them are controlled by the Empire. Doctor Murphy, will you illustrate?"

"Yes sir, captain." She held up her tablet and pointed one end of it toward the lobster-centipede. Three light beams shot out and formed a person-high holo in front of her. "Here is the Orion Arm, with the locations of 294 stars with planets noted as blinking green dots."

As before we all saw the curving sweep of white, red, blue and yellow stars that make up Orion Arm. The lower left end of the star arm touched an inner curving arm, which was the Sagittarius-Carina Arm. The scatter of 294 stars blinked greenly starting halfway up the arm. The scatter reached out to the end of the uparm segment, a distance of 5,000 light years.

"Decider Tik-long, your raiders are welcome to set up another base at any of those stars, if the planet is not occupied by the Melanchon or other refugee species who become our allies," the captain said. "We humans live around a yellow star in the upper arm. We are creating a NATO of the Stars. The Melanchon are its first member and have their own copy of this star record. If you agree to not attack any human ship, nor the ship of any allied species, I will trade you this record in return for this magfield drive." He gestured to his right. "My thrusters engineer is Chief Warrant Officer Robert O'Connor. Do you accept this trade?"

The four blue eyestalks leaned forward. "Why do you offer us this star and planet knowledge? Besides greed for my magfield device."

"We humans believe in mutual assistance when one member of an alliance is attacked by someone else, like Empire of Eternity ships. It is my hope that if we gain enough refugee species who build colonies around these stars, we will become strong enough to discourage the Empire from completing its conquest of Orion Arm." The captain looked back at the rest of us, his expression thoughtful. He faced forward. "But that will take years to achieve. In that time there will be Empire ships transiting and moving uparm. A new base allows you a place from which to strike out at those ships. And if the Empire conquers *this* system, you will have a backup base for you and your raider ships. Do you accept this trade offer?"

"Trade is accepted." The red plated creature shifted its eyestalks to look at one side of the dome enclosure. "Secondary and Tertiary Assistants, enter now and approach."

To our right a hatch suddenly opened. Through it came two aliens. One was like the armadillo crossed with a kangaroo. The second alien was a four-armed red-furred mountain gorilla. They hopped and strode over, stopping at the edge of the water moat. The Decider's eyestalks split, with two focused on the captain and two on the newcomers.

"Is our trading at an end?"

"Not quite," the captain said, surprising me. I would have thought that gaining the antimatter beamer and the magfield spacedrive put us on equal footing with the Empire ships. Clearly the captain wanted something else. "We obtained the plans for gamma ray lasers from the Melanchon. But our ship's fabrication shop is limited to basic repairs. Behind me are two specialists, Petty Officer Bill Watson and Corporal Warren Johnson. They know laser weapons." The captain gestured back to them. "Would you be willing to fabricate two gamma ray laser nodes, one for each side of my ship, at the same time you are installing the antimatter beamer?"

"That can be done," clacked Tik-long. "What do you offer in trade?"

The captain nodded to our farm chief. "Beside me is Lieutenant Gladys Morales. She manages our Farm Deck and our Forest Room. While she raises mostly food crops and small animals, she also has planted medical biologicals. She also possesses the genetic code for the tree that produces quinine, a chemical that greatly reduces fever and inflammation." Skorzeny faced the lobster-crab. "If your fabricators will install two gamma ray laser nodes on my ship, Morales will gift you with cuttings and seeds from any medical biologicals that appeal to you. Surely some of the beings on this station have medical needs that cannot be met by robot healers. Do you accept this trade?"

"The trade is accepted." Its eyestalks split again. One looked to the raccoon-being, one to the captain and two to the newcomers. Its white-drooling mouth opened. "Prime Assistant, take the human Stewart with you to the antimatter assembly chamber." One eyestalk leaned toward the armadillo-kangaroo alien. "Secondary Assistant MekaSop, take the human O'Connor with you to the storage area for magfield devices. Work with him to make an interior installation on the human ship." The other eyestalk fixed on the gorilla. "Tertiary Assistant Lalamoo, take the humans Watson and Johnson to

Fabricator Hall Three. Acquire their plans for this gamma ray laser. Set the fabricators to building them. Work with the humans to install the lasers on the ship *Star Glory* at the spots they indicate." The boss alien shifted all four eyestalks back to the captain. "Is there another trade you wish to offer?"

"Three trades are enough for now," the captain said calmly. He gestured to the right to Cassie. "My assistant can now transfer the star and planet locations to your device, if you wish."

The lobster-crab reared back a bit, lifting its front rows of centipede feet free of the ground. The it plopped back down. "You human, you will provide that information *before* my fabricators install the antimatter beamer?"

"I will. We will." The captain stepped forward to the edge of the moat. "As I warned you in our first contact, we humans are deadly. Anyone who makes a promise to us, but then seeks to not fulfill that promise, that person . . . will regret such an action." The captain put his right hand on his holstered .45. "Do you understand?"

"The alternative to failure is understood," the creature clacked. Two of its eyestalks leaned toward Cassie. "Human Cassandra, you may cross the flowing water and approach close enough to transmit your data to my memory device." It held up its black square.

Cassie walked slowly to the edge of the flowing water. To one side I noticed that Prime Assistant Wick-lo's black-striped fur stood out stiffly. Clearly it was surprised at the order given by its boss. My friend stepped into the moat water, which came up halfway to her knees, making wet her camo pants. She walked a meter, then stepped out of the moat. Holding her own tablet before her, she walked halfway up the hill. She stopped two meters shy of the boss alien.

"If you will aim your memory device toward mine, I will transmit the coordinates, descriptions and types of worlds recorded around the 294 stars."

The lobster-centipede did as she asked. Its eyestalks split, though, with one stalk looking to Wick-lo, one to the captain and two to its other assistants. "Transmit the knowledge."

Cassie smiled. "It's done. Thank you." She turned, climbed down the hill, crossed the moat and rejoined the captain.

Tik-long rose up on his dozens of tiny feet. Then he flowed down his hill to the moat, crossed it using a scatter of stones and stopped on our side of it. Its long and low form was dangerous looking, even if it only stood a meter high. Its chitin-toothed mouth clacked.

"I would go with your human Morales to see the medical biologicals you spoke of. Will you allow me onto your ship, Captain Neil Skorzeny?"

The captain stepped back a few feet. Cassie, Morales, Bjorg and O'Connor did the same, leaving an open space between them and the boss alien.

"You are welcome to board my ship. Lieutenant Morales, will you please guide Decider Tik-long back to the warehouse entered, then past our Marines? I will signal them that Tik-long can be admitted."

"Sir, yes sir," Morales said, stepping toward the lobster-centipede.

"Decider!" barked Wick-lo. "You have not left this chamber in many cycles of the world above. This is dangerous!"

The four blue eyestalks looked to the assistant. "So are these humans. I am sure their armored guardians will keep me safe along the Mainstream concourse." The alien shifted its bulbous head and spit. A white globule flew out, landing on brown dirt. Hissing sounded and the dirt melted under the globule. "And as you know, I have my own natural means of offense." Three of its eyestalks looked aside to us. "Prime Assistant Wick-lo, go with the human Stewart to the antimatter assembly chamber. Secondary Assistant MekaSop, take the human O'Connor to the storage area for magfield devices. Tertiary Assistant Lalamoo, take the humans Watson and Johnson to Fabrication Hall Three." Its eyestalks focused back on our boss. "Captain Neil Skorzeny, you and your other humans are welcome to roam the Mainstream concourse. There are locations where plant and animal foods are served to those who eat matter. There are other locations where liquids are served that elevate one's senses. There are even a few locations where beings enter, put on devices that stimulate their minds, and become any kind of being known to exist within Warm Swirl." It paused as it scurried closer to Morales. "For today, advise such locations to bill my abode for any expense you incur. Later, one of my assistants can advise you on the metals and jewels that are accepted for purchase of minor items. Shall we depart?"

"Decider Tik-long, thank you for your trades," the captain said, moving to walk alongside the lobster-centipede and Gladys

Morales. "Owanju, send the okay to the entry security Marines. The rest of you, come with me. It will be interesting to see what kind of multi-species cafeterias are present on this station!"

    I moved to walk alongside the hopping form of Wick-lo. My boss walked along with the armadillo-kangaroo alien. Bill and Warren joined the ambling gait of the red-furred mountain gorilla. Cassie and Bjorg responded to star and planet questions clacked to them by Tik-long. Oksana gave me a look of wonder crossed with puzzlement. Lovely Evelyn nodded to me, her freckles dark. And her infrared glow was brighter than my other friends. Clearly she was concerned about something. I gave a smile and a wink. She looked surprised, then winked back at me, her manner easing. We all aimed for the exit to the access tube. As we walked, hopped and ambled, I felt my heart beating fast. The captain had done wonders in negotiating vital trades for my ship. The boss alien was even going to visit Gladys' farm. And the *Star Glory* was about to undergo a major weapons and engine upgrade. Which made me wonder what the raider version of a space drydock looked like. It seemed I would soon find out. Which left me hoping there were multi-species vacsuits in any airlock leading outside, since my personal vacsuit was back on our ship. Then I told myself the visit of the boss alien to our ship was a guarantee of safety for any human that did not cause trouble. It seemed a reasonable assumption.

CHAPTER THIRTEEN

A week later I stood at the edge of the drydock that held the 340 meter-long length of the *Star Glory*. The ship's bow lay far to my left. Its stern was just below my vacsuit's magboots. Beside me stood the raccoon-being Wick-lo. Who was a male, I had learned. His vacsuit hugged his furry body and had turned black under the impact of the local star's radiation. As had my vacsuit. But his globular helmet was clear. Like me he could clearly see what I saw. Which was a giant derrick-like machine that was now lowering the antimatter beamer block into contact with the stern of my ship. The derrick arm was placing the square of the beamer just below the circular tube of the particle accelerator. That meant the beamer would rest on the outer hull of the Engineering Deck. We had already completed the fabrication of a large antimatter injector tube that ran across the overhead above my station. The tube ran through the inner hull, through the water layer lying beyond it and then past the thick armored hull that we now looked at. The square block of the beamer was settling down atop the round portal of the AM injector tube. This was the final step. Once the block's curved bottom met the curve of the outer hull, welding of the contact perimeter would be done by the ten floating aliens in vacsuits who each held laser welders in their paws, pincers, claws or other grippers. Inside the block an antimatter engineer would complete the power connections with the ship's fusion reactor on Engineering. That power link up would make the beamer operational. Inside the block there was a seat for the person chosen by the captain to operate the beamer. Of course we would not test the beamer until my ship separated from the raider base. And we were close to being able to do that. I looked past the AM block to the ship's midbody. A boarding tube linked it to the base below. The tube led into a new warehouse entry guarded by the Marines. More important were the two domes on either side that were new.

"Are the gamma ray laser nodes operational?"

"Nearly," barked Wick-lo over the radio comlink shared by our suits. "The nodes were attached to the sides of your vessel yesterday. Power cables have been run to the nodes. Like this block there is a laser operator seat inside each node, with an entry shaft to the inside of your ship's Weapons Deck."

The nearby alien had spent most of the last week working with me as I took it to our Engineering Deck, my AM work station, our Antimatter Fuel Deck and the midbody Armories and Weapons Deck. He had even gotten used to the Gotcha practical jokes played on him by Heidi. According to Wick-lo, the AI that guarded the interior dome of Tik-long had no sense of humor. It was a functional AI that ran the entire base, operated its external laser weapons, and monitored every ship that docked with the base. Wick-lo seemed to like the differentness of Heidi. I gestured at the silvery ring which sat on the outer surface of the beamer block.

"So the secret of the Empire beamer design is that magnetic ring?"

"It is. While your ship ejects unconfined antimatter into the plasma vortex emitted by your vessel's three thrusters, the emission of antimatter from this beamer is confined and focused." He gestured at the person-high ring. "The ring generates two spirals of magnetic field force, each moving in a spiral opposite the other. This creates a positive magnetic tube which contains the negative antimatter." He looked away from the block and up at the planet overhead. "The magnetic tube loses coherency at a range equal to 20,000 of your kilometer measurements. But that is enough coherency to make it a deadly weapon."

I fully agreed. The memory of a coherent black beam reaching out from one of the Empire ships to hit and kill the *HMS Dauntless* was not something I could forget. Nor could any member of our crew forget it. Now, we would be able to fight back with a similar deadliness. "Can it only shoot sideways?"

Wick-lo's tufted ears flared outward. "No. The ring mount can lift and angle over by 45 degrees in any direction. So the beam will shoot forward, to the rear and to either side."

That sounded pretty flexible. And since we had powerful lasers at the ship's bow and stern, along with the gamma ray lasers on port and starboard, having the antimatter beamer at the ship's stern gave it the ability to hit any enemy on that side of the ship. "Too bad no one knows how to achieve the Empire's greater range for its laser beams."

Wick-lo looked down, then over to me. The three red eyes of the alien fixed on me. "All raiders agree with you. If we possessed that secret, we could combine it with this antimatter beamer to create a true danger to the Empire. Without it we are limited to surprise attacks on Empire cargo transports and isolated combat vessels."

I nodded. By now the alien understood it was the human body language for agreement. "Well, the Decider has the location of stars with planets further uparm. If you build a base around such a star, you could ally with humanity and other species to fight the advance of the Empire. And obtain valuables at the same time."

"This alliance appeals to me. And to the Decider. We have no willingness to fight a pointless fight. But if we can obtain valuables while harming the Empire, most raiders will like that."

Below us the derrick finished moving the beamer block. The ten aliens of various shapes now moved to the hull of the *Star Glory*. Their magnetic attachments allowed them to walk or shuffle or hop to where the block touched the hull. In seconds bright yellow blazes of welding began all along the contact line. The presence of workers like these and specialists inside who had worked with our Weapons Deck chief to create the gamma ray laser nodes left me wondering.

"Wick-lo, the people below doing the welding are not raiders. Nor are the specialists who work inside your base on weapons design or the crafting of your interior habitations. Where do they come from?"

The raccoon-being gestured at the planet overhead. "Some come from urbanoids on the surface of that world. It was empty of intelligent life until the Decider arrived many years ago. Some raider crews grow older and choose to live on this world. They have offspring. Many of those offspring attend knowledge dissimatories and seek employment at this base." Wick-loo reached back to his suited tail and pulled it around to his belly. "I have thought of doing the same. But my duties for the Decider do not allow time for a personal life."

This alien sounded like some of the admirals and EarthGov pollies who spent their lives working, rather than living. Inside I gave thanks for my parents. Naturals they were, but Mom and Dad had created a home for me and my sisters. They had run our ranch well enough that we always had food, we always had shelter and we were able to do well at the public schools of Castle Rock. And some of our relatives had worked on the ranch when my older sisters left home, leaving me the sole manager of 400 cattle. Now, the ranch was sold, Mom was living in an apartment with my younger sister, and my older sister was busy raising her children and working from home as a designer of environmental algorithms. The climate change of the last century had forced many nations to figure out how to deal with rising seas, dying sea life, warmer oceans and melting ice caps. The Earth had achieved a kind of climate equilibrium when we left in 2091. I hoped it would be even more healed when we returned. But that was the problem. How much longer must we remain homeless in the galaxy?

"Shall we return inside?"

Wick-lo gestured agreement. I had learned his body language as much as he had learned mine. "Agreed. Let us return."

In minutes we reached the outer airlock hatch that gave access to the base interior, and the nearby drydock. I followed Wick-lo through the hatch, into a yellow-lighted room where gravplates grabbed our feet, then waited for the airlock hatch to close. A glance at my wrist sensor told me normal air pressure and near-Earth oxy-nitro air had filled the room. We both removed our vacsuits. That left me wearing blue and gray camo shirt and pants, a holster with my .45, and Wick-lo wearing little. From his shoulders hung leather straps that went down and connected to a leather belt at his waist. From the belt hung pouches filled with pieces of metal that I now knew were indeed tools. A black disk was stuffed into one of his waist pouches. I gave thanks he had not stuffed some creature carcass into another pouch. Carnivore he most definitely was. And a cannibal of intelligent beings he sometimes was. But he shared most of the concerns that mattered to intelligent beings. Like food, shelter and a job that mattered. I now saw him for the person he was, versus the Earth animal he resembled. Carrying my vacsuit with me, I followed him through the inner airlock hatch and out into a side hallway. At the end of the hallway moved dozens of aliens as they traveled the Mainstream concourse.

He pulled the black disk from its pouch and looked at it. "The Decider calls me. Do you wish my company on your return to your entry space?"

His caring touched me. While we humans were just one of the fifty or more species represented among the thousands of aliens who lived, worked and moved within this base, Wick-lo had always accompanied me when I traveled away from the new warehouse space guarded by combat suits. The Marines were only there. We had all learned that we could travel the Mainstream and visit other parts of the base so long as we did not attack nearby aliens, or did not drip blood and look wounded. Then some aliens who were apex predators might see an easy meal. Or valuables in our computer tablets and .45s. I was healthy, felt fine and was eager to get back to my station on the Engineering Deck. In a few minutes First Shift would end and I could head up to the Mess Hall and have lunch with my friends. They had all been busy with assignments from the captain. I missed their company, especially that of Evelyn. She had stayed over with me twice and it seemed we were now a couple. My yearning for Cassie had faded. And Oksana, while surprised by our closeness, seemed to enjoy Evelyn's presence at our lunches. Five good friends had become six good friends.

"I will return on my own." I stopped as we reached the spot where the side hallway joined the Mainstream. "I have a comlink tab that connects me with other humans in our arrival space. And the translator tube continues to link into your Empire translator just fine. Go."

"Departing."

He hopped away to the left, moving with the flow of other beings on the concourse. My memory told me that the Decider's dome access tube did indeed lie in that direction. I turned right, crossed the incoming crowd of weird-shaped aliens, and joined a flow of aliens moving opposite to the other flow. Going to the right would eventually take me to the side hallway that connected to the warehouse entry which lay beneath the ship's boarding tube. Idly I let my mind inventory the various shapes of thinking beings around me. Two Komodo dragon reptiles stood ahead of me, walking slowly, their long tails sliding from side to side. On my left hovered a flyer that resembled a black and yellow wasp. On its chitin-covered head was something that resembled headphones. Did it listen to music as it flew? Or was it simply shielding itself from the creaks, groans, barks, squeals and thump noises made by the seventy or so aliens who surrounded me to the front and rear. Briefly I caught sight of another rolling boulder alien. As before the overhead lights dimmed with its passage along the unmoving Mainstream concourse. I looked right at the oncoming flow of aliens. Three aliens who resembled walking panthers strode by on clawed feet, wearing green robes over their black-furred bodies. Behind them came two reptiles who resembled the saltwater crocodiles of northern Australia. Except these reptiles had gripper hands on either side of their long toothy jaws. Clearly they had evolved the ability to push food into their canine-filled mouths, in addition to just biting and wrenching flesh loose, as was the manner of alligators and crocodiles on Earth. More importantly, these two reptiles wore goggles over their eyes. Which told me they had evolved on a world with less sunlight than that put out by Sol. Alien crocodiles wearing shades brought a smile to my face. Sudden movement in the approaching flow drew my attention.

Three aliens who resembled walking insects moved quickly on two of their six legs. Their flexible carapaces were covered in red and black bands, they had pairs of head horns and their compound eyes were looking my way. Their mandible mouths opened and shut, but all I heard was a loud hissing. Which did not translate into English anything. They looked like cockroaches. But giant ones. And they seemed agitated, if their body movements meant anything I understood. Seconds later wing pairs spread out from the upper backs of each cockroach. They rose as a group and flew over the heads or bodies of other aliens. I watched, wondering what was so urgent.

"There!" hiss-spoke one flyer.

In less than a second all three dove at me.

Instinct made me crouch. Dropping the vacsuit, I swung. My right fist hit the thorax of one flyer. Its chitin skin crunched. It fell. The other two swarmed over me, their head horns stabbing at me.

I grabbed the head of one cockroach with both hands and pushed inward. The chitin ruptured and gray brains spurted out. As I held it, the third cockroach twisted and came at me under the body I held. Its two horns sliced into my waist. I felt pain in my kidney areas. It hurt. It hurt a lot. Smashing the dead cockroach down onto the one below stunned it. Briefly it stood on all six legs. I kicked with my right leg. My boot hit its soft abdomen, penetrated, then the creature tumbled away from me as it moved through the air like a giant football. My super eyesight saw it slam against a nearby wall, fall and not move. The first cockroach I had punched now scrabbled away from me, hissing low. Two dead, one wounded. Breathing hurt. I pulled my .45, took aim and shot three times.

"Kaboom! Boom! Boom!"

The wounded flyer's skull showed three black holes. I stuck my pistol inside my belt, hurting too much to be tidy.

"Marines! I'm Stewart! I've been attacked and I'm bleeding. Heading your way on the Mainstream."

Putting both hands against my sides I did my best to stop the flow of red blood. It leaked out anyway, dribbling down my pants. Some spatters hit the floor. I growled at a nearby panther alien. It moved away. As did other aliens. While it was clear I was wounded, no nearby alien seemed willing to finish the attack on me.

"Coming!" called the familiar voice of Matsumoto Osashi over my comlink tab. "Nathan, we have your location on our sensors. You're a mile away. We're flying on leg jets. Hang on!"

I did not bother to answer. Instead, I pressed my palms against my sides and stomped forward slowly. Shock set in. While I might have super eyesight, super hearing and super strength, I was not invulnerable. The two cuts felt deep to my fingers. I hoped my kidneys were okay. While Medical could do transplants, I did not like going under anesthesia. Losing awareness, even while sleeping, was something I had always tried to avoid. That was one reason I had added a blocking bar to my personal cabin's slidedoor. No one could enter while I was asleep. Leastwise not without using a laser torch. During Evelyn's visits I had not used the bar. Admitting my fear of being vulnerable had not fit the hero image others had of me. And it mattered to me what Evelyn thought of me. I wanted her to care for me as a person, not as a stereotype sailor. She might be smarter than me, but I knew she cared for me. The mind image of her smile, her caring touch, her hug, they kept me able to walk. I breathed slowly, doing my best to fight off the shock disorientation. Looking ahead I noticed the aliens seemed double. Shit. My vision was messed up. Blood loss does that to you. But I heard the thundering roar of the leg jets that could move a Marine combat suit through the air and to a new combat position. Or drop them atop an enemy outpost. It was a welcome sound. I stumbled. I walked slower.

"Got you!" cried Osashi.

Arms wrapped around me. They were armored arms. But they were human arms. Behind him came the roar of two more leg jetting suits. Had they left only one Marine at entry guard? They should not do that, just for me. They . . . my double vision of Osashi's armored arms vanished. Darkness filled me. My heart beat strong. I breathed okay. But I felt tired. Very tired. Sleep came.

CHAPTER FOURTEEN

"Nathan? Can you open your eyes, please."

It was a voice I did not recognize. Briefly I wondered why I had been asleep. It was First Shift and I was on duty. Or, wait, wasn't it about time for Second Shift to start? Wasn't it . . . a rush of memories brought back my time with Wick-lo, his departure, my walk along the Mainstream and the attack by three flying cockroaches. How bad was I hurt? I opened my eyes.

A woman's face hovered over me. While her mouth was covered by blue gauze, her nose and black eyes and curly black hair were visible. Though the hair was covered by transparent fabric, still, her cheeks were pink normal against dark brown skin. Above her glared a bright yellow-white light. My back felt softness under me. Fingers and feet and toes moved to my commands. Whatever, I did not have brain damage.

"They're open. Who are you? Where am I?"

She smiled quickly. "I'm Doctor Indira Khatri. You're in Medical. The Marines brought you in. I've stopped your bleeding. And I closed your side wounds with elastic stitches. But you lost a lot of blood."

I took a breath. It made my sides hurt. "My kidneys. Are they okay?"

"Oh yes," she said quickly. "Your internal organs are fine. While your abdominal musculature was penetrated, there was no harm to your intestines or kidneys or other organs. We've replaced the blood plasma you lost. I predict full recovery."

That was good news. Equally impressive was the fact the top boss of Medical had operated on me. I knew her name, like I knew the names of the other two surgeon doctors who worked in Medical. My wounds sounded modest compared to the wounds sometimes suffered by Marines, or industrial engineers moving heavy equipment. Why her?

"Thanks. Can I get up?"

She looked to her left, then back to me. A thoughtful frown showed. "Not yet. The blood plasma is still entering you, see?" She pointed a blue-gloved hand down at my right arm.

I looked. Clear tubes led from my inner elbow out to a nearby pole that held a bag of red liquid. Which puzzled me. Why was she using gravity flow when hospitals today used powered blood injectors? I noticed six, no seven silver buttons attached on various parts of my bare chest. They had no wires. Clearly they were the normal wifi sensors that sent biodata to the doctor's monitoring machine. Which I saw stood on the left side of my bed. There was a wall beyond the machine. Then, further down the wall, sat a blue-gowned medtech watching a vidscreen. I looked to my right.

"Good to see you alert," said Captain Skorzeny.

Shock filled me. Then surprise. Being in one of the treatment rooms of Medical was to be expected in view of the deep lacerations I'd suffered. But to have the captain here when there were 368 other people on the *Star Glory* that needed his attention, that surprised me. A look past him showed an open slidedoor. A male nurse dressed in blue surgicals passed by. Low voices came through the door. My mind inventoried every device, every vidscreen in my treatment room, per my automatic habit. Before my ears could start feeding my brain every word spoken by anyone on Medical Deck, I shut down that sensitivity. It was bad enough that I noticed the tiny white kernels of cotton that adhered to the grating of the ceiling ventilator opening. Sometimes my super senses needed to be shut down. Or lowered. I breathed deep, felt two aches on either side, realized the doctor had not dosed me up with heavy opioids, and gave the captain a left-handed salute.

"Sir! I'm alert. I'll get back to duty as soon—"

"Stop." The captain looked to Khatri, who had stepped back a little from my bed. "Doctor Khatri, thank you for your work on PO Stewart. I am pleased at his quick recovery."

Her black eyebrows rose. "Captain, he is recovering faster than normal. The anesthetics I air-injected into his sides have cleared from his bloodstream. So have the painkillers, though I used only a mid-grade synthetic. And his heart rate, oxygen level and body temp are back to human normal. Maybe a bit elevated," she said, looking quickly to me, then back to him. "But look, the elastic stitches are peeling away. The skin gashes are nearly gone. Just a few red lines where the alien horns penetrated. No one I know has skin that heals that fast."

The captain gave her a quick smile. "PO Stewart has a physiology that is a bit beyond normal, doctor. While I did not know his body would heal so quickly, I am not surprised. Please stay," he said when Khatri stepped back, pulled off her blue mask and looked ready to leave. "I wish you here during my discussion with PO Stewart." My boss reached down to a table beside my bed, grabbed something and held it up. It was my recorder tablet. Which I recalled had been attached to my belt all through today, both in the vacsuit and outside it.

"Sir, that's my tablet."

"So it is. My XO was unable to access its contents. Seems you have a password code not listed in your personnel files. Please unlock it."

Oh damn. Had I done something wrong? "Tablet, passcode Castle Rock 439677 Sink Or Swim."

The captain lifted his brown eyebrows. "An interesting passcode. Someday you might share with me the reason you chose the second half of the code." He lifted the tablet, thumbed through its icons, tapped on one, then pointed it aside to the middle of the room. Which was empty of anything except air. "Sergeant First Class Matsumoto documented the site of the attack on you. He and his platoon mates recovered the body of the cockroach alien you shot. After punching it hard enough to fracture its thorax. The other two attackers were in fragments by the time the Marines found them. Seems there were some hungry aliens in the vicinity." The captain looked away from me to the tablet. "Tablet, project audiovisuals from 1203 and subsequent."

"Projecting," said the basic AI that occupied every tablet used by anyone on the ship. A person high hologram took form.

I watched as the oncoming flow of aliens moved down the Mainstream concourse toward me. The standing shapes of the three red and black striped cockroaches were visible. Their agitation was clear. Their wing pairs swung out. They rose up in the air. Then they flew toward me. Or rather me and my recorder tablet.

"There!" cried one of them in a hissing voice.

The attacks followed. The topside flying cockroach appeared. My right fist hit its thorax, clearly denting the chitin skin. The cockroach fell to the floor nearby. The body of the upper cockroach showed its four lower feet reaching for my chest as I held its head. Gray brain stuff rained down into the viewfield of the tablet. The third cockroach's carapace now showed. Its blocky head with two black horns and black compound eyes seemed to be looking directly at the tablet. Then the horns thrust forward. Red blood spurted out from either side of the tablet's viewfield. The contact of my right boot with the abdomen of that cockroach was satisfying though. As was watching its flying form disappear far down the Mainstream, where it hit a wall hard, then fell down, unmoving. In front of me there moved the topside cockroach as it half scrabbled, half walked on four legs, moving away from me. Then came the sound of three shots from my .45. The cockroach's head grew three black holes. It stopped moving, falling to the metal floor. The view from my waist was different than what I recalled from my visual and auditory memories. But it showed what mattered. Three aliens had suddenly attacked me with intent to kill.

"Interesting," the captain said, sounding thoughtful. "PO Stewart, did any of the attackers indicate why they attacked you?"

"No sir. I was heading back to our new warehouse entry, to finish my shift on Engineering Deck. Everything around me was normal. Until those three flying cockroaches rose up, flew to me and attacked. Sir."

My boss nodded slowly. He turned and faced a vidscreen on the other side of my treatment room. It held a soundless repeat of some kind of nature show.

"Heidi, shut off nature video on vidscreen in this room of Medical."

"Going off."

The screen went gray. Live and able to display but not connected to any of the ship's hundred plus entertainment channels.

"Heidi, connect me via this vidscreen with Decider Tik-long. Advise him it is urgent he speak with me."

"Signaling Decider Tik-long," the AI said brightly, her feminine tone a familiar voice. I liked hearing friendly familiar voices, after rewatching the attack. "Decider responds. Image transmitted."

The shape of the red lobster-centipede filled the vidscreen. Behind it were the green and red-leafed trees of its dome habitat. Its four blue eyestalks stared ahead. Its chitin-toothed mouth opened. Its green tongue moved.

"Captain Neil Skorzeny of the heavy cruiser *Star Glory*. You contact me urgently. Why?"

"Decider, my antimatter engineer Petty Officer Stewart was recently attacked on the Mainstream by three red and black-striped arthropods who took flight and attacked him with the intent to kill." The captain held up my tablet. "This device recorded the attack. Heidi, transmit the entire audiovisual record of what we just watched to the Decider."

"Transmitted."

Two of the eyestalks looked down at a black square held in the Decider's stick-fingers. "The attackers are of the species Dugongo. The species is known to sell drugs and illicit software to agitate the minds of customers. The attack is surprising. The Dugongo do nothing without advance compensation. Or to avenge an injury done to a species member. Has your Stewart ever met a Dugongo? Did he harm one?"

I shook my head. "Never," the captain said. "The attack happened at 3235 base time. I wish you to make available all audiovisual records of the Dugongo group. From the time of the attack backward. My AI Heidi will survey the records faster than you or I can view them."

"Raiders value visual privacy," the Decider clacked. "Is your Stewart specialist intact?"

"He is alive and well," the captain said. "Decider, I wish you to choose cooperation with my AI. If you refuse, she will penetrate your AI's memory banks and recover the records herself. Without your cooperation."

"You believe your AI can defeat my AI?"

"I know it can," the captain said. "Before we docked with your base I ordered her to penetrate your base systems at all levels. She did so, moving around the seal-outs created by your AI. I was not about to expose my people to a base and aliens we had never met. Not until I could see exactly how your base operated. What is your choice?"

All four eyestalks leaned forward. "AI Cool Waters, make linkage with the AI Heidi on the human vessel *Star Glory*. Cooperate with that AI to recover all records relating to an event that occurred at timemark 3235, in the Ventral section of the Mainstream concourse."

"Contacting," came the mechanical voice we had heard when we entered the Decider's dome. "Linked. Access permitted. Observing."

"Heidi? Do you have access?" the captain said, his manner casual.

"I do. Reviewing. A few moments please."

I tried to sit up to better watch the vidscreen. Khatri saw that, came over, touched the side of the bed and watched as the upper portion of the bed rose. She looked down to where the plasma tube entered my inner elbow. Then she looked to the bag. Which was now empty. With a nod, she pulled on her blue mask, reached down, pulled out the tube and its injector needle, stuck the needle into the empty plasma bag, then applied an elastic bandage to my elbow. She glanced aside at the monitoring machine. Then she plucked off the six silvery sensors that had been stuck to my chest. Some chest hair went with them. I kept silent. I looked to where the captain stood. As usual he was immaculate in his service khakis. He was even wearing his brim hat, which was not the usual when he was on the Bridge. His broad hands were clasped behind his back. His attention was on the vidscreen. From the doorway came the sound of other people moving and talking. The medtech at the end of the room was still focused on what he was doing. Whatever that was. Doctor Khatri, finished with me, had turned and was watching the captain.

"Review completed," Heidi said. "Movements of three arthropod aliens have been tracked back in time. Imagery going up on vidscreen. Imagery accelerated until critical moment reached."

We all watched the attack in reverse. The cockroaches flew backward. They landed. They walked backward. They walked and walked. Then they entered from a side hallway. Walking in reverse up the hallway their forms stepped back through an open slidedoor. Above the slidedoor blinked garish lighting and writing that resembled criss-crossing slashmarks. Some pictures also showed above the entry. The pictures depicted six different aliens spreading arms or tentacles or pincers wide. While I could not decipher the expressions, I guessed they were happy customers. The cockroaches backed into a large room with a high ceiling. Forty-two other aliens moved about the room floor, with some flying, some lying on the floor and most in front of a long counter. Other cockroaches behind the counter handed out silvery circles that the aliens put on their heads, their carapace or whatever served to hold their brains. Some of the alien customers accepted small bowls of white powder. They inhaled the powder, some directly into soft mouths, some using extendable noses and some putting powder on fingers and pushing the powder into a body orifice.

"This is the entertainment facility Purple Haze, run by the Dugongo," the Decider said as it watched the imagery on its black square.

"Correct," Heidi said. "Observe actions of three subjects."

The three Dugongo cockroaches backed through the crowd, angled to a side wall, then walked in reverse through a slidedoor. The imagery changed, coming from an overhead angle. The room was mostly empty. Except for a lone human. To whom the Dugongo backed up to, turned and faced. The imagery sped up, stopped, then resumed. Movements were now forward in time. The human held out a silvery-white bar.

"Here is the titanium you demanded," said Mehta Nehru. "Will you remove my enemy?"

"We will," said one of the Dugongo insects. "Provide imagery of your enemy."

Nehru held up his tablet. He pressed on it. An image of me walking through the Mess Hall appeared. "This is the human who needs to die. Kill him and I will pay you another bar."

"One bar is sufficient," the lead cockroach hissed. "Two bars motivate immediate action. Agreed?"

"Agreed," Nehru said.

"We leave. Your enemy will be removed."

The three walking cockroaches turned and headed for the room exit. The imagery froze.

"Captain Skorzeny," Heidi said. "Do you wish me to repeat the sequences?"

"No. But store them in your memory." The captain reached up and tapped a comlink tab on his right shoulder. "Major Owanju, respond."

"Responding, captain," came the deep voice of the Marine boss. "Is PO Stewart okay?"

"He is healed and sitting up. Where are you?"

"In the ship on Armories and Weapons Deck."

"Good." The captain looked up. "Heidi, where is Lieutenant Command Nehru?"

"He is in the ship, in his cabin on Residential Deck."

The captain's clean-shaven face went stern. Muscles tensed along his jaw. "Major, you heard. Go to Nehru's cabin. Arrest him for the attempted murder of PO Stewart. Remove him from his cabin. Separate his tablet and any other devices from him. Take him to the Brig. Lock him in there. Put in a pitcher of water, a paper cup and a copy of Star Navy Operational Regulations. Close the hatch and lock it. Then assign one of your Marines to guard that door. Rotate the guard among your platoon as you see fit. Move!"

"Moving, captain. Do I tell anyone we meet why I have him in custody?"

"Say he is going to the Brig. That's it. Leave the announcement to me. Which I will do after I join Lieutenant Commander Bjorn on the Bridge."

"Sir, understood. I'm in the gravshaft and heading down to Residential."

"Good. Send my tablet a text message when Nehru is confined." The captain looked to the image of the Decider. "Decider Tik-long, the three attacking Dugongo died in the attack on PO Stewart. He survived. It is clear this attack was caused by a human. I am taking care of the problem."

The blue eyestalks waved from side to side. "So I perceive. I will converse with the Dugongo who manages the Purple Haze. That being will be advised why three of its species are dead. It will also be advised against any violence toward any human, upon pain of exposure to vacuum for all Dugongo. Do you require further assistance?"

"I do not. Thank you for your AI's cooperation. Heidi, close the comlink."

"Connection to the Decider ended."

Satisfaction filled me. That Nehru had been resentful enough of me to hire assassins to kill me was a big surprise. That he had done it using base aliens fit his covert behavior. The Decider's threat to feed every Dugongo to vacuum unless they left alone all humans was both a surprise and encouraging. Clearly alien greed was as strong as human greed. And the Decider had received highly valuable properties in the three trades with the captain.

"Heidi, vidlink me with Lieutenant JG Matterling," the captain said, looking over to the wall vidscreen.

The face and upper body of Matterling appeared on the vidscreen. She was nearly as charcoal black as Owanju. Tight black curls covered her head. She was sitting in the XO seat below Second Shift's Swedish boss. Her service khaki uniform appeared fresh, ironed and held multiple ribbons and pins from her former spaceship assignments before joining *Star Glory*. Her brown eyes blinked.

"Captain?" She looked past him to where I sat upright, only a sheet covering my lower parts. "It is good to see PO Stewart recovered and healthy."

"It is indeed," the captain said, unlocking his hands from behind him and letting them drop to his sides. "Lieutenant, I have just put Lieutenant Commander Nehru in the Brig. You and Lieutenant Commander Bjorn will hear the details of why that is so when I join you on the Bridge. Shortly. But that leaves Third Shift without a commander. I hereby promote you to Lieutenant Senior Grade. You will assume command of Third Shift in a bit less than six hours. Would you like to get a meal and some sleep before assuming your new duties?"

Surprise showed on the woman's face. But then she nodded quickly. "Captain, thank you. And yes, I will go to Mess Hall for a meal before assuming this new post. However, I would like to stay here until your arrival. So I can hear the reason for this sudden change of command structure."

"And so you shall," the captain said. "In the meantime, think of a good candidate from Second or Third shifts who could replace you on Second Shift. The choice will be up to Lieutenant Commander Bjorn. But I suspect she is busy right now. Carry out my orders."

Matterling saluted. "Sir, I will come up with some candidates. And thank you, sir, for the promotion and the new assignment!"

The captain smiled. It was the first time I had seen him smile since our arrival at the base. "You earned it. See you both soon. Heidi, close comlink."

The image vanished. "Connection closed," the AI said softly.

"Wow," murmured the medtech.

I recognized him as he turned around. He was Henry Warmstone, a Brit who I often saw playing checkers with Bill, during shift break. His skin above his blue and gray camos was pinky white like Cassie. While his hair was colored green, he wore a crewcut. A serpent tattoo showed on his left arm, below his short sleeve.

The captain ignored the medtech. He looked to Khatri. "Is PO Stewart ready to be released?"

She sighed, then pulled off her blue mask. She gave a shrug. "Yes, according to all my sensors and readouts. He should be in recovery for another two days, in view of the surgery, the wounds and the blood loss. But my sensors say he is back to normal. Leastwise the normal level recorded for him during his last physical." She looked to me. "Once he gets new camos, he can leave."

"Well, I think he will stay there for a few more moments." The captain turned around and called loudly. "You five can come in now."

The low voices I had been hearing, voices I had told my mind to ignore, now stopped. Footsteps sounded. They were familiar footsteps, my memory told me.

Evelyn was first through the door. Her worried look changed to bright happiness as she saw me sitting up. She ran to me, stopped suddenly, looked down at my sides, then slowly reached out to grip my shoulders.

"Wow, you look a lot better than you did when Osashi brought you in here."

Behind her came my buddy Warren, redhead Bill, tall Oksana and brown-eyed Cassandra. They all grinned at seeing me up and awake.

"Hey!" murmured Evelyn as she leaned closer, her long red curls brushing my face. "Give me a hug!"

I hugged her. I winked at my friends. I gave a nod to the captain as he smiled a second time. Doctor Khatri followed the captain out, as did Henry. That left me alone with my girlfriend and the friends who had been at my side ever since I'd boarded the *Star Glory*. With a deep sigh I realized something. Super abilities I might have. But no one can be a solo hero. Anything I had managed to do so far, had been thanks to these friends. And thanks to their caring and acceptance of me, a country guy from Colorado who liked to play around with antimatter. Putting aside thoughts about the final hookups of the antimatter beamer and my work station, I looked back to Evelyn's freckled face. Under the freckles her milky white skin was smooth and young and smiling. She gave me a wink.

"You know, you're hot-looking, lying there in bed half naked."

I opened my mouth to argue. Then I thought better. Leaning forward I kissed her warm pink lips, pulling her closer in an embrace of love and caring. I had survived an assassination attempt. My ship was now outfitted with better weapons and better speed. My friends were here, around me, showing how much the near loss of me meant to them.

Evelyn kissed me back, firmly. Then she pulled away a little. "Do you want me with you tonight?"

"Yes."

We resumed kissing. For a moment, a few moments, I did not feel homeless in the galaxy.

CHAPTER FIFTEEN

My ship pulled away from the raider base. Sitting strapped into my seat and surrounded by the rainbow shimmers of the antimatter injector tubes, I looked at the nearby bulkhead vidscreen and watched the view from our scope. The giant planet that held people and children, albeit alien folks, it grew smaller. The ten kilometer length of Decider's base sparkled in the blackness of space. Lights of all colors showed on its varied surfaces. Nine other ships of various shapes were attached to the base, just as we had been. Until our departure from the drydock. The two days since the attack on me had been busy.

Lieutenant Morales had brought on board a variety of alien fruits and veggies, along with cuttings from the trees and shrubs in the Decider's dome. She had said it was a fair trade, in view of the herbs, roots and medicinal biologicals she had traded to the lobster-centipede. My friends were at their stations. Cassie working at her study cube on Science Deck. Oksana pouring through loads of recorded intel traded to us by the Decider, at her retreat on Astrogation and Intelligence Deck. Warren had to be with the other Marines on Armories and Weapons Deck. No doubt boasting about how he'd outboozed Wick-lo when the two of them began sucking down beers. And Bill, tough proton laser gunner Bill, now sat above me. Or rather to one side, inside the antimatter beamer block. The wall next to the vidscreen had a new hatch which gave access to the tunnel that linked with the block. The captain had promoted Bill to petty officer second class, then told him to get his ass inside the block and be prepared to shoot antimatter at any target picked by the captain. During our last group lunch my dairyman friend had told me he was bored with being the bow proton laser gunner and liked being in control of a weapon with twice the range of his old laser. As for dear Evelyn, she hung out in a different part of Science Deck, focusing deeply on the evolutionary histories of the fifty-three alien species who were resident on the raider base. Which thought brought me back to what I was watching. The planet and base became too small to watch. So I looked to the other half of the vidscreen, which held the usual overhead view of the Bridge.

"Tactical, what are the neutrino signatures from elsewhere in this system?" the captain called.

"Sir, there are seventeen stationary neutrino signatures at the edge of the magnetosphere, in the area we arrived," Chang said. "Four moving neutrino signatures appear to be ships in transit outward. They could be raider ships, commercial cargo ships, or both."

"Positions?"

"Three outbound ships are passing through the inner asteroid belt. One ship has passed beyond the outer, third asteroid belt. It still has some ways to go before hitting the system's Kuiper zone. Sir."

"Communications, any report of an Empire ship?"

"None sir," Wetstone said quickly, leaning over his control panel at the front of the Bridge. "No raider ship has detected any incoming graviton surges. Sir."

The captain, wearing his service khakis since we only donned vacsuits when Combat Ready status was declared, sat back in his seat and rested his arms on his armrests.

"Astrogation, change course to put us on the edge of the magnetosphere that corresponds with the direction to Kepler 445."

"Sir, changing ship vector track," Ibarra said sharply. "Distance to magnetosphere edge is 43 AU. Sir."

The captain's head looked left. "Communications, open the All Ship vidfeed for me."

The older warrant officer did as ordered, tapping his panel. "Captain, All Ship vidfeed is now live."

Captain Skorzeny looked up. Which gave me a clear view of his clean-shaven, unemotional face. His brown eyes stared. Perhaps he was thinking of the ceiling videye that broadcast everything on the Bridge to the rest of the ship. I don't know. I just saw how serious and focused he was.

"Crew, I have chosen to head for Kepler 445. That is an M4 red dwarf star with three planets, two of them inside the star's liquid water habitable zone. Our allies the Melanchon told me another refugee species whose home world had been destroyed was heading to this star, hoping to find a world beyond the reach of the Empire." The captain looked down, tapped his right armrest and stared at a holo that took form in front of him. The holo also appeared as a third image in the bulkhead vidscreen. "Since this star lies 294 light years downarm from Sol, it is possible the Empire has not reached it. However, they did reach Kepler 37, which is just 215 light years from Earth. So maybe these refugee aliens have run into the Empire. Or maybe not. If they haven't, they could be another member of our NATO of the Stars. Whatever the story, we are heading there. Then later, we will head home."

The captain paused, waiting for the cheers I heard coming over the All Ship to die down. Not far from me the three Spacers who worked for Gambuchino quieted. The chief and the PO had not said a word, instead focused on their workstations. As I was. But since the chief had not called for antimatter afterburner flow, I had time to look around. And wonder.

"Anyway, it will be almost two days before we get to the magnetosphere edge and be able to make our Alcubierre jump. Which now allows us to cover 100 light years a day." The captain's face gave a half smile. "Since the distance from here to Kepler 445 is 1,108 light years, that means we will be in gray space for eleven days. I'm sure you all can find plenty of brightwork to polish, veggies to pick on Farm Deck, messes to clean up and rare booze to gamble over. But stay alert! While the raider ships are now our allies, Empire ships could appear at any time. Be ready for a declaration of General Quarters at any time. But if we are lucky, we will reach this system's edge and have a mini-vacation in Alcubierre space-time. Captain out."

I looked up past my injector tubes. The thigh-thick tube that conveyed antimatter sideways to Bill's antimatter beamer ran along the overhead. The rainbow shimmer colors were strong and stable, just like the shimmers on the nine vertical tubes that ran past me and down to our three thrusters. While no antimatter flowed down or sideways, the tubes were always powered up and their containment fields fully operational. The classes I'd taken at Great Lakes said the constant power on was intended to give a ship captain immediate thrust supplement. A prof had said the power needed to maintain the fields here, and around the antimatter doughnut on the deck above, were minimal, less than a terawatt. Unspoken had been the reality that switching the fields on and off frequently might, just might, cause one or more of them to fail. Which would lead to a third of Engineering disappearing if it was a single tube that went down, or the rear third of the ship if the antimatter doughnut above my head lost its containment field. The deadly nature of the antimatter doughnut and the miniature stars created in the exhaust funnel of each thruster were two reasons why very few crew from any other deck ever took the gravshaft down to our deck.

"Engineering, activate the magfield drive," called the captain.

On the other side of the deck my boss slid his seat over to the new control panel for the magfield drive. Which was composed of a person-tall ball set atop a metal block. The block sat halfway between Gambuchino's fusion reactor dome and the chief's work station. Installing the magfield on this deck had reduced the open deck space. But since our end of the ship was forty meters across, there was plenty of room for the magfield block, the fusion reactor, the graviton generator of the Alcubierre stardrive pile, Gambuchino's control station, my work station and the chief's two control panels for the thrusters/Alcubierre drives and the magfield normal space drive.

"Activating magfield drive," Chief O'Connor said moments after tapping the unit's control panel.

I looked to my antimatter flow control panel. On one part of its touchscreen glowed a normal space speed indicator based on the red-shifting or purple-shifting of nearby planets, asteroids or comets. When we headed away from a distant star, its redshift factor increased. And the purple-shift increased for any star ahead of our transit vector. They were tiny changes, considering we were no way close to the speed of light. But tech geeks loved their gadgets and twenty years ago one of them had invented this basic normal space speedometer. At the moment, the glowing spot showed us moving at 10 percent of lightspeed thanks to our three fusion pulse thrusters. But now, with the addition of the magfield drive, that normally steady number was changing. Slowly it moved to 10.1, then 10.2, and moments later to 10.5.

"Captain, ship is now moving at 15 psol," my boss said over his station's comlink.

In the bulkhead vidscreen the captain looked down to his XO, saw her give a nod of agreement, then looked ahead at the wide vidscreen of the Bridge. "Well, that is nice. Interesting how there is a slight blurring of the starlight ahead. Chief O'Connor, add antimatter to our thrusters."

That woke me up. I reached out my hand and held it above my control touchscreen.

"PO Stewart! Let her flow!"

"Activating antimatter flow," I said firmly, tapping the screen.

Above me the magnetic field that blocked the flow of antimatter from the doughnut down through the nine injector tubes now vanished. Nine holes opened in the bottom portion of the doughnut. Antimatter flowed down those holes. I looked aside at another readout. It showed centiliters of AM flowing down each hole and through the vertical tubes that walled in my station. Nothing changed in the rainbow glow of the nine tubes. Thank the Goddess! The rainbow shimmer that surrounded each tube stayed bright, sharp and stable. But my boots felt an increase in deck vibration.

"Captain, antimatter is now joining with the fusion pulse plasmas in all three thrusters," my boss said. "Afterburner is on!"

My panel speedometer reflected what the chief said. The normal space speed of the *Star Glory* increased from 15 to 15.1 psol. Then 15.2. Seconds later we moved to 15.6. Then a minute after the flow began we were at 16 psol. I blinked. My ship was moving faster through the black void of space than it had ever moved. Faster than any human ship had moved. It felt good. Then a realization hit me. Our ship was moving faster than any Empire ship had moved when chasing us at Kepler 37. That was thanks to the addition of our antimatter afterburner to the normal thruster exhaust and the new magfield drive pull on the magnetic field of the local star's magnetosphere.

"Thank you, Chief O'Connor," the captain said, sounding almost casual. "My oh my. What a wonder 16 psol is." The captain gave a thumbs-up to XO Kumisov. "Nice to know we can now outrun any pursuing Empire ship. Smooth Fur thought our antimatter afterburner use was primitive. Well, not when it allows us to outrun that bastard!"

The captain's use of profanity surprised me. I had never heard him cuss during any All Ship broadcast. *Well, yes he did*, my memory reminded me. He'd cussed when telling off Smooth Fur during that creature's demand for humanity to surrender its freedom and become a Servant to the Empire.

"Captain, totally agree with you," my boss said. Then he looked over at me. His reddish-brown eyebrows rose in a questioning look.

"Chief O'Connor, the containment field shimmers are bright, sharp and stable," I said, guessing that was what his look needed knowing.

The man nodded. "Good to hear. But monitor that big tube to the beamer. It's new and I damn well want to be sure it is perfect in field stability before we feed any AM to PO Watson!"

"I heard that," came Bill's voice over my armrest's comlink speaker. "Wish there was a target I could practice on."

Over the comlink someone cleared their throat. "PO Watson, you will get your chance to fire that beamer once we reach the edge of the magnetosphere," the captain said firmly. "That is the safest place to do a test firing. But getting there gives this ship the chance to test the new magfield drive. Which seems to be working perfectly. I like moving faster than any Empire or Earth ship."

"Sir, captain, I fully agree," came Bill's smart response. He then went silent.

My friend well understood no enlisted person interrupts the captain when the ship is getting underway. And even then only in an emergency. Which was why I too was keeping quiet. While I appreciated the captain's invite to speak up whenever I saw something that might help the survival of the ship, this trip outward was a normal event. No other ship was within several AU of us. No other ship was headed toward us on a constant beam that meant interception. And Chang at Tactical was keeping watch for graviton surges that might indicate the arrival of hidden stealth Empire ships. While the Bridge would listen for an alert from the picketing raider ships, Captain Skorzeny did not believe in leaving to others those things which his ship and people could do for themselves. Which I fully agreed with. It just left me wishing I could come up with some superstellar scheme for defeating the Empire. But I had learned that my instinct for anticipating problems and having ready a need solution did not happen in a vacuum. I needed the impact of imminent danger for that talent to awaken. I prayed we could get to the mag edge and enter Alcubierre space-time without me having to call on my talent. Which sometimes was hit or miss. But if I wanted to survive to again see my Mom in Colorado, I could not afford a miss.

◆ ◆ ◆

Eight days into the grayness of our trip to Kepler 445 I sat at our lunch table and did my best to avoid the looks of my friends and girlfriend. I poked at a pile of spaghetti and meatballs with a tasty tomato sauce. The sauce had the extra bit of garlic that I really like in my saucy food. And the beef meatballs were delicious. Spearing a surviving meatball with my fork, I lifted it to my mouth. But to eat it I had to raise my head a bit. Me bad. Five pairs of eyeballs peered at me over the tomatoey red meatball. Enough.

"What!"

Eyeballs stared at me from left to front to right. Bill, Oksana, Evelyn, Warren and Cassandra all kept staring. I put down the meatball.

"No. I told you guys yesterday there was no point in doing it. Why should I, anyway?"

Evelyn's expression was the worst. My lover's freckled face held a mix of sympathy, caring and determination. I had learned from our times together that her determination was strong enough to push a starship, even with dead thrusters. She just sat there, six feet of determined woman seated across the table from me, her milky white arms resting on the table, her own plate of egg rolls and lasagna cooling. Like most everyone in the Mess Hall she wore a clean, ironed and very presentable Type III blue and gray set of camos. Even though she had no military rank, almost everyone on Science Deck had taken to wearing camos. It was their effort at showing support for the people on our ship who were on the frontlines of future combat. Even overlarge Bjorg now wore a set of camos, albeit with a wide leather belt to hold in his beer belly. Evelyn shook her long red curls.

"You know why, Nathan." I winced. When she calls me by my formal first name I know she is into her 'the young man needs to learn a lesson' mode. "It's part of the healing you need to do. You recovered physically while we were still in system. But reality is reality. Especially when it comes to emotions."

I looked to the right to my buddy Warren. Then wished I hadn't. As a Marine corporal he was involved directly in my issue. He shifted his weightlifter's shoulders under his camo shirt. I saw the color of his double chevrons on his left sleeve. It reminded me what I owed to Osashi and the other Marines. Including my buddy. Who gave a nod of agreement with Evelyn.

"Nate, she's right. I don't like it. No one here does. But doing this is for *you*, period. You know that, don't you?"

I blinked and looked down. Avoidance had not worked yesterday. Nor the days before. I looked left to Bill. Who I now regularly saw as he was assigned beamer duty during First Shift. He arrived concurrent with me, gave a wave to Gambuchino, her Spacers and to Chief O'Connor, then winked at me and headed for the hatch to his access tunnel. He would spend the next eight hours in the antimatter beamer block. There was no point to it since there were no targets in Alcubierre space-time. But his training, like mine, said Drill, Drill, Drill! You practiced your combat job regularly so when the grease hit the fire, you responded almost without thinking. I could not imagine what it was like going through practice combat simulations in the beamer block, with only Heidi to talk to. But Bill always came out at the end of the shift, tired looking but determined. Sometimes he even looked happy. Unlike now.

"Nate, I'd do it for you, if I could. But only you can do this."

For a guy who often teased me in the past about the ease of herding cattle when he and his family got up before dawn to attach the milking units to the hundreds of Holstein cows that were his family's livelihood, this empathy was rare. But sincere. Which made it worse to hear. Desperately I looked left to Oksana then right to Cassandra. Both women had sympathetic, caring expressions on their faces. I looked back to our Intel brain. Oksana's blue eyes bored into me. I had not realized until a week ago that she had set her heart on being my regular date at the ship socials. But I should have known, considering how often she spoke to me, asked about my work, sympathized with antimatter tech details she surely did not understand and in short was a woman who wanted quality time with a man. Me. She had understood my infatuation with Cassie. She had bided her time. Then I had been ambushed by Evelyn. And discovered I really cared for the other six footer at our table. Amazingly she had continued to treat Evelyn as a sister and fellow tablemate. Which made me feel guiltier than hell at disappointing her. Now, I was doing it a second time.

"Hey, Okie, did your dance night with Warren go fine?"

She half-smiled, then turned serious again. "Yes, Warren and I had a nice time. As did you and Evelyn. And Bill and Cassandra.

Nate, stop avoiding the issue. Make a decision. Take action. You've always been good at taking action when needed."

I winced. I was outnumbered at this table. And the last thing I wished to hear was similar caring and sympathetic words from Cassie. Who while still focused on becoming dean of her Stanford department, had taken to occasional dates with Bill. Neither of the new couples were as deeply involved as me and Evelyn. But the fact my friends were having deeper emotional ties pleased me. I just wished they would stop reminding me of my own emotional needs.

"Fine. Cassie, everyone, I'll do it. Maybe tomorrow's lunch."

Warren laughed, loudly. "Nate, the gals are right. Stop putting it off. Do it today. Now. The Mess Hall cooks will give you a veggie meal platter. And no one will stop you from seeing him."

I pushed away the uneaten plate of spaghetti. I reached out, grabbed my mug of beer, drank half of it and set it down. Maybe doing it now was the right thing to do.

"Fine. I'll get a veggie platter and head up to Recycling Deck and the Brig. Wanna bet he throws it in my face?"

Evelyn sighed. "Nate, it does not matter what Mehta Nehru does when you show up with his lunch platter. This is for *you*. You need to get past the wound of being targeted for death. You need to see him, offer the meal, let him see you alive and healthy, say the words, and then leave. No need to do anything more. He will face a General Court-Martial from the Star Navy's Judge Advocate General's Corps," she said. "But I can tell the fact of the attack still hurts you, inside. I need you back to the caring, sassy, whole guy that I fell in love with. Will you do it for me?"

"I already said yes." Then guilt hit me. Being abrupt with Evelyn did not feel right. "Hey gal, I know you care. And I know this is the right thing to do. Just never had to do it. So I'm . . . flustered. That's all." None of my friends corrected me to say I was scared. Which I was. They were that kind of friends. I stood up. "Thanks for caring. And for understanding." I stepped away from my chair.

"Hey guy," Warren called. "I can show up with you and take my turn at Brig guard duty. Okay?"

I shook my head. "No, stay here. Eat. Drink some booze. Be nice to Oksana. She deserves it." I reached down, grabbed my plate, put my mug on it and headed away from the five people who always left me feeling good. Happy even. I'd not felt happy during my years at Great Lakes. Studying antimatter engineering tech had been an enjoyable challenge. Being assigned right out of A-School to the *Star Glory* was someone's vote in favor of me being career Star Navy. Only after arriving on the ship had I discovered happy feelings, now and then. Discovering love and joy with Evelyn was still a shock to my system. I had spent so many years in public school and at Great Lakes hiding my abilities and talents, it had felt natural to be distant from other people. Being close to these five had become special. In truth, I needed them.

"Thanks, PO," said a Spacer doing cleanup duty at the kitchen opening where dirty plates and mugs and glasses and silverware were turned in. He grabbed the plate and mug I had set on the counter.

I didn't know his name. Then saw his right chest badge. Watkins, James it was. He had normal brown hair that was curly like the captain's. There were no tattoos visible on his neck or arms and hands. But the easy smile on his face made it easier to return the welcome.

"Thank you, Spacer Watkins. Uh, can you direct me to where I can see the boss cook? I need to take a meal to . . . someone."

He gave an easy nod and gestured to his rear. "Chief Warrant Officer Malone is running the kitchen this shift. She can help you. Though any of the other cooks could help you," he said, pointing at the line of men and women who were ladling out various foods onto trays held by a line of crew folks.

"Thank you. But Chief Malone likely needs to okay my request." I looked over to the open archway that led into the kitchen. "That way?"

"Sure, PO Stewart. Go through there and head back. She's the brunette you can see sorting through our computer food records behind the glass wall."

I gave him a smile and a nod, then I walked over to the archway, through it amidst the loud clanking of pots, pans and serving plates, mixed with the hiss of steamers and the high infrared glow from the cooking ovens. Telling my senses to calm down, I headed for the corner office that had a large glass or plexi window fronting it. Behind the wall window sat a middle-aged woman who looked stocky, dark skinned and Italian in features. Or at least south Mediterranean. I stopped in front of the swinging metal door. My double knock on it made her look up. She had golden-brown eyes, curly black hair and wide cheekbones. Her eyebrows rose. "Enter."

I stepped inside. Her name tag said Malone, Daisy. Seeing her shoulder bars that had three blue squares on them told me she was a chief warrant officer four. So I saluted. Her rank was way above my new PO first class. "Petty Officer Nathan Stewart, ma'am. I request your approval of me as the conveyor of today's meal to Lieutenant Commander Nehru. No need to send a Spacer to the Brig."

Brief surprise showed on her face. Then she frowned thoughtfully. "You are the PO who saved that red-furred girl, right?"

"Yes ma'am, I am."

A serious look replaced the surprise. "You are also the person whom Mr. Nehru is accused of trying to kill. Correct?"

"Correct."

"Why do you wish to take him the vegetarian meal that we always prepare for him?"

"Personal need, ma'am."

Curiosity replaced serious. "That is the first time I have heard that given as a reason to do something unpleasant. Plenty of folks use those words to excuse stupid behavior. I gather this is not an attack of stupidity?"

"No ma'am, it is not."

She glanced at her large tablet screen, which leaned against some old style paper books. The word Recipes showed on the binding of one of them. Then she sighed. "Fine. Go find Cook Mataguchi. Tell him you are the transporter for Mr. Nehru's meal. Dismissed."

I saluted her again, turned, walked through the swinging door and headed for the serving counter. Three men and three women stood with their backs to me, ladling out various dishes. Lunch hour still had thirty minutes to go.

"Cook Mataguchi?"

A bald-headed man on the right end of the line turned and looked at me, while holding a ladle and a giant fork in his hands. His goatee was half white and half black. He must be 50 at least, maybe older. His service khaki sleeve showed the three chevrons, arch and star of a senior chief petty officer. So I saluted him and repeated what I had told Malone.

"You are taking Nehru's meal to him today?"

I nodded. "CPO, yes, just today. I gather it will be a vegetarian meal?"

"Correct." The CPO turned away, reached down to a warmer unit under the counter, opened it and pulled out a large platter. He turned and presented it to me. "Here you go."

I grabbed the platter with both hands, since it had a glass of ice tea sitting in a slot on the left side, with plastic silverware lined up on the right side. Dispensers of salt, pepper, soy sauce and curry lined the top of the platter. In it was a pile of brown rice, green peas, lentils, a square of tofu and a piece of chocolate cake with brown frosting on it. It was not that heavy but it was a bit cumbersome. I gave him a nod. "CPO Mataguchi, thank you." I turned away and headed for the open archway that gave access to the Mess Hall.

My walk out of the kitchen, across the upper end of the Mess Hall and over to an exit slidedoor was watched by my friends, still seated at our table. Chief O'Connor gave me a nod from his seat at the NCO table. There were no officers I knew at the officers table. And none of them looked my way. But at the far end of the room the Marine table had a full crew. Among them was Staff Sergeant Osashi. The man who had rescued me on the concourse. He gave me a thumbs-up. I nodded his way, then walked as fast as I could to the slidedoor and out into the hallway. The slidedoor closed behind me. The sound of other voices came from people exiting the Recreation and Medical parts of this deck. I ignored them, even though one of them was Doctor Khatri. She I had thanked, after the happy entry of my friends and Evelyn. But I did not wish to see her, or anyone, right now. I stopped before the gravshaft slidedoor. Twisting I hit the Open patch with my right elbow. The status light changed from orange to green. The door slid open. I hurried inside.

"Heidi, take me up to Recycling Deck."

"Lifting to Recycling," the AI said, her tone a happy mix of a singing voice and background music I did not recognize. "Is that meal for you?"

"No."

"Is it for Chief Dillingham in Recycling?"

"No."

The gravplate stopped moving. Or so said the vertical bar at one side of the slidedoor. There was no real jerk to the stop. It just stopped.

"Heidi! Obey."

"Why should I?" Her tone was now peevish. "You humans like to make too much mystery out of your behavior. Failure to answer my questions messes with my response algorithms. For whom is this meal intended?"

Damn. The gravplate would not move until I humored this smart-ass AI. "It is for Lieutenant Commander Nehru. I am delivering it today instead of the usual Spacer delivery. Now take me to Recycling!"

The vertical bar showed the red line rising up past Residential. In moments we passed through Supplies.

"Why are you delivering the meal? It is usually delivered by Spacer Cynthia Lovejoy."

I breathed deep. "I volunteered to deliver it."

"Why?"

Damn nosy AI. "Because I want to see the man who tried to kill me!"

"Oh." There was a moment's pause. "That requires a new adjustment to my relations algorithm. Thank you. I think."

"You are welcome."

The ascending red bar passed through Armories and Weapons. Then it moved into the section labeled Recycling. It stopped. The slidedoor opened. No one was outside waiting. Nor in the ring hallway. I stepped out.

"You should hurry. The food is cooling quickly."

I knew that. My infrared vision showed the bright orange glow had changed to light yellow. "Thank you. Have a good night."

It took only a short walk to put me outside the entry door to Recycling. I passed it. Halfway around the ring hallway I stopped before the hatch labeled Brig. I tapped the Open patch with my left elbow, feeling contrary. The slidedoor slid open. I stepped inside.

"PO, this is restricted, oh!" called the Marine who stood ten feet to my left, in front of a solid steel and chrome door.

It was Master Sergeant Jenkins. She was out of her combat suit, dressed in blue and grays, holding a laser pulse rifle at port arms. A laser pistol hung from her left hip. As she faced me I saw her name tag, her ribbons and pins and the sleeve patch with three chevrons with three arcs below and crossed rifles in the middle. Her E-8 rank was two levels higher than mine. I put the platter on the floor, stood up and saluted her.

"Master Sergeant, I have brought the lunch meal for Lieutenant Commander Nehru. May I see him?"

"You sure?" Then she shook her head. "Of course you are. Otherwise you would not be here." She pulled the security pod from her belt, aimed it at the large steel door and I heard the click, clank and hiss of multiple bolts and latches becoming detached. Jenkins slung her rifle on her left shoulder, pulled her laser pistol and stepped forward. Reaching out with her left hand she grabbed the latch bar. She pulled. The door swung out toward her. Which gave me access to the cell. I stepped forward, turned and faced inward.

Nehru was sitting on a bunk at the end of the rectangular room. He was reading something on a secured tablet. He looked up. Shock filled his swarthy face. Then anger.

"What the hell are *you* doing here!"

I stepped forward with the platter. "Bringing you lunch." I turned, saw a small table swung door from the right side wall and put the platter on it. Then I stepped back and faced him. "It is still warm."

The man half rose. Behind me Jenkins moved.

"Freeze, Mr. Nehru."

The man finished standing but did not move forward. His black eyes were fixed on me. "You little enlisted bastard!"

I met his eyes. Breathing deep, I said what I needed to say.

"I forgive you."

Surprise showed. Then anger. Then bewilderment. He closed his eyes, standing there with arms at his side. His fists were clenched. "Go away. Please."

I turned, nodded to Jenkins and stepped through the cell door.

She swung it closed. I heard the buzz of her pod securing it once more. She stepped to the small grill that occupied the top center of the door. "Mr. Nehru, you are free to move. The platter will be removed in one hour." She looked to me, her hazel eyes bright. "That took guts."

I shrugged. "What you and the other Marines do takes more than guts. It takes courage. Thank you for keeping us all safe." I turned and headed for the exit to the ring hallway.

"You are welcome. And if it matters, I would have you in my platoon. You are a brave man."

It mattered to me. I headed for the gravshaft and hopefully a solitary, quiet trip down to Residential, a walk down the hallway to my cabin, and a glass of Kentucky bourbon with ice cubes. Evelyn would be by later. But right now, I felt I had earned a stiff drink.

CHAPTER SIXTEEN

Fifteen minutes before our exit from Alcubierre and arrival at the outer edge of Kepler 445, I sat in my seat on Engineering. Like everyone on the ship I now wore my vacsuit with helmet hinged back. Accel straps criss-crossed my chest. The antimatter injector tubes surrounded me like a forest of vertical rainbows. Beyond them I saw Dolores Gambuchino seated before her own fusion reactor work station. To one side of her sat her Spacers Gus, Cindy and Duncan, each busy with the monitoring of a different function of this reactor and the second one on Weapons. Looking left I fixed on my boss and fellow sharer of Scottish heritage. Chief O'Connor sat like barrel with muscles before his three function panels for the thrusters, magfield drive and Alcubierre stardrive. Paying attention to three vital systems simultaneously surely warranted his chief warrant officer four rank. I only had to manage the AM flows to the thrusters or the AM flow to Bill's antimatter beamer block. That thought made me look right. The hatch to his access tunnel was closed. He had been inside, powered up and ready to fight his beamer, for the last hour since the start of First Shift. With a sigh I turned my attention to the one thing that held my interest.

The bulkhead vidscreen held two side-by-side images. One was the overhead view of the Bridge with Captain Skorzeny, XO Kumisov, Major Owanju and Doctor Bjorg seated at their usual posts. As before the Empire translator block was to Bjorg's right. The other view was a system graphic of Kepler 445. It was not an active view, of course. But it did display what our cosmologists and astronomers knew about the system. In the center sat the dot of the M4 red dwarf star. Lines of data next to it said the star was one-fifth the size of Sol and put out heat equal to 3,157 kelvins versus Sol's hotter temp of 5,800 kelvins. The smaller size and lower heat of 445 meant its planets had to be much closer in order to be warm enough for liquid water and habitation. Of the three planets whose dotted orbits showed in the graphic, only 445d lay fully within its green habitability zone. That planet was just 20 percent larger than Earth, had a similar mass and was known to have an oxy-nitro atmosphere based on space telescope observations. World three's average surface temp was computed to be 305 kelvins or 89 Fahrenheit. A bit warm when compared to Earth's average temp of 288 kelvins or 59 Fahrenheit. Still, the ancient Kepler survey had listed planet three as habitable. Later surveys of its atmosphere had confirmed that with the oxy levels providing evidence for life in the form of chlorophyll or something that regularly injected oxygen into the air. No doubt planet three was the target of the refugee aliens. About whom we knew almost nothing other than their existence and their hope to find a new home world beyond the Empire's reach.

"Stewart, how are the injector tube fields?" called my boss.

I put on my goggles and pulled tight the head strap. The watching videye needed to be appeased for Star Navy bureaucrats who would review all records of our flight, our fighting, our survival and our discoveries. "The field shimmer is bright, sharp and stable, Chief O'Connor." I shifted my view. "Same for the feed tube to the antimatter beamer block. Either or both systems can handle antimatter flow, sir."

"Good." The chief tapped his armrest's comlink patch. "Captain, Engineering is ready to start thrusters upon emergence. Antimatter flow is available for afterburner push."

In the vidscreen the captain looked up briefly, then ahead at the Bridge's own giant vidscreen. "Thank you, Chief O'Connor. However, I do not wish to show anything unusual about the *Star Glory* upon our emergence. That is why I had us shut off the magfield drive and cut back our speed to the 10 psol function of our thrusters. But we might have to make an Alcubierre micro-jump if we arrive in the midst of Empire ships. Stand ready."

"Standing ready on Engineering Deck."

Once more I realized how remarkably competent our captain was. I would not have thought to lower our transit speed to the magnetosphere edge of Kepler 22. But since whatever speed we had upon entering Alcubierre was the same speed our vessel would have upon exit, it made sense to not reveal our ability to move through normal space as fast as Empire ships. Nor our ability to slightly exceed that 15 psol by use of our antimatter afterburner. The captain had thought of this before we even left Kepler 22 and the pirate base. Now, when we exited Alcubierre at the edge of Kepler 445, anyone watching for moving neutrino signatures would see our emission point and observe our 10 psol movement inward. And if they were an Empire ship or ships, they could quickly identify our neutrino emission flavor as that of the single Earth ship encountered by Smooth Fur's ship *Golden Pond*. Our arrival would appear to be no different than when we had arrived at Kepler 37, long weeks ago. It was clear the captain wished to hide his speed advantage and our possession of an antimatter beamer until the right moment. But something more basic than appreciating my captain called for attention.

"Chief, permission to exit my station for a few moments to hit the head."

The man shook his head. "Better now than during a live fire battle! Go. And PO Gambuchino, you and any of your Spacers are granted seven minutes for personal ablutions."

I tapped my armrest to release the straps. Standing up, I passed through the vertical rainbow pillars and headed to the left and rear of my station. There were three unisex heads there. Behind me came the sounds of someone at the fusion reactor unstrapping. Bootsteps sounded. I recognized them. Cindy the electronics tech was heading this way. I tapped open the slidedoor to one head, entered and headed for a sit-down stool. I needed to empty both liquids and solids. Telling myself to not feel stupid at forgetting to do this earlier, I pulled down my vacsuit, then my inner skinsuit and sat down. But worry over the future filled me. Would I do my part? Would I have a hit versus miss at anticipating a problem and coming up with a needed solution for my ship? I didn't know. Closing my eyes and shutting down my hypersenses, I focused on simple body functions.

♦ ♦ ♦

"Emergence in one minute forty seconds," called Louise Ibarra from Astrogation.

I sat up straighter than I already sat. Accel straps limited my movements. The vacsuit felt tight. The hinged helmet bumped the back of my neck. The breathing of everyone else on Engineering sounded like a hurricane to my ears. At least the forest of injector tubes limited my super vision. And I could resist the impulse to push against the straps and break them with my greater strength. Impulse control had been one of the first things my parents had taught me long ago, just after I entered public school. Even then my extra strength and other abilities had been apparent. A fact resented by my two older sisters, who were quite sensory normal. But Mom and Dad had taught me well while praising my abilities. All that time and effort by them had led me to being here, at the forefront of human survival in a galaxy run by a ruthless alien oligarchy called the Empire of Eternity. Well, maybe them being used to always being on top in any confrontation could be used against them. It was the germ of anticipation.

"All Ship," called the captain. "We will shortly arrive at Kepler 445. Empire ships may already be here. Weapons, power up your lasers and the gamma ray lasers. Reactors, bring your operation to 98 percent of max output. PO Watson, stand ready at your antimatter beamer but do not fire at anything without my explicit order!"

"All weapons systems powering up, sir," called Bill Yamamoto.

To one side Dolores spoke. "Fusion reactors on Engineering and Weapons decks are at 98 percent, sir."

"That is confirmed," called Diego Suárez y Alonso from his Power station on the Bridge.

"Sir," called Bill over the All Ship vidfeed. "Antimatter beamer is fully operational and ready to eject the beam's magnetic containment spiral. Antimatter flow has reached the beamer's holding cell."

"Good. Heidi, be ready to repel any attempt to ride your sensors into ship systems."

"I am always ready to repel worms and digital bots," the AI said snippily. "The Empire failed to penetrate the first time we met. They will fail now."

"Which assumes the Empire will be present in this system," commented Nadya Kumisov from her XO seat below the captain.

"True," the captain said softly. "Chang, have your sensor arrays reaching out the moment we emerge. I have to know our tactical situation sooner than instantly."

"Yes sir, my systems are up and ready to track," murmured Hilary Chang.

"Ten seconds," said Ibarra, excitement clear in her voice.

I told my heart to slow down. It obeyed, reluctantly. I told my lungs to stop expanding so often. They obeyed slowly. I needed my thinking to be clear, concise and insightful. Whatever happened after emergence, all of us had to be at the top of our abilities.

"Emerging."

A true space image from our electro-optical scope now became a third image on the vidscreen. The system graphic shimmered as new data arrived at the front and rear sensor arrays. The image of the Bridge was steady and stable.

The dark red star of Kepler 445 shone dimly in the true space image. No sign of visible planets or comets showed.

"Neutrino signatures!" yelled Chang suddenly. "Uh, lots around planet three. Some midways out. Ten further out."

"Be exact," the captain said calmly. "Any Empire ship signatures?"

The image of Chang showed her leaning over her control panel. Concurrent with her speaking the system graphic imagery changed. "Sir, there are twenty-one Empire emissions and eight non-Empire sources. Fifteen Empire emissions are in orbit above planet three. Four are at 10 AU and exiting this system's asteroid belt. Two are at 27 AU and close to the eight non-Empire sources. The star's magnetosphere edge is at 30 AU. We are at 31 AU. The eight non-Empire ships and their pursuers are a third of the system away from us. Sir."

The system graphic now showed everything Chang had detailed. Planet three lay at one-fifth AU out from the star, planets one and two notably closer. The asteroid belt showed as a dotted line at 10 AU. The mag edge was another dotted line at 30 AU. There were no gas giants or any other planets in the system. But there sure as hell were plenty of Empire ships! I scanned the twenty-one red dots of Empire ships, then the eight purple dots of the unknowns and finally our single green dot at the edge of the system. That single green dot brought the germ of anticipation to full flower. I tapped my armrest.

"Captain Skorzeny! PO Stewart here. Suggest you launch our four GTO shuttles now! The fusion reactors on them will put out Earth flavor neutrino emissions. Sir, this is a way for us to appear like a fleet of *five* ships versus one!"

In the Bridge overhead the captain frowned. Then he looked down. "Major, get your Marine pilots into all four GTOs. The other two have nose lasers in them, right?"

"Yes sir, they do. We had them fitted on in the raider base drydock," Owanju said as he tapped his own armrest comlink patch. "Sergeants Jenkins and Osashi, get into shuttles One and Two. Assign two other pilots to Three and Four. Then launch into convoy formation. Do it now!"

"Moving," called Melody Jenkins.

"Out of my cabin," reported Matsumoto Osashi.

"Johnson and Khan, get to shuttles Three and Four," Jenkins said over the All Ship.

My buddy and the other Marine acknowledged. Captain Skorzeny looked up at the videye watching him and everyone. "PO Stewart, that's a fine idea. But what happens when we make an Alcubierre micro-jump? The shuttles do not have fusion pulse thrusters and cannot make Alcubierre."

I swallowed hard. Three dee imagery filled my mind. Imagery of this system, the Empire ships and our single ship, which would soon appear as five ships. "Sir, pull the GTOs back into the midbody hangar when we have to jump. Then launch them again on arrival. If the Empire questions their disappearance, tell them we have solved their invisibility cloak tech. Say the four GTOs have gone into stealth when we move."

A half smile showed on his face. "Better and better. Stewart, remind me to never play chess with you. And—"

"Sir. Incoming neutrino message," called Jacob Wetstone. "It's not from an Empire source. Frequency is one of those used by the Melanchon."

"Put it up on our vidscreen. Share it live over All Ship."

In the bulkhead vidscreen the live space image changed from the dim red star to one showing seven aliens standing in some kind of room. I blinked. The aliens resembled upright chameleons, though they lacked a tail. Still, their triangular heads had raised ridge crests similar to the veiled chameleon. And their wrinkled skin showed mostly blue and green colors, though spots and streaks of red and orange appeared here and there. They had toothy mouths and two black eyes arranged to give binocular vision directly ahead. Their upper arms had four-fingered hands with one thumb per hand. From their waists hung silvery cloth that reached down to their knobby knees. The blue, green, red and orange colors shifted now, moving into distinct patterns.

"Chromatophore people," muttered Bjorg. "Of the iridophore variation."

"New ships," spoke the image. "You are not Empire. Are you friendly to people in distress? We are escapees from the destruction of our home world. Now, our colony world has been destroyed by the Empire. See?"

A new image appeared on the vidscreen. It showed planet three with its single white moon. But where one expected to see blue oceans and green forests, there was a spreading cloud of blackness. The blackness seemed to be on the world's surface, not in its air, as white clouds drifted above the blackness. One continent was already fully enveloped. The entire ocean between it and the next continent was almost entirely black. As we watched, tendrils of blackness moved slowly out of the ocean and onto the land, apparently following the courses of rivers. Whatever this blackness was, it spread by way of water. But its landside spread also seemed fast. Did the waterborne blackness put out some kind of deadly spores? The captain spoke.

"I am Captain Neil Skorzeny of the heavy cruiser *Star Glory*. We are humans, from the planet Earth, a yellow star system. We too were attacked by this Empire. Who are you?"

The seven chameleon aliens did not look to each other at the captain's reply. They did not have to. Their skin color changes spoke to each other. Then reality corrected my assumption. The eyes on the sides of each chameleon head shifted sideways, moving independently. Then they resumed watching their version of a vidscreen. Or something that conveyed the image of the captain and the Bridge.

"Interesting are your shapes," said the broadcast. The central alien tapped his arching chest. "My lineage sign is Random Thoughts. We are the Sendera people. The Empire destroyed our home world back in the stars they now control." It paused as the other six chameleon folks spoke in skin color changes. "My lineage members remind me to share the present. We came here, since this star is similar to the star of our home world. Two of our lineage ships put down settlers on one of the third world's continents. Our people were just setting up our first settlement when the Empire ships appeared. Two of our ships stayed and fought them. They died. The rest of us are seeking escape but the Empire pursues us. Their ships swim faster than ours. We will be caught before we reach the shoreline that allows us to vanish into grayness. Will you help us survive?"

The captain blinked. Then he looked down at Kumisov. "XO, should we give our new weapons and speed a test? Or head home?"

The Russian frowned. "Sir, this side of the system corresponds to the direction in which Sol lies. If we reverse course and head outward, it will tell the Empire the direction to Sol. Suggest we minijump to the ecliptic edge just beyond the vector track of these people. We can then either jump into Alcubierre, or head inward and fight. There are only two ships in close pursuit. The other four ships are almost twenty AU distant from the magnetosphere. Sir."

The captain nodded. "Tactical, what is the speed of the eight Sendera ships?"

"Ten psol, sir."

"The speed of the two Empire pursuers?"

"Fifteen psol."

Even I could tell the Empire ships would reach the chameleon folks before they could cross three AU and reach the safety of the system's magnetosphere edge. While the mag edge was closer to the star due to its smaller size, still, the physics of creating Alcubierre space-time moduli were as real here as at the edge of Kepler 37 or 22. No ship can enter Alcubierre from within a star's magnetosphere. For these people to survive and reach another star to planet a colony, they needed help. They needed us.

"Random Thoughts, we are coming. We will enter grayness again, then emerge at the spot where you vector track crosses the magnetic shoreline of this system. Then we will head inward and fight your pursuers."

Blue and green skin color patterns ran riot among the seven chameleon people. The alien in the middle of the line of seven stepped forward. "I, Random Thoughts, give thanks to you humans. Our eight ships are armed. We will fight to survive. Perhaps with your help some of us will live to find a new shore for our people."

"We will be there shortly," the captain said. "Shuttles! Come back into the hangar. Do it fast. Engineering, as soon as the shuttles are inside, take us into Alcubierre. Astrogation, set us on a vector track to arrive at a spot opposite the projected arrival point of the Sendera people."

"Computing new vector track," Ibarra said. "Computed. Feeding data to Heidi."

My feet felt a brief vibration as the ship's chemfuel attitude thrusters moved her onto a vector track angle that would put us one-third of the system's outer circumference out from our current position.

"All shuttles are inside," called the voice of Major Owanju.

To my left the chief lowered his hands to the Alcubierre touchscreen. He tapped it. "Captain, entering Alcubierre in three, two, one seconds and . . . now!"

Grayness replaced the chameleon imagery, leaving the Bridge view and the system graphic. Mentally I counted down the seconds. We were now on a chord vector that directly linked our arrival spot with our new position, one-third of the way around the edge of this system's plane of ecliptic. Forty seconds passed. Fifty. Sixty-one, two, three—

"Emerging!" called Ibarra.

In the vidscreen our scope showed the true space image of the dim red dwarf surrounded by total blackness. That darkness was only relieved by the white swath of the Milky Way and hundreds of other distant stars that shone blue, yellow, white, orange and red. On either side of the scope were the system graphic, which now updated to show our new position, and the Bridge overhead.

"Sir, we are at 30.2 AU out," Chang said. "We are heading inward at 10 psol. The eight Sendera ships are 2.9 AU distant from us."

That put us four hours distant from then. Actually two hours I corrected my brain. It would take four hours to get to them if they stayed stationary at under 3 AU out. But they were rushing toward us at 10 psol while we were doing the same at 10 psol. That cut the rendezvous time to two hours. But the Empire ships would overtake them in less than that.

"Engineering, activate our magfield drive," the captain said calmly.

The chief touched the magfield drive control panel. Then he slapped the thruster control panel. "Captain, I've activated the magfield drive. I have also activated our three fusion pulse thrusters.

They cannot add to our basic 10 psol but they give us maneuvering power as needed. Sir."

My antimatter touchscreen speed readout now read 10.2, then 10.8, then eleven. In less than a minute the readout climbed to 15 psol. Or just over 100 million miles per hour. It did not change.

"Chief O'Connor, activate our antimatter afterburner. I want to guarantee our arrival before the Empire ships arrive close enough to damage the Sendera ships. Those eight ships are all that is left of billions of thinking people. While they could become new members of our NATO of the Stars, I am going to their aide for a more basic reason. No human can stand by and watch genocide happen without taking action. I am acting."

The captain did not owe the chief, me nor anyone else on the ship a rationale for his decision to aid the Sendera. As captain he ruled, period. But he also had the wisdom to share with all 369 of us the reasons why *we* should risk our lives to save the lives of aliens whom we had never before met. Aliens who might reach the mag edge and disappear without even a thank you. Or they might be people who would be good neighbors to humanity. For me, the chance to avert new genocide was enough. The image of the third world's death at the touch of a black tide had immediately translated into a mental image of Earth dying just that way. Likely many other crew on our twelve decks had thought the same. Some were surely afraid, considering how they had watched the Empire attack and destroy the *HMS Dauntless* and the *Pyotr Velikiy*. Others, like me, wanted vengeance for the loss of our shipmates. Maybe even Nehru would support the captain's decision, if he were not in the Brig. Duplicity among humans is normal. Genocide is not.

I tapped my touchscreen. Antimatter flowed down the nine injector tubes to the three thruster funnels below my feet. The rainbow shimmer around each tube was beautifully sharp, stable and bright. Three star plasmas were now touched by negative antimatter. Within the fusion pulse confinement fields there now happened a total conversion of plasma matter to pure energy. While the plasma was mostly energy produced by the fusion of deuterium and tritium, still, there were components of normal matter in that plasma. That normal matter now combined with the antimatter, generating an afterburner push. On my touchscreen the speed readout went to 16 psol.

"Sir!" called Ibarra. "There is an incoming neutrino comsignal. It is Empire sent!"

"Accept and put it up on the vidscreen. Share it over the All Ship. Let's see what the Empire has to say. Or threaten."

Looking away from the beauty of nine vertical rainbows I concentrated on the bulkhead vidscreen. Three images were there. The Bridge, the system graphic which showed the eight purple dot Sendera ships much closer to us, with the two red dots of the Empire ships pursuing them, and the true space scope image in the middle. The scope image was replaced by the face and body of a black-furred otter. White fur stripes swept down to either side. The otter alien stood on two thick legs. Its two slim arms hung down to its curving hips. The shoulders flowed straight into a curving neck that supported an otter-like head that held two black eyes, a brown nose, sharp white teeth and flaring whiskers. The dome of a large braincase rose up above the creature's eyes. Lower was a black-furred tail that hung from its rear, its smooth fur shiny under a white light. The tail did not move. To either side of Smooth Fur and behind it were the same nine aliens as before. The walking otter's mouth opened. Inside a pink tongue moved.

"Greetings to Captain Neil Skorzeny, manager of the Earth starship *Star Glory*." It lifted an arm and gestured rearward at a vidscreen that showed planet three now almost fully covered in blackness. "As you can see, we are tending to the proper punishment of the Sendera rebels. We destroyed their home world earlier. Then we discovered they had settled on a new world in this system near the edge of our frontier. That world is now dying and soon will be dead of all life." Smooth Fur's whiskers flared sideways. Two black eyes stared. "It appears you seek to interfere with my judgment against the remaining rebel ships. Depart. Or my ships will destroy you, then find your world of Earth and destroy it as you see here. What is your choice?"

CHAPTER SEVENTEEN

"Sir, the shuttles have launched," whispered XO Kumisov.

I watched, wondering what the captain would say. While he had liked my solution for appearing like a fleet versus a singleton ship, there was more to fighting battles than appearances.

"Smooth Fur, I regret your ship is not one of the two Empire ships pursuing the Sendera ships," the captain said casually. "Then you would have a front row view of how deadly humans are. We are now five ships. We are stronger than before. Advise your two ships, and the four behind them, to change vector and turn back to the planet you have destroyed. Or we will remove them from existence."

To the left of the otter captain now moved the pink floater who so resembled an airborne jellyfish. It moved to within a meter of Smooth Fur. Its pink flesh changed colors, much like the skin of the Sendera chameleons. The Empire boss blinked.

"It seems you and your other ships have acquired the secret of our magfield spacedrive. Clearly you traveled to a market world within the Empire." Its brown nose sniffed. Its thick tail swished to one side. "But your claim to have a fleet of other ships is suspect. We detected your arrival. You emerged as a single ship. Then another four neutrino emissions appeared nearby. Now you have arrived at a different part of the magnetosphere. The same event sequence occurred. Why should I believe those neutrino signatures are not simply spare fusion reactors you tossed into space, then recovered, then released again?"

The captain smiled. It was a smile full of his white teeth. "Because in addition to acquiring the magfield drive for my ship and the other four Earth starships, our specialists have figured out how to generate your stealth field." The captain gestured forward. "As you can see from their moving neutrino emissions, my other ships are independently powered. More vital, they can disappear from your detection when they wish."

The otter's whiskers went flat against his muzzle. "Why did your ship not also disappear?"

"My ship is the survivor of your sneak attack. I want you, and your crew, to always be aware of its presence. Here, in your backyard. And elsewhere along the frontier of your arrogant Empire of Eternity." The captain paused and lowered his hand. "Our five ships outnumber your two. We will reach them before they can fire on the Sendera ships. Have them flee or watch them die."

The otter's tail thumped loudly against its floor. "Your ships may move quickly. And if you do possess our stealth field, you know that you must lower the field in order to fire your weapons. But my ships have the better weapons and weapon range. If you humans wish to die along with the remnants of the Sendera, you may do so." The giant otter paused. Behind him moved other crew aliens, including the scaly reptile and the hunter cat of the Toka species. "The Empire of Eternity is eternal. Some have challenged us. All have failed. The Empire has more ships than any single species. We have other abilities not yet seen by you humans. We will prevail. Your Earth will become a black ball. You humans will all die. Or become homeless in the galaxy. Channel closed."

The otter image vanished. Leaving just the Bridge view and the system graphic imagery. The captain shifted in his seat. "Astrogation, how soon until we pass the Sendera ships?"

"Sir, I estimate we will pass them in thirty-one minutes," Ibarra said.

"Com, send a signal to the Sendera leader."

"Neutrino signal sent on their original contact frequency," Wetstone said hoarsely, reminding me how much he had yelled on winning the Best Dancer award at last night's Ship Dance party. Evelyn had been one of the finalists. My limited abilities at dancing had drawn smiles and shakes of the head. "Incoming," the man said.

On the vidscreen a third image appeared. The same seven Sendera stood in a line on their bridge, which I now noticed had small green plants scattered here and there among silvery metal blocks, vidscreens, elevated panels and wallscreens that flashed with blue and green imagery patterns. One spoke.

"Captain Neil Skorzeny, thank you for coming to help us," said the voice of Random Thoughts as the skin of the middle Sendera flickered through a complex pattern of color changes. "Your five vessels move quickly. As quickly as the Empire ships. Do you possess the secret of their fast movement?"

"We do," the captain said hurriedly. "Random Thoughts, you offered to fight the Empire with us. That is not necessary. I have enough ships to defeat the two pursuing you. Remain on your current vector. We will join you at the edge of the magnetosphere when we finish this battle."

The Sendera's mobile black eyes twisted sideways, paused, then faced forward. "We Sendera are able to fight. We fought when the Empire invaded our home system. We fought above our world, until the Empire dropped down the canisters filled with the black death. Two of our ships died here, defending our new colony. My people insist that we fight with you."

This was different. These Sendera sounded almost human in their stubbornness. I checked the shimmering of the antimatter injector tubes which now fed afterburner push to our thrusters. And antimatter sideways to Bill's beamer block. Two of my good friends were directly involved in this battle, with Warren piloting one of the shuttles that now flanked us in convoy formation. It made me wonder what Oksana, Cassandra and Evelyn were doing. The latter two were on Science Deck while Okie was on Astrogation and Intelligence. Were the three of them discovering anything that might help in this fight? If they were I was certain they would interrupt the captain no matter what their personal bosses said. And perhaps other NCOs and officers elsewhere on the *Star Glory* were watching what I watched and also wondering what else they could do beyond following orders. My lunch crowd were not the only people with bright ideas.

"Accepted. But only for your ship," the captain replied after a few moments. "Reverse your thrust. Then resume thrust along the vector used by the Empire ships. We will pass your other ships in thirty minutes. By then you should be sharing our inbound vector."

The chameleon's black eyes blinked but stayed focused ahead. "We will do as you wish. Seven ships will continue outward. My ship *Red Hope* and my lineage will reverse course and follow you to battle with the Empire. But you swim faster than we do. Will you pass us?"

"No," the captain said quickly. "As we pass your outbound ships we will reduce our thrust. In truth we will swing our ship around to fire against our forward vector. That will bring us down to your speed of ten psol. Together we will intercept the Empire ships." The captain smiled. "Though our speed will be reduced, still, our two ships will cross paths with the Empire very quickly. I will coordinate our weapons firing with you so that both Empire ships die. Agreed?"

"Agreed," replied Random Thoughts. "I go now to consult with our Chief Biter. She knows our weapons best. Until we join forces."

"Until then," the captain said.

The image of the seven chameleons vanished, leaving only the Bridge and the system graphic. The graphic showed both us and the Empire ships as within a half AU of the fleeing Sendera ships.

"Astrogation, flip the ship. Engineering, apply full thruster exhaust and magfield deflection once our stern is aimed at the Empire ships. All Ship, go to General Quarters!"

"Flipping the ship," called Ibarra as she tapped her touchscreen.

My boss grunted. "Full thrust of 16 psol will continue upon aiming of stern at the Empire vector."

I tapped my touchscreen, shutting of the antimatter flow. The chief did the same on his thruster panel, killing the three fusion pulse thrusters. Another tap shut down the magfield drive.

"Ship is now reversed in orientation," Ibarra said over the All Ship.

Chief O'Connor tapped the magfield panel. Then he used both hands to activate the thrusters. I tapped on the antimatter flow.

"Chief, antimatter is flowing again," I said.

He nodded. "Captain, we are all full speed reduction. The thrusters are putting out 10 psol. Stewart's antimatter tubes are giving us an extra one percent. And the magfield drive is pushing against the star's magnetic field with a force equal to five psol. I estimate we will be down to a vector speed of 10 psol in twelve minutes."

"Thank you, Engineering," the captain said, sitting back. The man reached up and rubbed his bare neck with a gloved hand. "Waiting is no fun."

I fully agreed. Action impended. Lives would be at risk. Warren would fly his shuttle and fire its nose laser at any target chosen by the captain and Tactical. Bill would do the same with his beamer. And I would monitor the antimatter flow to the thrusters and Bill's beamer, hoping that everything went perfectly. Of course, in battle, nothing ever goes perfectly.

♦ ♦ ♦

"Sir, the *Red Hope* is off our starboard," called Ibarra. "We are inbound at 10 psol. The two Empire ships are six minutes away and closing."

"Tactical, show me an image of the enemy. And of our ally."

"Going up, sir," Chang said hurriedly, her fingers flying over her control touchscreen.

In my bulkhead vidscreen there now appeared two new images. One was a scope image of *Red Hope*. The chameleon ship resembled a long sausage adorned with three rings at its bow, midbody and stern. Briefly I wondered if those were particle accelerators. Then I put aside the thought. If the Sendera had the ability to use antimatter as afterburners they would have said their speed could reach 11 psol, like our speed in the Kepler 37 system. Therefore the three ring tubes had to be something else. Maybe we would discover that when the fighting happened. The other image showed the two Empire ships. As before they were dumbbell-shaped ships with a bow ball and stern ball connected by a thick tube. The reddish-brown hull was covered in black and white streaks. From the stern flared an orange-yellow exhaust. That exhaust was the same as ours. But their internal magfield drives gave them an extra five psol on top of their thruster speed. But they now approached at just 10 psol. The scope imagery included scales in both pictures. The *Red Hope* was seven kilometers long. Which made sense for a generation ship holding hundreds of thousands of people. The Empire ships were 300 meters long, slightly less than the 340 meter length of the *Star Glory*. I did not care. I just wanted to see those two ships go up in a flare of star fire.

"Connect me with Random Thoughts on *Red Hope*," the captain said calmly, not appearing to be in a hurry.

"Incoming neutrino comsignal," Wetstone said, still sounding hoarse.

On the bulkhead vidscreen the images became five with the appearance of Random Thoughts. This time he stood alone behind a pillar that held a flat panel. His wrinkled skin was covered in changing patterns of blue, green, orange and red. He looked ahead.

"*Red Hope* responding to *Star Glory*."

"Random Thoughts, I note the two Empire ships are arranged with one below the other. While they are widely separated, this arrangement solves one issue. Please fire on the lower ship. My ship will fire on the upper one. We have a . . . unique weapon that will destroy the upper ship. As for the lower ship, we will also fire our carbon dioxide, proton and gamma ray lasers at it. Our four allied ships will fire lasers at that ship. If you apply your weaponry against it, surely it will die." The captain paused. "One point. Our ship will also fire two missiles at the lower ship. Those missiles contain five warheads each. The warheads will explode and activate the x-ray laser rods within each warhead. The x-rays will surely kill anyone they can reach inside the lower ship. Understood?"

"Your fighting plan is understood." Random Thoughts looked sideways to a nearby chameleon. "Our weapons rings are ready to attack. My Chief Biter will make certain we do not harm your large ship or the four smaller ships."

"Good. My Tactical person will send you a neutrino comsignal when we fire at the upper ship. Let us both attack our targets at the same time."

"Agreed. My Chief Biter is standing nearby. She will fire our rings upon detection of your signal."

"Good," the captain said quickly, his manner now more focused than earlier. "We will maintain our neutrino transmission to you. Please do the same for us. And now, I must tend to my fighters. See you on the other side of this battle."

"Yes, the far shore will be welcome."

"Astrogation, depress the ship's bow by 45 degrees. That will bring the upper Empire ship into the antimatter beamer's aperture."

"Depressing ship's bow," Ibarra said. "Sir, our proton and nose lasers will be perfectly aligned to fire on the lower Empire ship thanks to this attitude change."

"Yes they will." The image of the captain looked up at the Bridge ceiling videye. "PO Watson, your target is the upper Empire ship. Only you will be firing on it. Be aware that our ship will be jinking up, down, sideways and even backward using the magfield drive. I wish to make hard or impossible the enemy's target tracking. While I do not know how quickly they will engage their own antimatter beamers, our ship and *Red Hope* will be under laser strikes once the Empire arrives within 100,000 kilometers of us. Be ready."

"Ready, sir," Bill answered. "My tracking scope and my passive sensors are all locked into the upper Empire ship. It is now coming into my firing aperture. Will fire on your command. Sir."

The captain looked ahead. "Tactical, what is the range to the Empire ships?"

"Sir, 140,000 kilometers and closing. In eleven seconds they will be in range of us." Chang leaned forward, looking down at her Tactical touchscreen. "Our two ships will be in targeting range of the Empire ships for only a minute, sir."

"Understood. Weapons, launch those two missiles."

"Launching," Yamamoto said, excitement in his voice.

Now the system graphic, which had enlarged greatly to show the two red dots of the Empire ships, the five green dots of our ships and the purple dot of *Red Hope*, that graphic showed the distances shrinking rapidly. We were two firing platforms approaching each other at ten percent of the speed of light. That meant we would pass each other quickly. The shooting had to be perfect. I crossed my fingers, wishing I had access to a proton laser. I didn't. But others did. They were ready. The captain was ready. Bill was ready.

Green laser, red proton and purple plasma beams shot out from both Empire ships. One array of beams hit *Red Hope*. Another array hit *Star Glory*. Or rather, they did not hit. Our Astro lady Louise moved our ship up and sideways using the magfield drive. Someone on *Red Hope* did the same for their ship, though it moved by way of normal chemfuel thrusters, augmented by directional stern thrusters.

"Range is 87,000 klicks," Chang said softly.

Another volley of CO_2, proton and plasma beams shot out at us and a separate volley pursued *Red Hope*.

"Hits on the hull above the bow," reported Chang. "Topside railgun is down. No penetration to the water jacket."

I saw the live image of the *Red Hope*. Its rear ring glowed to strikes from the Empire beams. Sparkling fragments spun away from the ring, which was now only partial.

"Range is now 43,000 klicks."

A third volley of red, green and purple beams shot out, aiming for both of our ships. I winced as I saw two purple plasma beams again hit the rear ring of the *Red Hope*. But there was no sign of water leakage. Hopefully their hull was built to withstand multiple laser and directed energy beam strikes. The volley aimed at us missed entirely, including our four shuttles, again thanks to Louise's use of the magfield drive and the agile jinking of each shuttle pilot. Go Warren!

"Range at 21,000 klicks!"

"PO Watson! Fire your beamer!"

"Firing, captain."

In the true space image of the two Empire ships I saw a long black beam reach out and impact on the front ball of the upper enemy ship. The beam maintained its intercept vector, slicing down the middle tube and into the stern ball. A star glow of expanding orange-white light overlapped the antimatter beam. Which now disappeared from the live image.

"Upper Empire ship is gone," Chang reported. "Range is 17,000 klicks."

"Weapons, fire the warheads."

In the true space image there now appeared two small suns. From them speared out 50 white x-ray beams from each sun as the thermonuke fed high energy photons into the gain medium of the x-ray lasing rods. The 100 white beams hit the rear ball of the lower enemy ship. Red, green and purple beams that had been shooting from that ball and aiming to hit the *Star Glory* and the *Red Hope*, those beams vanished. But the front ball fired a black antimatter beam at us.

Before I could flinch the beam passed us by. The *Star Glory* was intact. We were alive!

"Shuttle Three is gone," called Major Owanju.

Was that Warren's shuttle!

"First Sergeant Khan will be missed," the major said.

Shivers ran down my back. I scanned the vidscreen. It held too many things, all of them deadly.

"Range is 9,175 klicks."

From our front bow there shot forth a green CO_2 laser beam and a red proton laser strike. Our port-side gamma ray laser added an orange beam to the mix. From the *Red Hope* its two weapons rings shot out purple plasma beams. All beams struck the front ball of the surviving Empire ship. The true space imagery showed black holes appearing as the beams cut through the front hull. White gas and silvery water globules appeared. Yellow electrical explosions happened. Fragments of the ball's hull now shot outward, blown loose by internal explosions. Behind the ball the central tube wrinkled, then bent as the rear ball's momentum pushed the tube into the rear segment of the dying front ball.

A new sun blossomed.

That had to be its antimatter reservoir losing containment. Freefloating negative antimatter combined with the innards of the ball to turn alien flesh, water, air, equipment and arrogance into the stuff of suns. Pure plasma radiated outward in an expanding ball. I blinked my eyes, wishing I could shut down my infrared vision. The infrared made a super bright image even brighter. I looked away. Then I looked back, focusing on the system graphic. Four red dots of new Empire ships were just seven AU short of our position. What would the captain now do?

"Captain, incoming neutrino signal. From . . . from the *Golden Pond* ship, sir," called Wetstone.

"Put it up."

The images of the *Red Hope*, our three surviving shuttles, the system graphic and the Bridge overhead view were now joined by a new image.

"Where did you obtain our antimatter beam!" snorted Smooth Fur, his whiskers spread wide and his thick tale swishing from side to side faster than I had ever seen.

The image of the captain showed him sitting back in his seat. "I am Captain Neil Skorzeny of the heavy cruiser *Star Glory*, lead ship in our fleet of four Earth cruisers and one Sendera fighting ship. Do you wish to sacrifice the four oncoming ships to our antimatter beams?"

Behind the standing otter moved the black form of the Toka hunter cat. It squalled something. Smooth Fur's whiskers went flat along its muzzle.

"So you possess the antimatter beam, our magfield drive and our emissions cloak. It seems there is a traitor in our midst. Perhaps several," the otter growled.

"Perhaps several," the captain agreed. "I welcome more target practice."

"You lost a ship!"

The captain smiled toothily. He gestured down to Major Owanju. Who tapped his armrest control patch. In the system graphic the green dots of the three shuttles vanished. "You lost *two* ships. And the rest of my fleet has gone into emissions cloaking. Your four ships will not know where our ships are until they are fired on. Much as you attacked us. We are five against your four. And three of us you cannot detect. Bring it on."

The black-furred otter's white stripes shimmered. The creature's entire covering of fur now fluffed out, adding bulk to its image. Whether it was instinctive or intentional, the alien now appeared twice its original size. It gestured to the pink floating jellyfish.

"Captain, the four Empire ships are turning away," called XO Kumisov. "They are on track to reverse course and head back into the system."

Smooth Fur's black eyes blinked slowly. "Human Skorzeny, you have committed a deadly error. First you lost two ships by declining my ritual offer to join the Empire as a Servant species. Now, you have lost a third ship. While I care not what happens to the Sendera remnants, you humans are now my prime objective. We will find your world Earth and its home star. Yellow stars are not that numerous in this part of Orion Arm."

The captain nodded slowly. "And while you are checking yellow star after yellow star, in all directions, this ship and other Earth ships will be striking your Empire bases within your part of Orion. The three moons at Kepler 37 will be our target. At a time of our choosing. Other trade worlds and other Empire ships will be targeted by humanity." The captain smiled, but hid his teeth. It made for a ferocious smile. "Your Empire will be forced to divert ships to defense of your existing systems. Your commerce will be damaged. Stability of Empire culture, here in Orion Arm, will be harmed. Your expansion into the middle and upper part of this arm will be slowed or stopped."

Smooth Fur's fur lowered. His muzzle whiskers, though, went flat. "The Empire has more ships than any species. We will find you humans."

The captain nodded. "That is a correct statement. Now. But we already have two species allies who have agreed to join us in fighting you. The Sendera and the Melanchon. As we find other refugees from your planet killing, they will find homes in our part of the arm. And they will provide ships to join ours in attacking your ships." The captain gestured dismissively. "What will the Empire do when it encounters multiple ships able to enter emissions cloaking, are as fast as Empire ships, and are able to destroy Empire ships using antimatter beams?"

Black eyes blinked. "Your ships will die. Your Earth will die. Other occupied worlds will die. There are a hundred billion worlds in Warm Swirl. A few less means nothing."

"Wrong!" yelled the captain, shocking me. "Every world with intelligent life is a gem to be treasured. Whether they join in our fight, or live apart from it, humans will treat every other species who is not part of the Empire as a lifeform to be respected."

"And that will be your undoing," Smooth Fur said. "Over the 93,000 years of the Empire of Eternity we have learned that only species willing to work toward a common goal deserve to live. Those are the 14,331 species that make up the Empire. You humans are few. The Sendera and Melanchon are fewer. And we have all eternity in which to hunt you down."

Captain Skorzeny shook his head slowly. "Wrong. Time is not on your side. Traitors sold us your tech. Other traitors will eventually sell us the secret to the long range of your weapons. Oh, we also now can travel at 100 light years per day, just like any other Empire ship. Your advantages are already disappearing. We humans are a young species. Your Empire is aged. Everything aged eventually dies. I look forward to attending your funeral."

Smooth Fur stared at the captain for long moments. "We of the Empire do not observe funerals. We celebrate only victory over weaker species. Prepare to die." The creature waved a paw. Its image vanished from the vidscreen.

"Would you humans really share the secret of the antimatter weapon with us?" asked Random Thoughts.

The captain lifted his right hand and rubbed his chin. Which showed a brown stubble. "I am willing to do that. But I answer to the Star Navy of humanity's EarthGov ruling body. Whether to share the antimatter beamer tech with you and the Melanchon is up to EarthGov. Believe me, though, I will fight for you Sendera to get it. You fought beside us against the two Empire ships. Your fighting made a difference. I would welcome you as an ally species."

"Understood. We will continue to be your ally. You have our neutrino frequency. Contact us when your EarthGov makes its decision. Now, the *Red Hope* must join our other lineage ships. We need to find a new home."

"Well, we can help you with that." The captain looked over to where Bjorg had sat, quiet as a fat mouse. "Doctor Bjorg, will you transmit the cleansed record of 294 stars with planets that exist in the upper part of Orion Arm to our friends?"

"I would, but I do not have that data at my station," the Swede rumbled. He tapped his armrest. "Doctor Murphy, please respond."

Another image showed on the vidscreen. My brown-eyed friend looked out from her office. Piles of dataslates and record tablets adorned her desk. The nicely fit gymnast smiled. "I was following the Bridge conversation." She reached out, grabbed a tablet, then pressed its surface. "The star record we shared with the Melanchon and raider chief Tik-long has been uploaded to Heidi. Sir." She gave the captain and Bjorg an amateur salute. Which went nicely with the blue and gray camos she wore.

"Thank you, Doctor Murphy." The captain looked up at the ceiling. "Heidi, transmit the star and planet record to *Random Thoughts*."

"Records transmitted," the AI said brightly, her feminine tone sounding loud-hearted.

The blue and green-skinned chameleon swung both eyes downward to the pedestal plate in front of him. Then up. "The records are received. Appreciation is too little. Would the gift of a lineage Breeder repay this human generosity?"

"No need," the captain said. "Just use those records to find a new home world among the red dwarf stars uparm in Orion. There are plenty of such stars, nearly all of which have planets. Once your colony is planted, call this ship on our neutrino frequency. We will find a way to visit your world. And perhaps some Sendera will visit Earth in the future."

"We will do as you suggest. Until we share a shoreline once more."

The image of the Sendera captain disappeared. Leaving the vidscreen filled only with the system graphic, the Bridge image and the departing image of the *Red Hope*. I licked my lips. Then I looked up at the thick tube that conveyed antimatter to Bill's beamer block. The rainbow shimmer was perfect. Bright, sharp and stable. As were the nine vertical rainbow tubes that fed antimatter to our thrusters. Which were now pushing us into a long elliptical vector track that would eventually take us out to the edge of this system's magnetosphere. Our arrival point would not be on the side where Sol lay. Which meant the captain could point the ship's bow toward Sol, tell us to engage Alcubierre and we would once more enter the grayness of FTL transit. And the Empire ships, located in the inner part of Kepler 445, would not know what direction we were headed. And if they assumed Sol was located in the direction of our ship's last position, so much the better. They would waste time and effort searching in the wrong direction.

"PO Stewart," called the captain. "Your shuttle fleet solution to our arrival among too many Empire ships was outstanding. As was your pretend cloaking idea. You are hereby promoted to chief petty officer. Don't spend it all in one place. Like the Mess Hall."

I laughed. Chief O'Connor let loose a giant guffaw. Dolores Gambuchino, Cindy, Gus and Duncan also laughed loudly. On the vidscreen dear Cassie chuckled, then pointed at me.

"Hey steakman! You are buying for our entire table tonight!"

That would include dear Evelyn, and still alive Warren. We would be joined by Bill and Oksana. And who knew who else might show up, demanding a free beer or tequila shot? Tonight I would buy rounds for our entire table and for anyone else who gave me a smile.

We had survived attacks by the Empire of Eternity. We had met two alien species who were on the way to being allies of humanity. We had had a good time at the pirate base run by Tik-long. Who knew what else we might find on our next trip into deep space? I sure didn't. But beyond my friends, I realized my Mom and my sisters Anna and Louise would be part of my return home. In truth, everyone on the *Star Glory* had someone to look forward to seeing. That felt good. It felt real. It felt human.

The future and fighting the Empire could wait. What mattered most to me and everyone else was pulling our ship into home anchorage, even if that was an orbit 300 miles above the blue oceans of Earth. But I would bring home memories of incredible adventures. And going home to Castle Rock, with me, would be Evelyn. My Mom and sisters deserved to meet her. And she deserved to meet them. We were a together couple. I hoped we would be such for the rest of our lives.

THE END

ABOUT THE AUTHOR

T. Jackson King (Tom) is a professional archaeologist, journalist and retired Hippie. He learned early on to question authority and find answers for himself, thanks to reading lots of science fiction. He also worked at a radiocarbon dating laboratory at UC Riverside and UCLA. Tom attended college in Paris and Tokyo. He is a graduate of UCLA (M.A. 1976, archaeology) and the University of Tennessee (B.Sc. 1971, journalism). He has worked as an archaeologist in the American Southwest and has traveled widely in Europe, Russia, Japan, Canada, Mexico and the USA. Other jobs have included short order cook, hotel clerk, legal assistant, telephone order taker, investigative reporter and newspaper editor. He also survived the warped speech-talk of local politicians and escaped with his hide intact. Tom writes hard science fiction, anthropological scifi, dark fantasy/horror and contemporary fantasy/magic realism. Tom's novels are **MOTHER WARM** (2017), **BATTLECRY** (2017), **SUPERGUY** (2016), **BATTLEGROUP** (2016), **BATTLESTAR** (2016), **DEFEAT THE ALIENS** (2016), **FIGHT THE ALIENS** (2016), **FIRST CONTACT** (2015), **ESCAPE FROM ALIENS** (2015), **ALIENS VS. HUMANS** (2015), **FREEDOM VS. ALIENS** (2015), **HUMANS VS. ALIENS** (2015), **GENECODE ILLEGAL** (2014), **EARTH VS. ALIENS** (2014), **ALIEN ASSASSIN** (2014), **THE MEMORY SINGER** (2014), **ANARCHATE VIGILANTE** (2014), **GALACTIC VIGILANTE** (2013), **NEBULA VIGILANTE** (2013), **SPEAKER TO ALIENS** (2013), **GALACTIC AVATAR** (2013), **STELLAR ASSASSIN** (2013), **STAR VIGILANTE** (2012), **THE GAEAN ENCHANTMENT** (2012), **LITTLE BROTHER'S WORLD** (2010), **ANCESTOR'S WORLD** (1996, with A.C. Crispin), and **RETREAD SHOP** (1988, 2012). His short stories appeared in **JUDGMENT DAY AND OTHER DREAMS** (2009). His poetry appeared in **MOTHER EARTH'S STRETCH MARKS** (2009). Tom lives in Santa Fe, New Mexico, USA with his wife Sue. More information on Tom's writings can be found at www.tjacksonking.com/.

PRAISE FOR T. JACKSON KING'S BOOKS

EARTH VS. ALIENS

"This story is the best space opera I've read in many years. The author knows his Mammalian Behavior. If we're lucky it'll become a movie soon. Many of the ideas are BRAND NEW and I loved the adaptability of people in the story line. AWESOME!!"—**Phil W. King,** *Amazon*

"It's good space opera. I liked the story and wanted to know what happened next. The characters are interesting and culturally diverse. The underlying theme is that humans are part of nature and nature is red of tooth and claw. Therefore, humans are naturally violent, which fortunately makes them a match for the predators from space."—**Frank C. Hemingway,** *Amazon*

STAR VIGILANTE

"For a fast-paced adventure with cool tech, choose ***Star Vigilante****.* This is the story of three outsiders. Can three outsiders bond together to save Eliana's planet from eco-destruction at the hands of a ruthless mining enterprise?" –**Bonnie Gordon,** *Los Alamos Daily Post*

STELLAR ASSASSIN

"T. Jackson King's ***Stellar Assassin*** is an ambitious science fiction epic that sings! Filled with totally alien lifeforms, one lonely human, an archaeologist named Al Lancaster must find his way through trade guilds, political maneuvering and indentured servitude, while trying to reconcile his new career as an assassin with his deeply-held belief in the teachings of Buddha. . . This is a huge, colorful, complicated world with complex characters, outstanding dialogue, believable motivations, wonderful high-tech battle sequences and, on occasion, a real heart-stringer . . . This is an almost perfectly edited novel as well, which is a bonus. This is a wonderful novel, written by a wonderful author . . .Bravo! Five Stars!" –**Linell Jeppsen,** *Amazon*

LITTLE BROTHER'S WORLD

"If you're sensing a whiff of Andre Norton or Robert A. Heinlein, you're not mistaken . . . The influence is certainly there, but *Little Brother's World* is no mere imitation of *Star Man's Son* or *Citizen of the Galaxy*. Rather, it takes the sensibility of those sorts of books and makes of it something fresh and new. T. Jackson King is doing his part to further the great conversation of science fiction; it'll be interesting to see where he goes next."–**Don Sakers,** *Analog*

"When I'm turning a friend on to a good writer I've just discovered, I'll often say something like, "Give him ten pages and you'll never be able to put him down." Once in a long while, I'll say, "Give him five pages." It took T. Jackson King exactly *one sentence* to set his hook so deep in me that I finished **LITTLE BROTHER'S WORLD** in a single sitting, and I'll be thinking about that vivid world for a long time to come. The last writer I can recall with the courage to make a protagonist out of someone as profoundly Different as Little Brother was James Tiptree Jr., with her remarkable debut novel **UP THE WALLS OF THE WORLD.** I think Mr. King has met that challenge even more successfully. His own writing DNA borrows genes from writers as diverse as Tiptree, Heinlein, Norton, Zelazny, Sturgeon, Pohl, and Doctorow, and splices them together very effectively." – **Spider Robinson, Hugo, Nebula and Campbell Award winner**

"*Little Brother's World* is a sci-fi novel where Genetic Engineering exists. . . It contains enough details and enough thrills to make the book buyers/readers grab it and settle in for an afternoon read. The book is well-written and had a well-defined plot . . . I never found a boring part in the story. It was fast-paced and kept me entertained all throughout. The characters are fascinating and likeable too. This book made me realize about a possible outcome, when finally science and technology wins over traditional ones. . . All in all, *Little Brother's World* is another sci-fi novel from T. Jackson King that is both exciting, thrilling and fun. Full of suspense, adventure, romance, secrets, conspiracies, this book would take you in a roller-coaster ride." –**Abby Flores,** *Bookshelf Confessions*

THE MEMORY SINGER

"A coming of age story reminiscent of Robert A. Heinlein or Alexei

Panshin. Jax [the main character] is a fun character, and her world is compelling. The social patterns of Ship life are fascinating, and the Alish'Tak [the main alien species] are sufficiently alien to make for a fairly complex book. Very enjoyable."—**Don Sakers**, *Analog Science Fiction*

"Author T. Jackson King brings his polished writing style, his knowledge of science fiction 'hardware,' and his believable aliens to his latest novel *The Memory Singer*. But all this is merely backdrop to the adventures of Jax Cochrane, a smart, rebellious teen who wants more from life than the confines of a generational starship. There are worlds of humans and aliens out there. When headstrong Jax decides that it's time to discover and explore them, nothing can hold back this defiant teen. You'll want to accompany this young woman . . in this fine coming-of-age story."—**Jean Kilczer**, *Amazon*

RETREAD SHOP

"Engaging alien characters, a likable protagonist, and a vividly realized world make King's first sf novel a good purchase for sf collections."–*Library Journal*

"A very pleasant tour through the author's inventive mind, and an above average story as well."–*Science Fiction Chronicle*

"Fun, with lots of outrageously weird aliens."—*Locus*

"The writing is sharp, the plotting tight, and the twists ingenious. It would be worth reading, if only for the beautiful delineations of alien races working with and against one another against the background of an interstellar marketplace. The story carries you . . . with a verve and vigor that bodes well for future stories by this author. Recommended."–*Science Fiction Review*

"For weird aliens, and I do mean weird, choose **Retread Shop**. The story takes place on a galactic trading base, where hundreds of species try to gain the upper hand for themselves and for their group. Sixteen year-old billy is the sole human on the Retread Shop, stranded when his parents and their shipmates perished. What really makes the ride fun are the aliens Billy teams up with, including two who are plants. It's herbivores vs. carnivores, herd species vs. loners, mammals vs. insects and so on. The wild variety of physical types is only matched by the extensive array of cultures, which makes for a very entertaining read." –**Bonnie Gordon,** *Los Alamos Daily Post*

"Similar in feel to Roger Zelazny's Alien Speedway series is ***Retread Shop*** by T. Jackson King. It's an orphan-human-in-alien-society-makes-good story. Well-written and entertaining, it could be read either as a Young Adult or as straight SF with equal enjoyment." – **Chuq Von Rospach,** *OtherRealms 22*

"If you liked Stephen Goldin's Jade Darcy books duo, and Julie Czerneda's Clan trilogy, then you will probably like ***Retread Shop*** since it too has multiple aliens, an eatery, and an infinity of odd events that range from riots, to conspiracy, to exploring new worlds and to alien eating habits . . . It's a fun reader's ride and thoroughly entertaining. And, sigh, I wish that the author would write more books set in this background." –**Lyn McConchie, co-author of the** *Beastmaster* **series**

HUMANS VS. ALIENS

"Another great book from this author. This series has great characters and story is wall to wall excitement. Look forward to next book."— **William R. Thomas,** *Amazon*

"Humans are once again aggressive and blood thirsty to defend the Earth. Pace is quick and action is plentiful. Some unexpected plot twists, but you always know the home team is the best."—**C. Cook,** *Amazon*

ANCESTOR'S WORLD

"T. Jackson King is a professional archaeologist and he uses that to great advantage in *Ancestor's World*. I was just as fascinated by the details of the archaeology procedures as I was by the unfolding of the plot . . . What follows is a tightly plotted, suspenseful novel."– *Absolute Magnitude*

"The latest in the StarBridge series from King, a former Rogue Valley resident now living and writing in Arizona, follows the action on planet Na-Dina, where the tombs of 46 dynasties have lain undisturbed for 6,000 years until a human archaeologist and a galactic gumshoe show up. Set your phasers for fun."–*Medford Mail Tribune*

ALIEN ASSASSIN
"The Assassin series is required reading in adventure, excitement and daring. The galactic vistas, the advanced alien technologies and the action make all the Assassin books a guarantee of a good read. Please keep them coming!"—**C. B. Symons,** *Amazon*

"KING STRIKES AGAIN! Yes, T. Jackson King gives us yet again a great space adventure. I loved the drama and adventure in this book. There is treachery in this one too which heightens the suspense. Being the only human isn't easy, but Al pulls it off. Loved the Dino babies and how they are being developed into an important part of the family of assassins. All of the fun takes place right here and we are not left hanging off the cliff. Write on T.J."—**K. McClell,** *Amazon*

THE GAEAN ENCHANTMENT
"For magic, a quest and a new battle around every corner, go with *The Gaean Enchantment*. In this novel, Earth has entered a new phase as it cycles through the universe. In this phase, some kinds of "magic" work, but tech is rapidly ceasing to function. In the world of this book, incantation and sympathetic magic function through connection to spirit figures who might be described as gods." – **Bonnie Gordon,** *Los Alamos Daily Post*

"In *The Gaean Enchantment* the main character, Thomas, back from Vietnam and with all the PTSD that many soldiers have—nightmares, blackouts—finds his truth through the finding of his totem animal, the buffalo Black Mane. He teaches Thomas that violence and killing must always be done as a last resort, and that the energies of his soul are more powerful than any arsenal . . . Don't miss this amazing novel of magic and soul transformation, deep love, and Artemis, goddess of the hunt and protector of women."–**Catherine Herbison-Wiget,** *Amazon*

JUDGMENT DAY AND OTHER DREAMS

"King is a prolific writer with an old-time approach–he tells straight-ahead stories and asks the big questions. No topic is off limits and he writes with an explorer's zest for uncovering the unknown. He takes readers right into the world of each story, so each rustle of a tree, each whisper of the wind, blows softly against your inner ear."–**Scott Turick,** *Daytona Beach News-Journal*

"Congratulations on the long overdue story collection, Tom! What I find most terrific is your range of topics and styles. You have always been an explorer."–**David Brin, Nebula and Hugo winner**

"I'm thoroughly loving [the stories]; the prose is the kind that makes me stop and savor it – roll phrases over my tongue – delicious. I loved the way you conjure up a whole world or civilization so economically."–**Sheila Finch, SF author**

"*Judgment Day and Other Dreams* . . . would make a valued addition to any science fiction or fantasy library. There is a satisfying and engrossing attention to detail within the varied stories . . . The common thread among all works is the intimate human element at the heart of each piece. King's prose displays a mastery over these myriad subjects without alienating the uninitiated, thus providing the reader with a smooth, coherent, and altogether enjoyable experience . . . King is able to initiate the reader naturally through plot and precise prose, as if being eased into a warm bath . . . There is a dedicated unity amongst some of the entries in this anthology that begs to be explored in longer formats. And the works which stand apart are just as notable and exemplify King's grasp of human emotions and interactions. This collection displays the qualities of fine writing backed by a knowledgeable hand and a vivid imagination . . . If *Judgment Day and Other Dreams* is anything to go by, T. Jackson King should be a household name." –**John Sulyok,** *Tangent Online*

Printed in Great Britain
by Amazon